June Thomson, an ex-teacher, lives in St Albans, Hertford-shire. She is the author of fourteen previous Inspector Finch novels.

'Superior . . . faultless as ever in plot and execution'
Irish Times

'An accomplished author at her best'
Mail on Sunday

'A sure sense of timing and an unerring way of creating suspense'
Woman & Home

'The setting is scrupulously described, middle-class motives and manners meticulously analysed, with a careful, economical exactitude that answers all the questions that were posed'
Daily Telegraph

'Another stylish detective story from a writer with an increasingly prestigious reputation'
Annabel

D1322263

Also by June Thomson

ROSEMARY FOR REMEMBRANCE
and published by Corgi Books

THE SPOILS OF TIME

June Thomson

CORGI BOOKS

THE SPOILS OF TIME
A CORGI BOOK   0 552 13591 7

Originally published in Great Britain by
Constable & Co Ltd

PRINTING HISTORY
Constable edition published 1989
Corgi edition published 1990

This book is set in 10/11½ Palatino
by Kestrel Data, Exeter

Corgi Books are published by Transworld Publishers Ltd,
61-63 Uxbridge Road, Ealing, London W5 5SA, in Australia by
Transworld Publishers (Australia) Pty Ltd, 15-23 Helles Avenue,
Moorebank, NSW 2170, and in New Zealand by Transworld
Publishers (N.Z.) Ltd, Cnr Moselle and Waipareira Avenues,
Henderson, Auckland.

Printed in Great Britain by
BPCC Hazell Books
Aylesbury, Bucks, England
Member of BPCC Ltd.

In memory of Lilian,
with my best love

1

Detective Chief Inspector Jack Finch noticed her as soon as he and Detective Sergeant Boyce walked into Divisional Headquarters in Chelmsford.

She was sitting on one of the bench seats just inside the swing doors in the public part of the entrance hall under the notice-board with its posters about stolen cars and the Identikit picture of the man wanted for rape over at Witham. It was difficult not to pick her out. She was very old for one thing; in her eighties, Finch estimated, and wearing, despite the heat of that late July afternoon, a bright red woollen coat with a little collar of black fur and a matching pill-box hat, of a style that had been fashionable in the 'forties. Underneath its bit of limp black veiling, hennaed hair and a tiny, heavily-powdered face with its carefully drawn in lipsticked mouth gave her the grotesque and comical appearance of a small, wizened, female clown.

And yet she wasn't without presence, even her own form of dignity. She sat bolt upright, clutching a worn black patent leather handbag on her lap like a defensive weapon and, as Finch and Boyce entered, she shot the pair of them a look of intense and quizzical interest from very sharp dark eyes, summing them up and then dismissing them, especially Finch who, because it was a warm day and there hadn't been much on the books apart from an interview with a suspected burglar, had thought it fit to wear an open-necked shirt and a shabby linen jacket which had seen far better days.

But Mills, the uniformed Sergeant on duty behind

the desk, evidently wasn't impressed with her. He was moving pieces of paper about on the counter top, clipping some together and reading over others with a look of such heavy and scowling intensity that Finch suspected it was a ploy to keep the old lady at arm's length and dissuade her from bothering him any further.

It was evident, too, from the amused, God-help-us-all expression he exchanged with Boyce as he unlocked the security door, allowing the two plain-clothes officers to pass into the corridor beyond, that the Detective Sergeant had encountered her before.

'Who is she?' Finch asked as he and Boyce went up the stairs to the Chief Inspector's first-floor office.

But Boyce wasn't much help.

'Lord knows. She was here yesterday afternoon when I went to the canteen. Something to do with her brother who she says has gone missing. According to Mills, she wants a senior officer put on the case and a couple of men sent up to London to trace him. Mills told her – Get in touch with the Salvation Army. They'll find him if anyone can. But she wasn't having any. Seems to think it's our job. So what do you want done about Pierson?' he added, reverting to the more immediate and professional subject of their interview that afternoon. 'Shall I get his alibi checked?'

'Yes; do that, Tom. Kyle and Muir can handle it. And send Barney and a WPC round to talk to the girlfriend. Pierson himself may be a tough nut to crack but he's always had a weakness for little dollybirds with more sex-appeal than sense. She may be worth leaning on.'

When Boyce had left to carry out these instructions, Finch settled himself down at his desk although with no great sense of urgency. Like Sergeant Mills downstairs, he felt he was merely moving pieces of

8

paper about to give himself the illusion of being fully occupied.

The most recent major crime, the murders at Morton Grange school, had been satisfactorily cleared up, an arrest made and the bulk of the papers sent off to the DPP. All that remained to be done was the correlation of some minor written evidence and the tidying up of the files, work which could have been left until he returned from the few days' leave he was due to start the following morning.

As for Pierson, Boyce himself could deal with him perfectly adequately.

His own thoughts occupied him more than the contents of the papers in front of him although he went through the motions, stapling this bit to that, rearranging the order of others, from time to time glancing across at the window where the sun, slipping round to that side of the building, was beginning to gild the slate roofs of the houses opposite and to give the chimney-pots and the television aerials a glamour quite out of keeping with their prosaic, everyday shapes.

He was thinking of Marion Greave, a preoccupation which seemed to be externalized by the white vapour trail drawn across the sky by some invisible plane and of the same colour and texture as the narrow bands of cloud which faintly marbled the otherwise immaculate blue expanse.

Marion was returning by air today from Crete; perhaps had already arrived. He had no idea what time her flight was due to arrive at Gatwick. She might even already be at the hotel in London where he had arranged to meet her the following day.

Tomorrow!

Giving up all pretence at work, he shoved the folders to one side and, leaning his elbows on the desk, watched the plane's unseen progress until it passed beyond the

9

edge of the window-frame and all that remained was its vapour ribbon, slowly dissolving into small puffs of pale flocculation.

It was absurd to be so happy at his age. He was a middle-aged bachelor, well past the age of passion, or so he had imagined, living alone now that his widowed sister, who had kept house for him, had recently remarried. Falling in love was the last thing he had thought of doing. As he acknowledged himself, he was not exactly designed for romance. Stocky, fresh-faced, open-featured, his appearance betrayed his country background and upbringing. He hardly looked like a professional policeman, let alone a lover.

And then he had met Marion Greave who had acted as locum on a case when Pardoe, the regular police pathologist, had been on leave, and had fallen head over heels in love with her like any adolescent, attracted by her air of quiet independence and self-sufficiency. So, he could hardly complain, could he, when she had turned down his proposal of marriage, preferring him as a friend rather than as a husband?

He had not seen her for some considerable time, not since she had moved to Leeds to take up a post as a hospital pathologist. Over the months, they had kept in touch intermittently by letter, the latest of which, written before she had left for a holiday in Crete with a colleague, had suggested that they meet at her hotel on her return to London, where she was planning to spend a few days before the end of her leave.

In the letter, she had not specified who the colleague was and it was none of Finch's business to ask. He was only grateful for the chance of meeting her again face to face after so long a time, the prospect of which filled him with such idiotic joy that he caught himself smiling broadly at the least provocation, like a schoolboy anticipating the end of term.

At half past five, he gave up any further pretence at work and, shoving the folders into the filing cabinet, he slung his jacket over one shoulder and made for the door.

To his surprise the old lady was still seated in the entrance foyer when he went downstairs. Although he had not given her any thought since that brief conversation about her with Boyce, he had imagined that she would have given up and left hours ago.

'What's her name?' he asked *sotto voce* of Mills, leaning one elbow on the counter and taking care not to look in her direction.

'Laud, sir. Kitty.'

'Mrs?'

Mills raised one shoulder, indicating that he wasn't sure and he didn't much care either. It was the end of a long, hot afternoon in which nothing much had happened and the Sergeant preferred to keep it that way until he went off duty.

Even so, Finch might have ignored her. He was on his way home where he intended spending a leisurely evening ironing a clean shirt for the following day, polishing his shoes and making sure that his one decent suit, back from the dry-cleaner's, was free of any of those exasperating little paper labels which tend to be pinned on to garments in the most unlikely places.

But, his hand on the swing-door in the act of pushing it open, he changed his mind and walked back.

'Can I give you a lift somewhere?' he asked her.

She had turned to watch his approach, her expression changing from one of hope that someone was at last taking notice of her to disappointment that it was only him after all.

She said, 'Thanks very much but I'm waiting to see someone in charge.'

Mills took the opportunity to shove his oar in, anxious

to get rid of her and, at the same time, to put her straight about Finch's exact professional status.

'That's Detective Chief Inspector Finch,' he told her.

She perked up at once, smiling and rearranging her head to a more becoming angle.

'Well, now,' she said, her voice taking on a warmer note, 'that's ever so kind of you, Chief Inspector. I'm here about my brother. You see, I haven't heard from him for weeks now and I'm so worried . . .'

She had risen to her feet as she had been speaking, her skinny little legs, which put Finch in mind of a sparrow's, trembling with the effort.

'Whoops!' she added, laughing as she clutched at the arm he held out for her. 'Drunk again! Whatever will the nice Sergeant think of me?'

She gave Mills a look of bright-eyed malevolence which he ignored with massive indifference, lowering his head once more to study the papers on the counter-top.

Finch smiled down at her, amused at the situation which gave an unexpected twist to the end of an otherwise ordinary day and added to his end-of-term feeling. School was out and the rules really didn't matter a damn any more.

'Let me drive you home,' he suggested. 'We can talk on the way.'

She kept hold of his arm as he escorted her to the carpark where he packed her carefully into the front passenger seat, helping her into the safety belt and clipping it into place. It had been a slow business walking her to the car and she seemed fussed by this last attention, embarrassed, Finch guessed, by her own frailty and her need for his assistance.

'All these damned contraptions!' she said snappily.

'Tell me about your brother,' Finch asked to take her mind off the seat-belt as he started the engine.

Apart from giving him her address, she had said

nothing on their walk to the carpark, concentrating her attention on gripping his arm and keeping upright on a pair of high-heeled patent leather shoes which, judging by the film of dust over their cracked toe-caps, she hadn't worn for years but had dug out from the back of a cupboard for just this occasion.

She said, 'I've told you, he's gone missing. I haven't heard a dicky bird from him for ages and his landlady's said he's not there any more. I got in touch with her, you see, dear, when he didn't send for my birthday, not so much as a card. He's never missed before. So, thinking he might be ill, I dropped her a line. She wrote back to say he left about five months ago and, as he hadn't turned up and there was rent owing, she'd let his room, the rotten cow. I've got her letter here.'

She was plunging about in her shabby handbag among a litter of old envelopes, crumpled handkerchiefs and odds and ends of make-up, releasing a small cloud of powder grains, smelling sweetly-stale, into the interior of the car.

She was still rummaging around when Finch drew up outside her address in Digby Road, a short street of terrace houses a few minutes' drive from Divisional Headquarters.

'You'll come in for a cup of tea,' she added, making it a statement rather than a question.

'All right,' he agreed. She hadn't given him much option. Besides, he was still amused by the situation and intrigued as well by her story which she hadn't had time to finish. How old was the brother, for one thing? Like her, in his eighties? And who was she anyway? In their brief conversation, he hadn't even established her name with any certainty.

He made a move in that direction as she found her latch-key, and fitted it into the front door.

'You're Mrs Laud?' he asked.

13

'Miss, actually,' she corrected him, 'although I always call myself Mrs. Sounds more respectable, doesn't it?'

She gave him a look of saucy conspiracy over her shoulder, hinting at a less reputable past as he followed her into a narrow hall almost entirely taken up by a bike.

'Belongs to them upstairs,' she said by way of an apology as they edged past it.

The hall itself had been crudely converted into an entrance for two separate flats, the side of the staircase covered in with hardboard, while two doors, one at the foot of the stairs, the other at the opening of the downstairs passageway, had been set into thin, plaster-board partitions. Another door on the left, which should have led directly into the front room, had been sealed off by the simple method of nailing another sheet of painted hardboard over it. A strip of worn red turkey carpet covered the lino. The air smelt hot and heavily spicy from which Finch deduced that the occupants of the upstairs flat and the owners of the bicycle were probably Indian.

'Although strictly speaking,' she went on, unlocking the passage door and leading the way into a back room, 'the name's Dixon. Laud's my stage name. But don't worry, dear. You can call me Kitty.'

It was said with a warm magnanimity, accompanied by a theatrical sweep of her arm as if she were introducing him to her *alter ego* in the form of dozens of glossy black and white photographs of herself which stood about on the furniture and lined the walls.

'I'll put the kettle on,' she added. 'Make yourself at home.'

And with another gracious gesture, she indicated chairs and a sofa, inviting Finch to take a seat although her exit from the room was somewhat marred by her parting comment, 'God, I can't wait to get these bloody shoes off my feet!'

She was gone for several minutes, long enough for

Finch to stroll about and examine at least some of the photographs, not all of which were just of her. In the majority of them she was accompanied by a man; her brother most probably, judging by a strong family likeness – similar small, fine-boned features, bright dark eyes, smilingly crinkled, an expression of roguish charm. In all of them, they were wearing evening dress, the man in white tie and tails, a carnation in his buttonhole, Kitty in a variety of gowns from the knee-length skirt and dropped waist of the 'twenties to the romantic look of the early 'fifties with a heart-shaped neckline and yards of swathed tulle. Her hairstyles altered, too, with the dresses, the neatly cropped shingle, with semicircular spit curls decorating the cheekbones, changing to the peek-aboo made fashionable during the war by Veronica Lake.

The furniture had the same rubbed, dated look of her shoes and handbag. But it didn't seem to matter. Apart from the photographs, there was too much else in the room to divert the eye – a shabby silk shawl thrown over the back of an armchair, a pierrot doll occupying a corner of the sofa, a collection of fans stuffed behind the hideous dark oak overmantel, below which a painted vase full of ostrich feathers almost hid from view an elderly gas-fire, its chromium fittings turned rusty with age.

Through the sash window, looped about with dingy lace and velvet curtains, the hems of which trailed across a worn cotton carpet, Finch had a glimpse of a backyard, bright with yellow dandelions, their diaphanous seedheads floating lazily in the hot, still air.

But the garden was an irrelevance. The outdoors had no significance here at all. It was the room and its contents which clamoured for attention, especially the photographs which smiled and lured and postured on every side.

Finch had paused to examine two of those on the mantelpiece, one of Kitty on her own, languorously

15

glamorous in white fur, the other of her and her partner posed at a grand piano, the man at the keyboard, Kitty gracefully draped across its lid, one foot in a satin slipper swinging free, when Kitty herself entered the room, carrying a tray which she dumped down on a low table in front of the sofa, sweeping aside the newspapers and magazines which littered its surface.

'That's Hal,' she said. 'My brother. The one I was telling you about.'

During her absence, she had taken off her coat and hat, revealing a black crêpe de Chine dress with a bunch of crumpled, artificial parma violets pinned to one shoulder and a low V-shaped neckline which exposed too cruelly her scraggy neck, while the crippling high-heeled shoes had been replaced by a pair of comfy blue velveteen slippers with pompoms on the toes.

'Hal and Kitty Laud!' she went on, joining him in front of the fireplace, her voice vibrant with reminiscence. 'We used to do a variety act together. The Singing Lauds, that's what we were always billed as. Mostly musical comedy stuff, stage as well as films, especially the Astaire and Rogers songs. Hal played the piano beautifully and he had a lovely light tenor voice. We used to specialize in the more sophisticated numbers – "Lady be Good", "Stay as Sweet as You Are", "A Nightingale Sang in Berkeley Square." ' She hummed a few bars of the last tune, breaking off to exclaim with a laugh and a sigh, 'Oh, they don't write songs like that any more!' Turning back to the table, she added with a sudden brisk practicality, 'How do you like your tea, dear? As it comes?'

'That's fine,' Finch agreed, accepting the cup from her and sitting down on the sofa next to the pierrot doll.

Kitty took her own tea over to the armchair where, perched on its edge, she watched him over the brim of the cup with her bright, shrewd eyes, summing him up as she sipped at its contents.

16

'I've been dying for that all afternoon,' she announced before, putting down the cup, she continued, 'So you're going to help me find him?'

She seemed to take his agreement as a foregone conclusion, as she had done his acceptance of the invitation to tea. But Finch was less willing to comply on this occasion.

He compromised by saying, 'Tell me more about your brother. How old is he?'

'Seventy-nine. A couple of years younger than me, as a matter of fact.'

As she said it, she put her head on one side, clearly expecting a response, at which Finch obligingly remarked, with suitable incredulity, 'You're never eighty-one! I don't believe it!', a compliment which she received with a smile and a little, flirty shrug of the shoulders.

'It's true. But I like to keep myself looking young, dear. It's half the battle.'

'And your brother's been living in London?' Finch went on.

'That's right. In Clapham. I've found the letter from his landlady, by the way. It's on the tray by the tea-pot. You can read it if you like.'

As he picked it up and began to scan it, she continued to talk, distracting him from its contents although they seemed straightforward enough and covered most of what she had already told him.

Mr Dixon, the letter read, in a small, pinched writing, had left five months earlier, telling her he was going to stay with friends. As he hadn't returned and there was money owing on the rent, she, his landlady – Mrs Townsend, Finch assumed, glancing quickly at the signature – had been forced to let his room. She had her living to make the same as anyone else.

She concluded by stating that she had some luggage belonging to Mr Dixon, who seemed to be known to her by his real rather than his stage name, which she would like collected as soon as possible as she couldn't be expected to go on storing it. And it was no use asking for his present address because she didn't know it.

There was a disobliging tone to the letter which seemed to justify Kitty's description of her as a rotten cow.

Meanwhile Kitty was saying, 'We packed up the act in the 'fifties. Thanks to television, variety was finished by then, at least as we'd known it. Not like before the war when every town had its own theatre. The Bristol Empire, the Hippodrome at Darlington. We've played them all in our time. Mind you, we were never top billing but we weren't the dregs either. But things changed. No-one seemed to want glamour and romance any more. It was all those skiffle groups and rock and roll numbers. And we weren't the kind of turn that'd go down in the working-men's clubs or the holiday camps. "Time to hang up the tails," as Hal said. We weren't getting any younger either.'

'So you split up?' Finch asked. He replaced the letter in its envelope and propped it up again by the tea-pot, having made a mental note of the landlady's address, 14 Balmoral Road, as well as her name, but writing neither down in case Kitty construed it as a commitment on his part. 'What did you do instead?'

'Hal got married to a widow who ran a boarding-house in Bradford. We'd stayed there several times when we'd been playing the Alhambra. I'd no idea he was keen on her until he wrote and asked me to the wedding. I couldn't go though. I'd got a job then in London, running the ladies' cloakroom at the old Imperial before it was pulled down. But as it was a Wednesday, which meant missing the matinée as well as the evening performance, the manager wouldn't give me the time off and I didn't want to lose my job. You got a nice class of clientele in the dress circle in those days and besides,

18

the tips were good. Then, a few years later, she died.'

'Who did?' Finch asked momentarily losing the thread of her narrative.

'Her. Hal's wife. Poor old kid! He thought he'd found himself a cushy berth for life with her – cooked meals three times a day and nothing much to do except play the piano in the evenings to entertain the boarders. As it turned out, the place was mortgaged to the hilt and by the time *her* children had grabbed their share, all Hal was left with was a couple of hundred quid. But he never was lucky with money. Liked spending it too much. "In our game, darling," he used to say, "you've got to cut a bit of a dash." '

'Go on,' Finch said encouragingly. Although Kitty intended no criticism of her brother, by reading between the lines of her account he had begun to piece together in his mind a picture of Hal Laud or Dixon – talented, charming, clearly adored but undoubtedly self-centred, whose main aim in life as far as he could see, seemed to be, in Kitty's words, to 'cut a bit of a dash' while, at the same time, ensuring his own creature comforts.

'After she died and the will was sorted out,' Kitty resumed, 'he came to London, found digs and got himself a nice little job playing and singing in a West End club until it got too much for him. But he couldn't settle. He was always changing about from one address to the other. He always kept in touch though. I'd moved out of London by then. Rents were going sky-high and, once I'd lost my job at the theatre, I couldn't afford to go on living there. I'd got a friend who'd retired here – she used to be assistant to Marvo, the magician. Heard of him, have you, dear? No? Well, he was quite famous in his time but it doesn't matter. Anyway, Phoebe and me were company for one another. We used to meet up for a drink and a chat about the old days. Then she died, so here I am.'

19

On my own, the last sentence implied but it was said with a smile and without the least hint of self-pity.

'And you've no idea who these friends are your brother went to stay with?'

'No, dear, I haven't. If I had, I'd've got in touch with them like a shot. But Hal knows hundreds of people. He'd pick them up all over the place – bars, restaurants, at the races . . .'

'Races?' Finch asked, wondering if there were some dubious connection which might account for her brother's apparent disappearance.

'He used to take the train out to Epsom or Newmarket in the days when he could get about more. He always enjoyed a flutter. But it was the crowds and the excitement he really liked. I'll tell you something else he used to do. He'd wait outside a theatre for the interval, especially in the summer when the doors were opened and the audience came out on to the pavements for a breath of air. Then he'd nip upstairs to the circle bar and treat himself to a brandy and soda. He loved that, being back amongst the red plush and the gilding, even if nobody bothered to dress up any more. He always did. Never went anywhere without a white carnation in his buttonhole. You could say it was his trademark.'

She nodded across to the opposite wall where a particularly large glossy print of herself and her brother was hanging, both smiling, Kitty with a *diamanté* clip in her hair, Hal's cheek close to hers, the carnation gleaming immaculately white against his black lapel.

'When was the last time you heard from him?'

'Christmas. He never was one for writing letters but, give him his due, he never missed my birthdays or Christmas. Always sent me something nice, too; earrings or a silk scarf, knowing I like pretty things. Once it was a cheque for twenty-five quid.' She glowed briefly at the memory. 'And that's the point, you see, dear. It was my birthday three weeks ago and I didn't get a thing; not so much as a card. So I waited a few days and then wrote to his landlady.' Indicating the tray where the letter was propped up, she continued, 'I'd go up to London myself only I can't. It's my legs, see, dear.' She held them out for his inspection in their blue velveteen slippers. 'I can't rely on them not to let me down, especially on those damned escalators. It was as much as I could do to get round to the police station to report him missing. Not that your Sergeant seemed all that interested. "Get in touch with the Salvation Army," he told me. As if I would! Not that I've got anything against the Sally Army, don't get me wrong, but Hal'd have a fit if I sent them round after him. He's never been all that keen on God or anything like that.'

'But wouldn't he object more if the police turned up?' Finch asked, scenting a let-out.

'Not if it was done discreetly,' Kitty replied promptly. 'I'm sure you could manage it, dear. Just ask about, that's all you'd have to do. Then there's his luggage to consider. How on earth am I to get it down here? I can't lug it back on the train all by myself.'

She looked across at him appealingly and, much against his better judgement, Finch came to a decision.

Marion had asked him to meet her at her hotel at two o'clock the following afternoon, an arrangement which he had accepted although, given the choice, he would have preferred an earlier appointment so that he could have spent more time with her. But, as he was in no position to call the tune, he had agreed, applying for a few days' leave himself in the hope of further meetings with her in London before she had to return to Leeds.

Still, there was nothing to stop him driving to London in the morning and, by calling on Mrs Townsend in Clapham, making a few unofficial inquiries about the whereabouts of Hal Dixon. But, anxious not to raise

Kitty's hopes too high, he merely said, 'I'll see what I can do. But I'm making no promises.'

Even so she beamed at him.

'Oh, I know I can rely on you!' she assured him gaily. 'You've got that kind of face. I can always tell.' As he rose to his feet to replace his cup and saucer on the tray, she added unexpectedly, 'Married, are you, dear?'

The question came as a small shock to him and he stood in silence for a few moments.

'No,' he said at last.

'Then you ought to be. You'd make someone a lovely husband. Give me your cup.'

The request was as much a surprise as her question.

'Why?' he asked, handing it over and watching with baffled amusement as she tipped the dregs of tea into her own cup.

'I'll read your leaves. Phoebe, that friend of mine I was telling you about, Marvo's assistant, showed me how. Now let's see what they say. You'll be going on a journey. That's clear enough.'

'To London?' he asked with mock gravity.

But the irony was lost on her.

'It could be. The leaves never go into much detail. But there's someone here who's close to you. Very close; I can tell.' Then abruptly replacing the cup in its saucer, she said, 'Don't let any woman break your heart. We're not worth it.'

It was all nonsense, of course, but as he took his leave of her, having assured her of his return as soon as he had any news of her brother, and squeezed his way down the hall past the bicycle and out into the dusty heat of the late afternoon, he could not help feeling a small chill of foreboding at her words.

2

Number 14 Balmoral Road, Clapham, was, like Kitty's, a terrace house but more substantial than hers, being three-storeyed and having the benefit of a small front garden with a privet hedge and a view at the end of the road of the common with its grass and trees and the swirling traffic which circumnavigated it.

Parking the car and getting out, Finch surveyed its façade of yellowish brick and its neatly-netted windows. It looked clean and well-maintained but grudgingly so, the privet-hedge trimmed but the strip of garden containing nothing more than a row of French marigolds, sparsely distributed, the front door, despite its brightly polished knocker, sombre in dark green paint.

Three dustbins in the front garden, under their own little wooden shelter, and a row of bell-pushes by the door suggested multi-occupancy. Finch pressed the bottom one labelled 'Mrs Townsend' and waited.

The door was eventually opened a scant three inches by a middle-aged woman who peered round the crack and said 'Yes?' in the tone of one expecting an unwelcome visitor in the shape of a brush salesman or a Jehovah's Witness.

'Mrs Townsend?' Finch asked pleasantly. Had he been wearing a hat, he would have raised it. She had an air of rigid respectability, grey hair stiffly set, a cameo brooch, like an oval Cyclopean eye, pinned to the neck of her blouse. He could only be grateful that he had on his good suit and that his shoes were polished. 'I'm a friend of Mrs Laud, Mr Dixon's sister. I wonder if I could have a word with you about her brother?'

He had already decided on the way there not to present himself in his professional capacity but rather as a family friend. After all, it was an unofficial inquiry. Face to face with Mrs Townsend, he realized it had been a wise choice. Any mention of the word 'police' would have made her even more suspicious and on her guard.

As it was, she pressed her lips together at the inconvenience of his request although she opened the door another few inches and said unwillingly, 'You'd better come in then, I suppose, although,' showing him into the front room, 'I can't tell you much more about Mr Dixon than I've already written in my letter to Mrs Laud.'

The room was as neat and as unwelcoming as he had anticipated. As she indicated an armchair where he would be permitted to sit, Finch took a few rapid and surreptitious glances about him, noting the three piece suite covered in dark-mottled moquette and more gloomy patterns in the carpet and on the walls. The only bright objects in the room were a collection of brasses on the mantelshelf but even those were arranged joylessly, like trophies she was obliged to display rather than as ornaments to give pleasure.

She was saying, 'As I told Mrs Laud, Mr Dixon went away about five months ago. As usual, he sent a note and enough money to cover the rent for March. I waited until the second week in April, but, as I didn't hear anything more from him, I re-let his room.'

' "As usual"?' Finch repeated, picking up one of her earlier remarks. 'Has Mr Dixon been away before?'

'Oh, yes; on and off quite often; usually for only a few days although he was away once for six weeks but, as he wrote saying he still wanted his room and the rent was up to date, I kept it for him. But this last time, I really couldn't be expected to oblige. I had to find another tenant. Since my husband's death, I rely on the money from the bed-sitters.'

It was possible to read into her remarks and the tone of voice in which she spoke them, a little of Mrs Townsend's own background. Widowed and left with a large house but not enough money to maintain it, she had been forced unwillingly into letting out part of it as furnished rooms. But it was Hal Dixon's story he had come there to hear, not hers.

He said, 'And you've no idea where he went?'

'Only that he's staying with friends. He never left any forwarding address although he did once mention they lived somewhere down on the south coast; Bournemouth, I think he said.'

'So there was no address on the letters he sent?'

'No; they weren't proper letters in fact; just a few lines written on one of those notelet cards you can buy in packets.'

Her voice implied not only impatience at his questions but disapproval of Mr Dixon's informal method of communication.

Finch would have liked to ask more about these notes – their exact contents, the dates when they were received, whether or not she had noticed any details of the franking on the envelopes but he hesitated to do so in case he aroused her suspicions further. It was not the kind of inquiry that a mere friend of the family might be expected to make. There would be a more suitable occasion for such questions should Mr Dixon's apparent disappearance ever be made official, which he very much doubted. The fact that an elderly man had chosen of his own free will, it seemed, to stay with friends on the south coast without informing his landlady or his sister of their address was hardly likely to be the cause of a police investigation.

Instead, he continued with a casual air, hoping to

inveigle her into a more gossipy response although judging by her expression and the manner in which she was sitting with knees and ankles firmly pressed together, he was wasting his time, 'Tell me more about Mr Dixon. I've never met him, you see. I only know his sister.'

'Well, he was pleasant enough, I suppose,' Mrs Townsend ventured. 'I had no reason to complain.' It appeared to be all she was prepared to say. As Finch waited, head cocked encouragingly, she continued a little unwillingly, 'Respectable. Nicely spoken. I only let my rooms to older tenants, the sort I can rely on not to waste the hot water or leave the landing lights on all night.' As an afterthought, she added, 'I think he may have come into money.'

As a piece of information, it was like finding a nugget of gold. Finch immediately brightened.

'Really? What made you think that?'

'He began to go out more often. He's always enjoyed dressing up for an evening out somewhere, in the West End, I imagine – carnation in his buttonhole, that sort of thing. A bit of a dandy, to tell you the truth, but I understand he'd been on the stage.'

It was a long parenthesis for Mrs Townsend, spoken as if, now that Mr Dixon was no longer her tenant, she was free to voice her criticism not only of his antecedents but of the destination of his evening jaunts as well. Finch waited, still smiling, head cocked, for her to get to the point.

'But he'd begun to find the walk round to the tube station too much for him. Then, about three or four years ago, he started going out again once or twice a week on a regular basis – by mini-cab.'

'Mini-cab?' Finch exclaimed, echoing her disapproving surprise at the extravagance of such a mode of transport.

'I'd hear him ringing up to order one. There's a

pay-phone in the hall and, having the downstairs rooms, I couldn't help overhearing. Besides, the drivers used to come to the front door sometimes to ask for him.'

'And you think that he might have come in for a legacy?'

But he had lost her. Mrs Townsend folded her lips, obviously regretting her brief burst of loquacity.

'I really couldn't say,' she replied.

Finch took the hint and got to his feet.

'Thank you very much, Mrs Townsend. It's been most kind of you to spare the time. Naturally, his sister's worried about him but perhaps he'll get in touch with her soon – from Bournemouth, didn't you say?'

As he was speaking, she showed him out into the hall where, ignoring his remarks, intended to disarm, she suddenly announced, 'There's his suitcase. I hope you're going to take that with you, now you're here. I really can't be expected to go on keeping it indefinitely.'

The luggage. He had forgotten it and was surprised when he helped Mrs Townsend to retrieve it from the cupboard under the stairs. It was a large, old-fashioned case, evidently full, judging by its weight, and battered from travelling round the variety theatres with the Singing Lauds, he imagined, an assumption which seemed to be borne out by the remains of luggage labels still adhering to its sides and lid.

'He left all this?' he asked.

Mrs Townsend folded her lips more tightly.

'Expecting me not only to pack it up but to store it for him.'

'But what did he take away with him when he left?' Finch continued, allowing his surprise and curiosity to show.

'Just the one bag. I answered the door when the cab-driver called for him. Mr Dixon was coming down the stairs. He had a small attaché case with him and his raincoat over his arm. Naturally, I don't interfere with my tenants' rooms, except to look in once a week to leave fresh linen and to make sure they're being kept as clean as they should be. But once Mr Dixon's rent was overdue and I was thinking of re-letting, I went through his things and packed them up. They're all there, down to the paperback book on his bedside table. His sister won't find anything's missing.'

'I'm sure she won't,' Finch replied, smiling and nodding as Mrs Townsend opened the front door.

Heaving the suitcase on to the back seat of the car, he drove round the corner where he parked and where, out of sight of Mrs Townsend's front windows, he tried the catches. The case was unlocked and, lifting back the lid, he made a quick search of its contents.

Displayed on the top, no doubt to convey Mrs Townsend's disapproval, was the book of which she had spoken, a cheap, secondhand copy of a thriller with a smoking gun and a blonde in diaphanous camiknickers displayed on the cover.

The rest of the contents were tame enough; mostly clothes, including three suits, several shirts, underwear, two pairs of pyjamas, a dressing-gown with lapels of red, quilted silk; all of good quality, the suits bearing the labels of West End tailors, but most of them a little shabby and old-fashioned although the pyjamas and some of the shirts looked fairly new – and expensive, too.

Tucked in under the shirts was a small, velvet-lined jeweller's box which, when he opened it, Finch saw contained a pair of gold cufflinks inscribed with the letters H.D.

With the box open in his hand, Finch stared out through the windscreen at the scene in front of him, seeing neither the street, nor the houses, nor the dark brick Methodist church on the corner.

Hal Dixon's luggage posed more questions than it

answered. He had been absent now for five months. How had he managed for all that time when he seemed to have left the majority of his clothes at Mrs Townsend's? According to her, he had taken with him only a small attaché case, containing presumably his shaving-gear and perhaps a pair of pyjamas and a clean shirt which suggested that he had intended going away for a few days. But why then had he sent the rent for a further month and yet had said nothing in the accompanying note to Mrs Townsend about the reason for his change of plans nor made arrangements for more clothes to be forwarded to him?

There could, of course, be a perfectly logical explanation. Illness might account for his continuing absence, as Kitty herself had first thought when her brother had failed to get in touch with her for her birthday. As for the lack of any forwarding address, that could be put down to a natural reluctance on Hal Dixon's part to let his landlady, or even his sister, know exactly who the friends were with whom he appeared to have stayed on more than one occasion and with whom he was now presumably living. The fact, too, that Hal Dixon appeared to have come into money could also be accounted for rationally. He could very easily have been left a legacy, as Mrs Townsend seemed to think, perhaps by some admirer from his Variety days – a more likely explanation than a lucky flutter at the races which would have had to be a considerable sum if it had kept him in mini-cabs for the past three or four years, not to mention the new clothes and the jaunts to the West End.

All the same, Finch felt vaguely disturbed by the air of secrecy which seemed to surround Hal Dixon's activities, generated more by Dixon himself than the actual circumstances. An old gentleman is left some money and goes off to stay with friends. There was nothing inherently suspicious in that. What had given rise to concern was the fact that the two people who should have been informed of his whereabouts, his landlady and, more particularly, his sister seemed to have been kept deliberately in the dark. It was this which caused the nagging doubt.

Not that there was anything Finch could do about it. He could hardly involve the Bournemouth police, if that was where Hal Dixon was now living, in the search for an elderly man who, for reasons best known to himself, seemed to prefer no-one knew his present address. No doubt, he or the friends of his would eventually get in touch with Kitty.

As he started the car, it occurred to Finch that possibly the old boy had a secret love-nest somewhere down on the south coast where he kept an aged mistress. The idea amused him but less than it might have done on any other occasion. He was on his way to see Marion Greave, the thought of which filled him with that mixture of high hope and half-fearful, half-exultant anticipation which he last remembered feeling to this pitch of intensity as an adolescent. It was ridiculous, of course, but it put him in no mood to laugh at any form of love, even that imagined between a seventy-nine-year-old man and his putative mistress.

He arrived at her hotel much too early; a whole hour, in fact. After he parked the car, he walked past it on the other side of the road, looking straight ahead, apart from one quick oblique glance at it, and trying to appear like any other passer-by in case she might happen to look out of one of the windows and see him. That, too, was absurd. But he felt reassured that the hotel did really exist and that he had not come to the wrong address.

It was in Bloomsbury, in a side street near the British Museum, and, having established its exact location to his satisfaction, he went off and had lunch in a sandwich bar and then wandered about looking in the windows of the second-hand and antiquarian bookshops.

At four minutes before the appointed hour, the time he had estimated it would take him to walk back to her hotel by two o'clock, he set off in its direction in a state of surprised jubilation that the moment when he would see her again, so long anticipated, had actually arrived and that the traffic and the people and the buildings, even the pigeons walking along the gutter and fluttering upward whenever a car passed too near, were so ordinary and yet so transfigured.

The hotel, which he had hardly registered apart from its name when he had walked past it earlier, was, he saw now, attractively discreet with window-boxes of pink geraniums and trailing ivy and two bay trees in terracotta pots on either side of the front door. As he went up the steps, he noticed how their thick leaves glistened in the sun as if they had been painted over with light.

In contrast, the foyer was shadowy. He had a fleeting impression of a rich, dark carpet, soft underfoot, walls covered with a fleur-de-lis pattern, a white-painted staircase going up on the left with a small gilt lift beside it.

The next moment, he saw Marion, who had risen to her feet from a chair beside the reception desk, coming towards him to shake hands and saying something in greeting to which he replied although he had no idea of the exact words either of them spoke.

She looked, at first, unchanged; suntanned, of course, from her recent holiday in Crete but otherwise unaltered – the same short, dark, glossy hair; the same smile which puckered up her eyes and which gave her face, not conventionally pretty – even he recognized this – its amused appeal.

But, after the first moments of greeting when their hands parted and they stood a little awkwardly together, he was aware of a change in her. She looked, despite the smile and the eyes, subtly sad. He could not define it exactly but some shadow seemed to overlay her. A disappointment, perhaps. In him? The thought made him more awkward than he might otherwise have been.

She was saying, 'Shall we go out, Jack? It's too hot to stay in the hotel.'

Outside on the pavement, she suggested they went to the British Museum which, she explained, she hadn't had time to visit since her arrival late the previous day. Finch agreed, hiding his disappointment. He had hoped for the opportunity of a more intimate conversation with her which a public place like the British Museum was unlikely to supply.

As they walked in that direction, it occurred to him that this was the reason she had suggested it. He had the impression that she was keeping him at arm's length but in a kindly manner, unlike Sergeant Mill's treatment of Kitty Laud the day before. All the same, she talked almost too animatedly, describing Crete – the countryside had been superb – Knossos, fascinating – she really must read a great deal more about the Minoan civilization. Did he know anything about it?

'Not much,' Finch admitted. He felt obscurely *de trop*, without knowing exactly why. He noticed she said nothing about the colleague who had accompanied her on the holiday and never once, although he listened carefully, used the pronoun 'we'.

They crossed the wide forecourt which fronted the museum, crowded with tourists feeding the pigeons, taking photographs of one another or merely sitting on the benches in the sun, and passed through the revolving doors into the entrance hall where, to his surprise, she turned to the left towards the Assyrian galleries although, from her earlier comments about Knossos, he had imagined she might have chosen some other civilization closer to it in style and spirit.

32

For several minutes they walked about in silence, contemplating the sculptures, so militantly aggressive, so superbly self-assured. It was clearly not a part of the museum which attracted much attention for, apart from themselves and a few other visitors, the rooms were empty.

Finally they paused in a side gallery in front of a lighted cabinet full of artefacts where, after a rapid glance to left and right to make sure no-one was within earshot, she suddenly said, 'I think I ought to tell you, Jack, that I've been having an affair.'

She did not look at him as she spoke but continued to gaze straight ahead.

He said in quick distress, 'My dear, you don't have to tell me anything.'

'But I want to,' she replied. This time she turned to face him and he saw that the shadow which he had noticed before had deepened, leaving her features sharper and more angular. 'We've always been honest with one another in the past. I don't want to deceive you.' At that moment, someone entered the gallery and she said abruptly, 'Shall we move on?'

They walked together into other rooms and up a staircase past more sculpture and displays of pottery, into the Egyptian gallery with its painted mummy cases and through the Romano-British section while she told her story.

Finch listened in silence. It came to him fragmented, a sentence here in front of a caseful of Celtic jewellery, a few words when they paused momentarily to look at some bronze daggers before other visitors approached, forcing her to fall silent. Added together, the account was, he supposed bleakly, ordinary enough. One like it must have been repeated many times to many different people. But that knowledge did not prevent him from being cut to the heart all the same.

She had fallen in love with a colleague – a paediatrician at the hospital where she worked. Married, of course. That went almost without saying. They had been lovers for the past year, an affair which had culminated in their holiday together in Crete. It was there that she had decided to end it.

And when he asked her why, she replied, 'Because we were so happy. Absurd, isn't it, Jack? But I couldn't bear the thought of him going back to his wife and family. He had no intention of divorcing her and marrying me. Suddenly I couldn't take the lies and deceit any longer. We'd had to be so careful about the arrangements, travelling by different planes, making a joke about the coincidence we'd both be in the Mediterranean at the same time although I told everyone I was going to Cyprus. His excuse was that he wanted a couple of weeks alone to write up some research he'd been doing. Out there, it seemed so sordid and underhand. I can't explain why. Perhaps it had something to do with the sea and the sunlight.'

She gave him a wry, lop-sided smile as they stood side by side in front of a sloping cabinet of illuminated manuscripts, the cover to protect them from the light turned back, their faces reflected dimly in the glass above the pages laid open for their inspection. They had come almost full circle – physically in their tour of the museum for, through the tall doorway, Finch could see the entrance hall with its brightly-lit shop and the crowds of people moving to and fro; conversationally as well. The story had almost all been told.

Finch found himself gazing down at a Book of Hours with its tiny, exquisite illustrations of the Annunciation, and wondered what to say. At any moment, someone might enter, forcing them to move on, and the opportunity would be lost. And the loss would be more than the mere immediate chance to reply. Once they passed

34

through the doorway into the bustle of the hall, she would say goodbye at the entrance and walk away and the chance of ever seeing her again would go with her.

He said, concentrating on the ornate black lettering and the little blobs of gold leaf, so thick that they stood out proud above the vellum page, 'It doesn't make any difference, Marion. To us, I mean. To our relationship,' although, as he said it, he wondered what the hell he meant by 'relationship'. They had none; not in the sense that she meant it when she spoke of the man who had been her lover.

He had met her, fallen in love with her, proposed to her. And she had turned him down. Since then there had been nothing except an exchange of letters.

He had meant to say that he still loved her and, for that reason, would be prepared to settle for anything, rather than lose her altogether.

She had rested one hand on the edge of the cabinet and he put out his own hand to take her wrist.

'Please,' he said.

She was silent for several moments. To anyone entering the gallery, they would have appeared like any other pair of visitors, a rather ordinary couple, the woman in a green linen dress, dark hair tucked behind her ears, bending down to examine an illuminated script, the man, middle-aged and stocky, drawing her attention to some detail by touching her on the hand.

She straightened up.

'I don't know, Jack,' she replied. 'I have to work this out in my own way. I'm going back to Leeds tomorrow to hand in my resignation. After that I honestly don't know. There's a job advertised at St Margaret's, here in London. I might apply for it. Or I might go abroad. But I feel – and I don't mean this unkindly – I do genuinely value our friendship – that I need to be alone for a while to think things over. Give me time.'

She turned away before he could reply, walking quickly ahead of him, small and slim and very purposeful.

They parted as he had imagined, at the entrance of the museum, under the huge portico.

'Let's say goodbye here, Jack,' she said.

In the sunlight, very bright after the cool, shaded interior of the museum, she looked suddenly older and more strained. He saw the gathering of fine lines round her eyes and the small V-shaped crease between her brows.

He stood on the step above her, both of them hesitating to shake hands, she perhaps because the physical contact would imply some form of intimacy, he because the gesture was too final.

The next moment she had gone and, although he managed for the first few seconds to keep her in sight among the crowds, he lost her before she had crossed the forecourt and reached the tall wrought-iron gates.

3

At the same time that Finch stood watching Marion Greave walk away from him towards the gates of the British Museum, another couple were strolling across the lawn of a country house, under the cedar trees. They made an ill-assorted pair – the old man, legs stiffly splayed, jerking himself along with the aid of two sticks; the young woman, slim-hipped and boyish in jeans and a blue and white checked shirt, pacing slowly at his side although her contemporary, androgynous appearance was off-set by the femininity of her features and the cloud of shoulder-length dark hair which, because of the heat of the afternoon, was tied loosely back with a petersham ribbon.

Yes, she has the Aston good looks, Uncle Rollo decided, peering at her obliquely as he toiled on. First Constance. Then Rowena. And now Claudia. That hair. Those eyes. Extraordinary! Like one of Rossetti's women only finer-boned. Pity about the trousers, though. A damned pity.

They reached the bench at the far side of the lawn where Claudia helped him to sit down, propping his sticks against its arm. Facing them was the cream-painted, stucco façade of Beechcroft, Private Residential Home for the Elderly, where Uncle Rollo now lived. Along its terrace some of its other residents, less mobile than Uncle Rollo, could be seen displayed in wheelchairs among the tubs of glaring yellow and pink antirrhinums, Matron's figure among them, conspicuous in her white uniform, bending down solicitously to tuck a blanket in here or rearrange a cushion there.

'Poisonous bitch,' Uncle Rollo remarked with unexpected vehemence. 'She's only come out to look at you. Wonders what you're doing visiting me on a Wednesday afternoon. So why are you here, my dear? Something out of the ordinary's brought you down from London, hasn't it?'

Claudia turned to him with relief, reassured that the walk, which had been his idea, hadn't exhausted him as she had feared; glad, too, that the subject of her visit had been raised by him. But there never had been any beating about the bush with Uncle Rollo. All the same, it wasn't going to be easy to break the news to him.

He was seventy-eight; a once tall, rangy man, now bent over with arthritis but still managing to preserve that quality of alert, shrewd directness and the trick of looking at her sideways as he spoke, which she remembered from childhood, his lean, beaky profile like some intelligent bird of prey's.

Strictly speaking, he was only an honorary uncle, not a blood relation at all but, having been a boyhood friend and near neighbour of her grandfather for many years, he had become part of the family.

Even if she had wanted to, it was impossible to deceive him and she said, matching his directness with her own, 'It's grandfather, Uncle Rollo. Great-aunt Constance phoned me at lunchtime. He's very ill. I've arranged to go down to Howlett's to see him but I thought I'd call on you first to let you know.'

'Ah!' said Uncle Rollo. He was silent for several moments, then he asked, 'What's the matter with him?'

'He had a stroke yesterday morning. I gather he's not expected to live very long.' There seemed no way to break it to him more gently although she added, 'I'm so sorry it's bad news.'

In reply, he said abruptly, 'Give me my sticks,' and when she demurred, he went on, 'No, I wouldn't rather sit down, Claudia! I spend all my life these days sitting down. Let's walk.'

She helped him to his feet, waiting while he arranged his sticks before, she modifying her pace to his, they set off once more across the grass.

'So Constance is staying at Howlett's?' Uncle Rollo asked. 'I assume with that second husband of hers and his ghastly son?'

'Yes, I believe Teddy and Basil are both there.'

Uncle Rollo gave her one of his oblique looks.

'You realize that it was because of that damned Basil that your grandfather and I quarrelled?'

Claudia had heard the story several times before but she said 'Yes' encouragingly, knowing that, even more today, he would need to repeat it in order to explain or justify or to expiate some of the old bitterness which still surrounded the dispute which had separated the former friends.

'It was when I was thinking of selling up the farm and retiring,' Uncle Rollo began, using almost exactly the same words with which he had recounted the circumstances on other occasions. 'I'd arranged to buy an annuity with the capital; nothing spectacular but it would've given me enough in the way of income to cover the cost of my retirement. Naturally, I talked it over with your grandfather; put him in the picture. But he must have spoken of it to Basil. That annoyed me for a start. Edgar had no business discussing my affairs with an outsider. In the 'fifties, long before you were born, my dear, when he was thinking of selling off the gatehouse and some of the land, I didn't go blabbing about it to every Tom, Dick or Harry. Advised him against it, of course. Never part with land, I told him. It's a damned good investment. Not that he took any notice. Went

39

ahead and sold anyway. Strapped for cash at the time, I believe. But that's neither here nor there. To get back to the point. The next thing I knew, I had first Constance and then Teddy on the phone, advising me to invest in some scheme or other of Basil's which would bring me in a higher interest.

'Then your grandfather brought the subject up one evening when I'd called at Howlett's. So I had it out with him. Lost my temper, I'm afraid. It's none of your confounded business, I told him. He called me a stubborn old fool and we haven't spoken to each other since. Pity. But I blame Basil. And Constance, too, to a certain extent. A very strong-minded woman, your great-aunt. Likes to get her own way. Felt she had some right to meddle because we'd known each other from childhood although she probably meant it for the best.' He was silent for several moments and then continued, glancing sideways again at Claudia, this time with a wry look, half-amused, half-shamefaced, 'Damned good-looking woman in her day, your Great-aunt Constance. Don't mind admitting I fancied her myself. Told you about it, have I?'

'No, Uncle Rollo,' Claudia replied. He had but it didn't matter. Like the circumstances surrounding the quarrel with her grandfather, she could understand his need to turn over these old memories and, by examining them, perhaps come to terms with them at last.

'Proposed to her once,' he went on. 'In the garden at Howlett's by the pool. Lovely evening, I remember; her twenty-first birthday. Cleared it first with her father, of course – your great-grandfather. Got his blessing. But she turned me down. Married that first husband of hers instead – what was his name? I forget now. The old memory isn't what it used to be. Son of some minor baronet. Frightful wart. Looked just like the young Oscar Wilde. Pots of money, of course, otherwise Constance wouldn't have married him. Shrewd woman, Constance, where money's concerned. Not that it did her any good. Damned fellow spent it all on cards and drink. Died of the DTs in Monte Carlo before the war.'

He paused for a moment, resting on his sticks, his beaky profile turned to look at the house, his expression contemptuous, but whether at the fate of Great-aunt Constance's first husband, dying at Monte Carlo, or the prospect of his own death in the hygienic, highly-polished surroundings of Beechcroft, Claudia could not tell.

'Then the war broke out,' Uncle Rollo resumed, grasping his sticks and plodding forward once more across the lawn. 'Constance was kept busy in London driving an ambulance for the Red Cross while the War Office in their wisdom saw fit to pack me off abroad. And when I came back, it was too late.'

He broke off, lowering his head to concentrate on placing one foot in front of the other, leaving Claudia to fill in the details of his war-time posting as an Intelligence officer to India where, in the 'twenties and early 'thirties, he had spent several years as a tea planter, before coming back to England in 1936, on the death of his own father, to run the family farm at Easeden, near Howlett's. His return to England had been the occasion of the proposal, already described, to Constance, the younger sister of Claudia's grandfather.

Also unmentioned but implied in his last remark was Great-aunt Constance's second marriage after the war to Teddy Nugent, a wealthy widower and father of Basil. From earlier conversations with Uncle Rollo, Claudia had gathered that Teddy had made his fortune from dubious wartime black-market activities – that is, if Uncle Rollo's interpretation of the source of the Nugent money could be relied on – as well as land speculation during the building boom which followed.

But, as Uncle Rollo had said, Great-aunt Constance had

always been shrewd about where she bestowed her affections.

Uncle Rollo had never married. After the war, he had resumed the management of the family farm, left to the care of his mother and an elderly bailiff during his absence in India, until his own retirement seven years before when, crippled with arthritis, he had at last reluctantly conceded that he was beaten and, having sold up, returned to Beechcroft.

With an abrupt reversion to the original subject of her grandfather's illness, Uncle Rollo suddenly asked, 'What about your mother? Have you managed to get in touch with her? About your grandfather, I mean.' He cleared his throat awkwardly. 'I suppose if poor old Edgar's really on his last legs, she ought to be at his bedside. Only daughter and all that. Where is she now? Still in Florida with that Latin lover of hers?'

'I'm not sure,' Claudia confessed. Knowing Uncle Rollo's secret disappointment in her mother, the beautiful Rowena, Claudia was anxious to avoid too detailed an answer although some explanation would have to be given. 'I tried phoning their apartment after Great-aunt Constance rang me but the maid said they'd left for Jamaica three days ago for some fashion show Gino's involved with. I've telexed the hotel they're staying at, asking her to get in touch with me at Howlett's.'

'Pity,' Uncle Rollo replied.

To Claudia's relief, he said nothing more although the one word seemed to sum it all up, not just Claudia's failure to contact Rowena at such a crucial time but her parents' disastrous marriage and subsequent divorce, as well as her mother's succession of lovers, including the last, Gino, twelve years her junior, and in fact a talented fashion photographer; of Italian extraction, it was true, but hardly meriting Uncle Rollo's disapproval of him on that score alone, even though Claudia understood that his anger and disappointment could never be directed at Rowena herself but only at the men she had been involved with. This disapprobation included Claudia's own father who, in Uncle Rollo's eyes, had married her when she was far too young and had never properly appreciated her.

In order to forestall any query regarding her father, Claudia said quickly, 'I rang Daddy, too, but he won't be able to come. He's got some important meeting coming up in Brussels.'

They had reached the far side of the lawn where they sat down again in a small rustic summerhouse, its open side facing Beechcroft which Uncle Rollo contemplated in silence for several moments before remarking with that characteristic abruptness of his which had become more pronounced as he grew older, 'You're like her, you know.'

Rowena? Claudia wondered. Or was he referring again to Great-aunt Constance?

It could have been either because he continued, 'The Aston women always were a fine-looking bunch. Good figures. Lovely eyes. And style. That's what I admire in a woman – style. Can't beat it. Take Constance. She could dress in a potato sack and still look like a queen. Your mother, too. I remember her wedding reception at Howlett's.' And he repeated the word 'Pity!' with a sigh before adding, 'Don't make their mistakes, my dear.'

'Mistakes?' Claudia asked, startled by the depth of concern in his voice.

'Marrying the wrong man for the wrong reason: Constance for money; your mother for romance.'

'Is that why she married my father? For romance?'

It was difficult to believe it now; certainly of her father, Ralph Byrne, a senior Foreign Office man, middle-aged and conventional, who, for the sake of his family, had given up the diplomatic life of moving from one foreign posting to the next for a more settled career with the European Commission.

Of her mother, with her succession of lovers, it was easier to imagine. All her life, Claudia realized, Rowena had been searching for the exotic, in clothes, in places, in people, especially men.

'Older man, your father,' Uncle Rollo was continuing in explanation. 'Experienced. Serious. Dark good looks. Had a touch of the Anthony Edens about him. They met in London. He was just back from a posting in South America, I remember. Foreign embassies, diplomatic garden parties, all that bilge. Swept her off her feet. Only eighteen. I blame him. Shouldn't have expected her to settle down. Brussels!'

He gave the last word the same tone of outraged contempt with which he had earlier spoken of Monte Carlo.

Claudia was silent. His remarks touched her more deeply than she cared to admit. There was a quality of Rowena in herself, she realized. Why, after leaving Oxford, having graduated in Modern Languages, had she chosen to spend two years travelling abroad instead of finding herself a sensible job and starting a career? It had been fun, of course, staying with friends, first in Rome and then Athens, where she had met a party of Canadian students, among them Ross, and had joined them back-packing round the Greek islands. Fun, too, at least to begin with, to become Ross's lover. But Rowena wouldn't have made the mistake of falling in love with him nor of hoping for some commitment on his part.

It was still humiliating to remember how, the trip over, he had taken her to the airport at Corfu, kissed her goodbye and simply walked away, as if she, too, like her luggage had been checked in and could now be conveniently forgotten.

As if following her thoughts, Uncle Rollo suddenly

remarked, 'You ought to be thinking of marriage, Claudia.'

It was impossible that he knew about Ross. It had to be a shot in the dark. Or was it? Despite his age, Uncle Rollo was still very shrewd and observant. She was aware that he was studying her with that keen, oblique glance of his.

With a serenity which she did not really feel, she replied, 'Should I, darling? But I'm in no hurry to settle down, you know.'

'Sorry, my dear.' The apology came with his usual abruptness although he put one of his old, mottled hands on hers. 'Shouldn't have said that, Claudia. None of my damned business. Impertinent of me. But I have only your best interests at heart. I want to see you happy.' With another of his sudden changes of subject, although in this case the two were inextricably linked in Claudia's mind, he asked, 'So you're back in England for good now? No more gallivanting off to foreign parts?'

She had already explained to him on her previous visit three weeks before, shortly after her return from Corfu and on her way, on that occasion also, to Howlett's, that she had found herself a bed-sitter in Notting Hill and a temporary job in a bookshop, while she looked round for something more permanent. She doubted if he had forgotten; his memory seemed unimpaired. She assumed he asked the question partly to turn the conversation to a less personal topic and partly to confirm the facts, much in the same way as he had repeated the circumstances of the quarrel with her grandfather or his old passion for Great-aunt Constance, as if, as he grew older, he was anxious to establish for his own peace of mind that he could, after all, remember all the details.

'Yes, Uncle Rollo,' Claudia assured him. 'I'm working in London now, although Daddy's suggested I apply for

45

a post with the EEC. At the moment, I'm not sure what I'll do.'

'You mean because of this business with Edgar?' Uncle Rollo asked gruffly.

Although her grandfather's illness was only one minor aspect of Claudia's uncertainty about her future, she nodded as if in agreement.

'Does he ever mention me?' Uncle Rollo continued, this time not looking in her direction but staring fixedly across the lawn towards the terrace where two women assistants were already wheeling some of the chair-bound residents indoors in readiness, Claudia supposed, for tea.

It was better to keep as near as possible to the truth. He would only guess it from her voice or expression. But her reply would have to be suitably censored.

'No, not really, darling. I've noticed he's got much older and more frail since I've been away. Talking seems to tire him. And he never seems to want to refer to the past.'

Which wasn't strictly accurate. On the last occasion when she had seen her grandfather three weeks before, he had indeed talked about the past but not about Uncle Rollo. He had spoken instead of Helen, his wife and Claudia's grandmother, who had died before Claudia had been born, appealing to Great-aunt Constance for confirmation of his recollections.

The three of them had been seated in the drawing-room at Howlett's, Grandfather, despite the warmth of the afternoon, tucked up beneath a tartan travelling rug, his eyes turned towards the garden, one frail hand lying on top of the cover like a leaf which had blown in through the open window.

'I was thinking of the engagement party my father gave for Helen and me before the war. Do you remember it, Constance? The marquee out there on the lawn and the policeman on duty at the gates to direct the cars?'

And Great-aunt Constance had replied, 'Of course I remember it, Edgar. There were coloured lights in all the trees and champagne for breakfast. Oh, Claudia, they don't give parties like that any more!' – turning on her great-niece a look of such vivid and yearning nostalgia that Claudia had believed her.

Uncle Rollo was asking in a gruff voice to cover up his concern, 'Who's Edgar's doctor these days? Still that Callender chap?'

'No, not old Dr Callender. His son.'

'Robert?'

'Yes, I think that's his name.'

'Good thing!' Uncle Rollo announced emphatically. 'Old Callender must be seventy-one if he's a day. Long past it.'

It was hardly the moment to tell him that old Callender, as Uncle Rollo called him, had died two years before at the age of sixty-nine, nine years younger, in fact, than Uncle Rollo himself.

Instead, she replied, 'I don't think grandfather has needed to see any doctor until fairly recently. He's been so fit. Great-aunt Constance said he was still pottering about in the garden most mornings until he went down with bronchitis the winter after I went abroad. Since then, he hasn't been out of the house much, except to sit on the lawn if the weather's been fine and to be taken for an occasional drive to the village. And now, of course . . .'

The sound of a gong, announcing tea-time, came floating across from Beechcroft, saving her from any further reference to her grandfather's latest and presumably fatal illness. As a further reminder of the time, matron's white-clad figure came to the edge of the terrace where, making a megaphone of her hands, she called across to them.

'Tea-ee!'

'Stupid woman!' Uncle Rollo remarked. 'Treats me as

47

if I'm deaf.' Raising his own voice, he shouted back, 'All right! All right! I heard the damned gong.'

'I think we ought to go,' Claudia said, helping him to adjust his sticks and get to his feet. 'I promised Great-aunt Constance I'd be at Howlett's by four o'clock and there's still another twenty-minutes drive.'

They began to plod back again across the lawn, Uncle Rollo walking painfully at first as he got used to the unaccustomed motion after sitting for so long.

'Blasted legs!' he commented and then, without any further preamble, he added, 'Don't expect too much from your grandfather's estate, my dear. There's the house of course, Howlett's, but I doubt if there's much else. Your great-grandfather spent most of the family fortune having it built. Charming man but not very prudent where money was concerned. Wanted to make too big a splash socially. Pity, that. The Astons were rich enough before the war; hardly Rockefellers, of course, although your great-grandfather always believed they'd eventually make it into the millionaire class. That's the trouble with your family, Claudia. They're odd about money. Either like it too much, like Constance, or spend it too quickly like your great-grandfather. Sometimes both. Then, after the war . . .'

He broke off, unsure how much Claudia knew about the Aston story. Probably not all of it, he realized. Neither Constance nor Rowena, and certainly not Edgar, would have told her the whole truth. He was not even certain of the entire facts himself although he could make a shrewd guess at some of them.

The Aston fortune had been spent, and not all of it, as he had led Claudia to believe, on building Howlett Hall and entertaining the local gentry. On what exactly, he had no idea. Gambling was one possibility; if not on anything as crude as cards and horse-racing, then on unwise investments. Such an explanation would fit in

48

with what he knew about old Philip Aston, Edgar's father and Claudia's great-grandfather. He had been more than odd about money. He had been obsessed with the stuff; not just in the making and spending of it but on where it had come from. In his case, from trade; more specifically from the manufacture of farm implements. And when Philip Aston had set up the family business in the early 1900s, trade, whether you sold meat or threshing machines, was socially beyond the pale. Old Aston had been keenly aware of this fact. That Aston pride of his, which Edgar had inherited, had suffered badly. But money talks, as he had been fond of saying, and the bigger the fortune, the more respectability you could buy with it, if not for yourself then for your children and grandchildren.

It was more than likely that the Aston money had gone in trying to realize this dream; not just on Howlett Hall and laying out the gardens, nor on buying the right education for Edgar and Constance but on speculating in stocks and shares in the hope of a quick financial killing by which all of them, Aston himself as well as his family and generations of Astons yet unborn, could lift themselves out of trade and into the carriage class.

But old Philip Aston had not taken into account two factors; three, if you counted his own death in 1942. One had been the war. Ironic to think that the war which had swept away so much of the old class-consciousness should have brought about a down-turn in the Aston fortunes. The firm had been requisitioned and turned over to making parts for tanks, not tractors. The other factor which Philip Aston couldn't have foreseen was Edgar's change of attitude. Once his father was dead and the old man's energy was no longer there to drive him on, Edgar had lost much of his own vigour, selling up the business soon after the end of the war to a consortium, and retiring to Howlett Hall to live the life of a country gentleman – another irony because old Aston, who had always aspired to such a role for his son, would have heartily disapproved of what he would have seen as his son's lack of ambition.

Edgar had had his reasons. Helen, his wife, had been ill with cancer; in fact she had died in the early fifties. It was understandable that he should want to spend as much time as possible with her. And the war itself had taken its toll. Howlett Hall had been overrun with evacuees. Edgar himself had worked long hours at the factory.

All the same, it didn't alter the fact that the Aston fortune had never recovered. The family luck had finally run out.

What was that saying about rags to riches and back to rags again in three generations?

Hardly rags in their case. That was something of an exaggeration. But it was about this time that Edgar had started to sell off the property piecemeal, first the gatehouse and then some of the land, much to his, Saxby's, disapproval.

God knows what had happened to that money either. Constance must have taken her share of it, of course. As for the rest, he assumed Edgar must have frittered it away, perhaps like his father on dubious stock market deals which that ghastly stepson of Constance's had put him up to.

So much for old Aston's dream of the family millions. Pity.

Claudia was saying, 'I hadn't thought about the money.'

They had reached the bottom of the terrace where a ramp for wheelchairs led up the slope. Here Uncle Rollo paused.

'You mustn't take any notice of me, Claudia. I never was the soul of tact. Always spoke my mind. That's what

50

caused the trouble with your grandfather. Shan't change now, I'm afraid. Too old a dog. But don't underestimate money, my dear. It makes a difference. And you can be damned sure Constance has thought about it. Some of the estate's in trust to her. Did you know that?'

'No, I didn't but it really doesn't matter.'

'Humph!' Uncle Rollo managed to inject a wealth of amused irony into the exclamation.

Matron appeared above them on the ramp, accompanied by one of the assistants and he said hurriedly, 'Say goodbye to me here, my dear. I'd rather you didn't see me being lugged into tea like an old sack.' Leaning forward, he kissed her and Claudia felt his lips, dry and oddly cold against her cheek. 'Marry,' he went on. 'You ought to. But marry wisely. And call on your way back to tell me how Edgar is. Give him my . . .'

But Claudia was not to hear the last word. Matron laid claim to him, bustling down the ramp to take his right arm at the same time giving Claudia a bright, social smile which nevertheless assessed her appearance and probably, too, priced her blouse and jeans.

'Come along, Mr Saxby,' she announced loudly, cutting through his parting remark. 'Tea-time. We mustn't keep everyone waiting, must we?'

What had he meant to add, Claudia wondered, as she walked round the side of the terrace to the front drive where she had parked her car. His best wishes? Commiseration? Love, even?

It was impossible to tell.

Although she knew that he would prefer her not to, she glanced back as she reached the corner of the house and saw him, as he had described, being hoisted slowly up the ramp between matron and her assistant, bowed over his sticks but still, to her delight, managing to maintain that old, proud lift to his head, despite the indignity.

4

Nevertheless, the visit to Uncle Rollo left Claudia feeling low-spirited, a state of mind which the twelve-mile drive to Howlett's only marginally alleviated.

The countryside was at its best, lying replete and fulfilled under the bright sunshine and the pristine blue of the sky which one always remembers of childhood summers. The harvest was not yet in and the wheat was heavy with grain while the roadside verges were tall with grasses and wild flowers, scabious, ox-eye daisies, meadow-sweet, which she also recalled from childhood visits to her grandfather's house, driving down from London in the Rover with her parents, her father silent and serious behind the wheel, her mother in a light, summery dress, turning round eagerly in the front passenger seat to draw her attention to some feature of the landscape which she, Rowena, remembered from her own childhood.

'Look, Claudia, darling! Becket's wood. And the mill. Nothing's changed.'

But it had.

Pity, as Uncle Rollo would have said.

Not physically so much, Claudia thought as she changed down into second gear to negotiate the narrow bridge over the river Howe. The mill-house was still there; materially improved, in fact. The new owners had restored it and painted it and installed a swimming-pool where once there had been a small, nettle-ridden paddock, the old rough-coated horse which had once occupied it banished to God knows where.

It was a sense of the past and the mutability of the present which seemed to overlay the landscape and weigh heavily on her own spirits. Grandfather dying. Her parents divorced. Uncle Rollo so old. Great-aunt Constance, too. Even Uncle Rollo's remarks about her great-grandfather added to her sense of roots which, although they still went deep, no longer had quite so firm a grasp on the earth as they had once possessed.

Howlett Hall did nothing to raise her mood. Built by her great-grandfather earlier in the century with part of the family fortune of which Uncle Rollo had also spoken, it stood apart from the small town of Howlett, a monument to that Edwardian sense of Aston pride which had found expression in solid red brick and slate, in jutting gables and stone-trimmed windows and in little touches of architectural exuberance, inherited from the earlier Victorian age, apparent in the stained glass panels in the landing window and the pair of stone lions guarding the steps up to the front door.

When new, it must have been impressive – handsome, sedate, imposing, with its extensive grounds and gate-house built of the same solid brick. As a child, she had loved it. Visiting grandfather at Howlett's had been like coming home.

But since her return to England, she had become aware of the slow process of change and decay which she had never really noticed before. The gate-house had been sold off years before; so, too, had much of the land. Now, as she turned into the drive, she saw that the shrubbery which bordered it was untrimmed, the lawn in front of the house reverting to meadow, while the Virginia creeper which covered the walls seemed even more rampant than on her previous visit three weeks earlier. Tendrils were beginning to insinuate themselves over the porch and across the slates of the roof.

Even the stone lions which, as a child, she had regarded

as the guardians of the place, had not been spared. Parking the car and going up the steps with her suitcase, she ran her hand over the one on the left, feeling the once-smooth surface flaked and worn from the depredations of frost and rain.

Edie, grandfather's housekeeper, met her in the hall. She, too, had altered with the house. Claudia, who had never thought before about her age, considering her, along with the rest of the place, as fixed and immutable, like the furniture which year after year never changed position, saw with a small shock that, even in the past few weeks, she had grown gaunt and old. Caring for Claudia's grandfather had clearly taken its toll.

She must be in her late sixties, Claudia thought, putting down her suitcase and shaking hands. Edie had never once offered to kiss her, not even when Claudia had been a child. Although she had lived in the house long before Claudia had been born, at the time when her grandmother was still alive and Rowena, Claudia's mother, had been a child herself, Edie still preserved that air of keeping her distance and knowing her place.

'So you've arrived,' Edie said in her usual, faintly disapproving voice, as if no young woman these days could be relied on to be punctual. 'I've put you in the blue bedroom. Miss Constance and the others are in the drawing-room. I'll fetch the tea.'

'How is grandfather?' Claudia asked. But Edie, her thin back still ramrod straight under her dark dress and her flowered, cross-over apron, had already moved away towards the passage which led to the kitchen. It was not her province to answer such personal questions regarding the family.

At that moment, the drawing-room door opened and Great-aunt Constance emerged. Or rather, made her entrance, Claudia thought with amusement and immediately felt her mood lift. Great-aunt Constance defied time. Although, like grandfather, she must have been in her seventies, she remained ageless.

Swooping on Claudia in a tinkle of bracelets and a rustling of silk, she enfolded her in her arms.

'Oh, darling! I'm so glad you've come. Poor Edgar! So dreadfully, dreadfully sad.'

'How is he?'

Releasing Claudia, Great-aunt Constance touched her handkerchief to the corners of her mouth, her eyes big with tragedy.

'Very ill indeed. The doctor's with him now. The last two days have been a nightmare. Thank God Teddy and I were here. Edie had the sense to phone us yesterday when he was first taken ill. We drove down at once although Basil only arrived this morning. But come and sit down, darling. You must be exhausted.'

It was a good performance, Claudia thought wryly, as she followed Great-aunt Constance into the drawing-room, although the judgement was unkind. Constance was so accustomed to treating life as a theatrical production that it was expecting too much of her to start behaving naturally now although, underneath the studied poses, the lines spoken as if on stage, she no doubt felt real grief for her older brother.

She took up her position immediately they entered, collapsing gracefully into a corner of the sofa, her feet, in their little high-heeled shoes, raised along its seat, cushions behind her head, leaving Claudia to make the rounds and greet the other occupants of the room.

Teddy Nugent, Great-aunt Constance's second husband, rose promptly to his feet, offering Claudia a warm, plump hand to shake. He was a small man, shorter than Constance, and comfortably padded as if years of good living had gradually built up the layers of flesh as a piece of furniture acquires a patina, bestowing a deep, rich gloss to its surface. She rather liked him for his twinkling air of bonhomie and the good-natured tolerance with which he treated Great-aunt Constance even though she bullied him dreadfully.

She was not so sure about his son, Basil, whom she did not know so well, having met him less frequently. As Great-aunt Constance's stepson, he was even more of an outsider than Teddy whom even Edie, usually so protective of the Aston tribal boundaries, had accepted. Claudia wondered why he was there.

She had never felt at ease with him, largely because he was not at ease with himself. Taller than his father and more loosely padded, he had about him the air of the plump child grown shrewd and middle-aged, no longer the butt of others but still wary of any real or imagined slight against his dignity. It made him an uncomfortable companion.

'So sorry about your grandfather, Claudia,' Teddy said, taking her hand in both of his with what seemed genuine warmth and commiseration.

Basil merely said, 'Good afternoon, Claudia,' and shook hands perfunctorily before sitting down again. As Claudia seated herself opposite her great-aunt, she noticed Basil's brief-case, a splendid black leather object with brass fittings and a security lock, propped up against the side of his chair. It struck an ominous note, indicating that, as a financial consultant and, according to Great-aunt Constance, something of an expert in the City, Basil was there less as a quasi-relative than as a business adviser.

To be in at the death? she wondered and was relieved when the door opened and Edie entered, pushing the tea-trolley.

'Edie, you darling! Tea!' Great-aunt Constance exclaimed as if she had been languishing all afternoon for just such sustenance. Immediately recovering, she sat upright and, shaking back her bracelets, began to fill the cups from the big silver teapot, beckoning Teddy forward to distribute them round the room.

It gave Claudia time to adjust to the others' presence and the room itself which had subtly changed from her childhood memories of it although the furniture it contained was exactly the same. Large, comfortable sofas and armchairs, covered in glazed rose-patterned chintz to match the curtains, were grouped on a pale green carpet, also rose-wreathed, with a surrounding area of polished parquet flooring, exactly equidistant on all sides. Cream walls hung with seascapes, two glass-fronted cabinets of china in the chimney alcoves and a huge gilt mirror over the marble fireplace, carved with Doric columns, brought cooler, more watery tones and reflections into a setting which might otherwise have been too flowery although Claudia had always loved that rose-patterned room which seemed redolent of summer even when the garden, glimpsed through the tall windows, was covered with snow.

But she saw how shabby, in fact, it was – the roses faded to pale pink, the pile of the carpet by the door worn thin with use, the window panes partly obscured by insidious little tendrils of Virginia creeper which seemed intent on engulfing the whole house.

In contrast, the occupants of the room seemed, despite their age, to be too modern and band-box fresh – Great-aunt Constance with her fashionably styled, blue-rinsed hair, her jewellery and smart silk dress, the men in dark city suits and crisp, white shirts. Observing them, Claudia realized suddenly that all three of them were dressed in a form of half-mourning; Constance in grey, relieved only by a long, floating scarf of pink chiffon worn to hide the signs of ageing in her throat which not even her masseur had managed to disguise, Teddy and Basil in plain, dark ties which might almost have been black.

Claudia, conscious of being too casual in jeans and

blouse, began to dread the funeral, should grandfather die.

Great-aunt Constance was remarking to the room in general, 'I really don't know how we would have managed without Edie. She's been an absolute godsend.'

The comment was made just as Edie was leaving the room and was clearly intended to be heard by her. It was, Claudia supposed, offered as a sop for all Edie had done for grandfather. All the same, it seemed too fulsome and out of character.

'You know, of course,' Great-aunt Constance continued as the door closed, 'that Edie's nephew, Colin, has moved in to help with some of the chores.'

'Yes,' Claudia said. 'You mentioned him briefly the last time I was here but I didn't meet him. He had the day off. Until then, I didn't even know Edie had a nephew.'

'Yes, you did, darling. You must have heard about him. He's her sister's son, the one that was evacuated down here during the war. Of course, he was only a baby then. Anyway, the point is Colin was a hospital porter or orderly – something of the sort – so he's used to lifting patients. Naturally Edie can't be expected at her age to cope with anything like that so Colin's been able to take some of the heavy work off her shoulders.'

'How long has he been here?' Claudia asked. Very little had been said to her about Edie's nephew on her previous visit to Howlett's, although she remembered now vague references over the years to Edie's background, never fully explained and never referred to by Edie herself.

It seemed that, during the blitz on London, several families had been evacuated to Howlett's from London, among them Edie's sister. It was through this connection that Edie had been offered the post of housekeeper when the war ended. And here she still was, over forty years later, still looking after grandfather, almost but not quite one of the family.

Now that Great-aunt Constance had mentioned it, Claudia remembered there had been talk about a nephew in London whom Edie visited from time to time on her days off.

'When did you arrange for Colin Knapp to start work here, Teddy?' Great-aunt Constance turned to her husband but before he could reply, she had answered her own question. 'It must have been some time after Christmas. I remember we'd come down to spend a weekend with Edgar during the New Year. It was bitterly cold and there was poor Edie carrying those heavy coke hods about as well as logs for the fire in here and the dining-room. And even then Edgar could hardly get out of the bath on his own. I said to Teddy, didn't I, darling, something would have to be done otherwise Edie will be ill next and then how would we possibly cope without her? I know that woman from the village – Nancy whatever her name is – comes in to help with the cleaning but that's only two mornings a week so she was hardly the answer. Anyway, we discussed it with Edie and in the course of the conversation, the nephew was mentioned. It seemed he was looking for a job so Teddy suggested he came here.'

'Seemed a sensible idea,' Teddy himself put in. 'We couldn't have poor old Edie knocking herself up, could we?'

'Yes, I see,' Claudia said.

While realizing she was hardly being fair, she felt obscurely angry that so little had been said to her about these arrangements and that Constance and Teddy seemed to have made the decision between them. On the other hand, she, Claudia, had been out of the country, during which time her great-aunt and Teddy would have had to bear the whole burden of visiting grandfather and seeing to his welfare. All the same, it did not prevent her from feeling excluded.

At that moment, someone knocked briefly at the door and a tall, pleasant-looking, middle-aged man with a preoccupied air entered the room.

'Ah, Dr Callender!' Great-aunt Constance announced. 'You remember my great-niece, Claudia? And you'll join us for tea, of course.'

'Yes, I remember Claudia,' Dr Callender said, coming across the room to shake hands. 'We played tennis together one summer when you were staying here with your mother. You must have been about ten.'

Claudia also remembered the occasion. Robert Callender had seemed terribly old to her then, a doctor working in a London hospital and therefore a grown-up but one who had nevertheless treated her as an adult herself, not a child, which she had liked. She still found some of that open, generous quality in him now.

'And no thanks, I won't stay for tea, Mrs Nugent,' he continued, turning to Great-aunt Constance. 'I have another patient to visit this afternoon and I want to make arrangements for a nurse to stay with Mr Aston tonight. It's going to mean ringing round the agencies to find one. But I'll call again later this evening, after she's arrived, to make sure she's fully in the picture about Mr Aston's case.'

'How is grandfather?' Claudia asked, getting up from her chair.

'Not too well, I'm afraid,' he told her.

'May I see him?'

'As long as you don't stay longer than a few minutes. And don't expect him to answer you. The stroke's affected his speech although he may be able to hear you. It's difficult to tell.'

They were standing facing one another and for the first time he seemed to register her properly, no longer as the little girl he had once played tennis with but as a grown woman. For a few seconds, he looked startled and then, recovering himself, said a general goodbye to everyone in the room and left.

'Such a pleasant man!' Great-aunt Constance remarked almost before the door closed on him, in much the same way as she had commented on Edie. 'He's been so attentive to Edgar.'

It seemed that, now grandfather was dying, everyone was expected to be charming and complimentary about everyone else, as if any unpleasantness had to be covered over and disguised under a general cordiality.

Like flowers on a coffin, Claudia thought.

She said briskly, 'I'll take my suitcase up to my room,' and was aware as she closed the door behind her, of a silence on Great-aunt Constance's part.

Collecting her case which she had left in the hall, Claudia mounted the stairs. Halfway up, under a stained-glass window emblazoned with armorial shields, an attempt on her great-grandfather's part to suggest some ancient, aristocratic lineage for the Astons, the staircase divided on a landing, one flight continuing towards the central part of the house where the principal bedrooms were situated. The other, shorter flight of two steps only turned to the right towards a lesser wing, cut off from the main house by a soundproof, baize-covered door, designed originally to house the day and night nurseries and some of the domestic staff in the days of nannies, nursery maids and governesses. Two further staircases opened off this nursery wing, one descending to the kitchen quarters on the ground floor, the other leading up to more servants' bedrooms in the attics.

Grandfather's bedroom was in the front of the house. Claudia passed it on her way to her own room. Its door was closed and, although she paused outside it to listen, no sound emanated through its thick panels.

Her room faced the side lawn. It was large – too large, it seemed – and was furnished with a ponderous mahogany bedroom suite which had once been fashionable: a great wardrobe like several sarcophagi standing on end, a dressing-table resembling an altar and a double bed with heavy, carved head and foot-boards. It was called the blue bedroom by reason of the wallpaper – morning glories entwined on trellis; pretty enough but it did little to relieve the gloom of the rest of the furnishings. Claudia wished she had been put in the old night nursery which had always been her bedroom when she had stayed at Howlett's as a child.

She unpacked quickly, hanging the few clothes she had brought with her in the wardrobe where they dangled disconsolately in all that empty space, placed her toilet things by the old-fashioned basin in the corner with its broad marble surround and solid brass taps and, having changed out of her jeans into a more suitable cotton skirt, returned along the corridor to knock at her grandfather's door.

It was opened to her by a man in his forties – the nephew, Colin, Claudia assumed. Like his Aunt Edie, he was tall and long-faced but much heavier built and with an air about him of ingratiating familiarity which Claudia instantly disliked.

Closing the door softly behind him and coming out on to the landing to join her, he said, 'You must be the granddaughter, Claudia. Aunt Edie said you were expected some time this afternoon. Come to see your grandad, have you?'

'If I won't be disturbing him,' Claudia replied, trying to sound pleasant. 'I've been told not to stay too long.'

She felt resentful of his presence. He was wearing an open-necked shirt with the sleeves rolled up which gave him a casual, lounging appearance, hardly professional, although she realized that, having played no part in caring for her grandfather during her absence abroad, she was in no position to object to the man's introduction into the household.

The nephew – she could not bring herself to think of him as Colin – opened the door for her with something of a flourish, inviting her to enter, another small cause for dislike, but he had at least the sensitivity to remain on the landing while she went inside.

The room was in semi-darkness. Because it faced south, the curtains had been drawn against the bright afternoon sunlight. The bed stood opposite the door so that, on entering, she was confronted by it – so wide and high that the figure of her grandfather, propped up in it, seemed very small and shrunken amongst all that spread of white linen and patterned counterpane.

He had altered dreadfully since the last time she had seen him although even then she had noticed a change. In the two years she had been away, he had become an old man, his vigour spent. But that was nothing compared to his deterioration in the past three weeks. He was clearly dying.

His eyes were partly open but he did not register her presence, not even when she sat down on the chair beside the bed. One of his hands was lying on the top of the coverlet and, with a sudden surge of love and compassion, she covered it with hers and said softly, using the pet name for him from her childhood, 'It's me, Gramps. Claudia. I've come to see you, darling.'

There was no obvious response although she felt his hand stir faintly under hers and she thought his eyes, under the half-closed lids, seemed to brighten a little.

She sat with him for the five minutes stipulated by Dr Callender, sometimes silent, sometimes speaking to him about the family and the house – subjects which she thought might penetrate to some conscious part of his mind and evoke a reaction, however small. But there was no further indication that he heard her or even knew she was sitting beside him. When the time was up, she rose from her chair and, bending down, brushed her lips gently across his forehead before leaving the room.

The nephew was waiting outside on the landing, leaning against the banister rail. He had taken the opportunity of his absence from the room to light a cigarette, using a saucer from the Crown Derby tea-set as an ashtray.

He smiled at Claudia as she came out and seemed about to speak to her. But to her relief, the sound of some disturbance in the hall downstairs distracted them both.

Great-aunt Constance's voice could be heard exclaiming, 'Oh my God! The old fool!'

Brushing past the nephew, Claudia ran down the stairs to find Constance, who had evidently just emerged from the drawing-room with Teddy hard on her heels hurrying towards the front door which Edie was in the act of opening. Through its glass panels, a taxi could be glimpsed drawn up in front of the porch, its driver carefully assisting an old man from the back seat, a small suitcase in his other hand.

As the figure appeared, impatiently waving aside the driver's arm with a stick, Claudia saw his face.

It was Uncle Rollo.

5

Great-aunt Constance immediately took charge. Edie was despatched to make fresh tea, Claudia and Basil directed to assist Uncle Rollo into the drawing-room while Teddy was ordered to pay off the taxi and bring in the suitcase.

She stood centre stage in the middle of the hall, flourishing an arm first in this direction and then that before, stalking ahead of them, she took up her position on the sofa, so that, by the time Uncle Rollo was helped into the room, she was ready to receive him, seated bolt upright, her expression ominous.

'Such a lot of fuss!' Uncle Rollo protested crossly as Claudia and Basil lowered him into an armchair.

But he looked, Claudia thought, like a chastened child confronted by nanny, appalled by what he had done and yet determined to brazen if out if he could. Claudia was torn between the desire to laugh at the absurdity of the situation and very real anxiety about his physical state. The drive had clearly exhausted him. Breathing irregularly, his face ashen, he nevertheless clutched his sticks so fiercely that the knuckles bulged white.

'What on earth do you mean by turning up here?' Great-aunt Constance demanded.

The others had grouped themselves about her as if for a production of *Lear*, Teddy and Basil standing at each end of the sofa like a protesting chorus supporting Great-aunt Constance in her role as an outraged Goneril or Regan, with Claudia, who had perched on the arm of Uncle Rollo's chair, playing the part of the young Cordelia seated at the side of the aged king.

'I wanted to see Edgar,' Uncle Rollo explained, his bottom lip jutting out stubbornly. 'Make the quarrel up with him if I could before it's too late. Say I'm sorry and all that. So I rang up the George in Howlett to reserve a room and then ordered a taxi.'

'Does anyone at Beechcroft know you're here?'

'No,' Uncle Rollo admitted.

'You mean you were planning to spend the night away at a hotel without telling someone in charge?'

'I may be old, Constance,' Uncle Rollo said, 'but I'm not senile yet. And I'm not a child either. I don't have to ask permission before deciding to book myself into a hotel.'

Great-aunt Constance gave him a long look of mingled affection and exasperation and then turned to Teddy.

'Teddy,' she ordered, 'telephone Beechcroft at once. You'll find the number in the directory. Ask to speak to the matron. Explain that Mr Saxby is here with us and will most probably stay the night. Also ring the George and cancel Roland's booking.' As Teddy dutifully left the room to carry out these instructions, Great-aunt Constance continued, interrupting Uncle Rollo's protestations. 'No, Roland, you are certainly not returning to Beechcroft this evening nor are you spending the night at the George. Look at you! You're in no condition for either. Edie will get a room ready for you here and either Teddy or Basil will drive you back tomorrow morning when you're properly rested. As for seeing Edgar . . .'

'How is he?' Uncle Rollo asked, managing this time to override Great-aunt Constance.

Claudia saw her expression soften. It was significant, Claudia thought, that her great-aunt should lower her guard a little in Uncle Rollo's company as if she still saw in him the ardent young man, newly returned from India, who had proposed to her by the pool out there in the garden all those years before.

'Very ill indeed, I'm afraid.'

'But I'll be able to see him?'

For once, Great-aunt Constance looked uncertain and seemed about to turn to Basil for his advice.

'Constance,' Uncle Rollo said, and Claudia was relieved to hear that his voice had grown stronger, 'I'm not leaving this house until I've seen Edgar, even if it's for only a few moments.'

Claudia broke into the conversation on Uncle Rollo's behalf.

'Surely it won't do any harm?'

'But how will he manage the stairs?'

Claudia was about to point out that, if Uncle Rollo stayed the night, he'd have to get upstairs to his room anyway, when Uncle Rollo, banging a stick down on the carpet, intervened.

'I wish you women would stop discussing me as if I'm deaf! The damned matron at Beechcroft does exactly the same. Talks about me over my head. I'll manage the confounded stairs somehow. Claudia can help me. And so can he.'

This time the stick was jabbed in the direction of Basil who looked affronted although he murmured to Great-aunt Constance, 'I think Claudia's right. I can't see a short visit will do any harm.'

'There you are then,' Uncle Rollo said, surprised at this unexpected support from Basil. 'The matter's decided. I'll stay the night, as you suggest, Constance. Never cared much for the George anyway. And I'll see Edgar. Now where's the tea?'

As if on cue, Edie entered at this moment, carrying a tray with clean cups and a pot of fresh tea which she arranged on the trolley, listening with folded lips while Great-aunt Constance explained the situation to her. Mr

Saxby would be spending the night at Howlett's. Could a bedroom be made ready for him?

'Which one do you suggest, ,Edie?' Great-aunt Constance concluded, the appeal intended, Claudia suspected, to appease Edie for any inconvenience she might be put to by the presence of an unexpected extra guest. 'All the main bedrooms are occupied, apart from the one next to Edgar's and the nurse who'll be arriving later ought to be given that.'

'I don't mind moving out of mine,' Claudia put in.

'All this damned palaver!' Uncle Rollo protested, aware suddenly of the trouble he was putting everyone to on his behalf. 'I'll sleep on the sofa if it's necessary. Got used to roughing it when I was in India.'

'Don't talk nonsense, Roland,' Great-aunt Constance told him sharply. 'You'll do no such thing.'

She, too, seemed uncharacteristically flustered, the colour high in her face.

It was Edie who retrieved the situation.

'Mr Saxby can sleep in the night nursery,' she said, as if the matter were decided. 'There's fewer steps up to it and there's a bathroom next door.'

'Of course, Edie! What a splendid idea!' Great-aunt Constance exclaimed.

'I'll get the bed made up now,' Edie added, turning away to the door.

'Claudia can see to that,' Constance announced, resuming control of the situation. 'Basil, pour tea for Roland. Claudia, come with me.'

She swept Claudia out of the room in Edie's wake, leaving Basil to deal with the teapot, although once in the hall, where Teddy was in the act of replacing the telephone receiver, she abandoned Claudia for him.

'I want to talk to you, Teddy,' she announced. 'Come into the morning-room.'

As the door closed behind them, Claudia heard her

say, 'Roland's insisting on seeing Edgar. You'll have to speak to him, Teddy. I don't think it's at all wise . . .'

The rest of the conversation was lost as Claudia followed Edie down the passage which led from the hall towards the kitchen although she could guess its content. Between them, Great-aunt Constance and Teddy would try to dissuade Uncle Rollo from seeing her grandfather, a shame in Claudia's opinion, considering that Uncle Rollo had come with the express intention of apologizing to him.

The kitchen at Howlett's had always fascinated Claudia even though Edie had not encouraged her to enter it too often. It was her domain and a large part of its attraction had been that it was, so to speak, forbidden territory. Like the rest of Howlett's, it was virtually unchanged, with the big deal preparation table still standing in the centre of the room, its old-fashioned built-in cupboards for china occupying the whole of one side, and the frieze of black and white tiles, like a chess-board, which came half-way up the walls.

Opening off it were lesser pantries and larders, still equipped with the deep sinks and marble shelves which had probably been installed when the house was first built.

To Claudia as a child, it had been a place of mysterious culinary arts, almost alchemical in their complexity, for which the batteries of copper saucepans, the jelly moulds, the huge serving dishes – relics of earlier days when there had been many more mouths to feed, but still displayed on the shelves – had been the ritual vessels.

As she grew older, Claudia had realized that this reaction had been part of a childhood fantasy. Edie was a good, plain cook, nothing more, a fact which the cauliflower draining in a colander by the sink, and the chicken laid out on the table together with a packet of sage and onion stuffing, tended to confirm. It would be served up later at dinner with bread sauce, roast potatoes and probably frozen peas, the kitchen garden having ceased to be productive years ago, although Claudia could just remember the time when grandfather had employed a full-time gardener and there had been fresh strawberries and asparagus.

All the same, she felt inclined to linger even though Edie was saying, clearly wanting to get rid of her, 'You'll find clean sheets and pillowcases in the linen cupboard upstairs. Everything else you'll need is already on the bed.'

She spoke abruptly as if none of these arrangements met with her approval.

Feeling some apology was needed, Claudia said, 'I'm afraid you're being put to a lot of trouble.'

'That's what I'm here for,' Edie replied.

She had gone over to the sink to refill the kettle before placing it on the Aga stove.

'How long exactly have you been at Howlett's?' Claudia continued, curious about the part Edie played in the household, which she had never really considered before until Great-aunt Constance's remarks earlier in the afternoon had aroused her interest. Edie had always been there, her life inextricably but mysteriously bound up with the family's.

'Since the war,' Edie said.

'Wasn't your sister evacuated to Howlett's?'

'Yes, she was.'

It was not easy getting Edie to talk about herself but Claudia was determined not to be dissuaded.

'And you used to come here to visit her?'

Edie, who had been bending down to riddle the ashes out of the Aga, straightened up, her thin face flushed with the effort.

'When I could get a weekend off. When the war started, I volunteered for factory work. I got sent to a place in

70

Chelmsford, making parts for Spitfires. I'd cycle over. Your grandmother was alive then but run off her feet with the evacuees who'd been sent down from London to get away from the bombing. I used to give her a hand. When the war finished, she asked me if I'd like to stay on as housekeeper.'

It was said dismissively as if none of it really mattered although Claudia was struck by the implications behind the terse remarks. Edie, who must have been about twenty at the outbreak of war, had not only volunteered for factory work but had cycled the ten miles and back from Chelmsford in her free time to see her sister as well as helping with the evacuees. It was an aspect of Edie's life which seemed quite extraordinary to Claudia, part of the past which she had only experienced through old newsreel shots on the television.

'What was the war like?' she asked.

'Bombs. Black-out. Rationing,' Edie told her grimly. 'You were lucky if you got a fresh egg once a month. We used to queue up for everything – meat, soap, elastic even until that disappeared from the shops.'

'And what did you do before the war?'

'I was in service, in London.'

'But you didn't want to go back afterwards?'

'I preferred it here. I wasn't ordered about so much. There it was do this, do that. Hardly a thankyou. Your grandmother and Miss Constance were very kind. Miss Constance used to pass some of her things on to me, lovely silk blouses and coats from Harrods and places like that.'

As she was speaking, she was drying up the silver teapot which had been washed and up-ended on the draining-board, swaddling it as carefully as a baby in a clean tea-towel and patting its sides.

Suddenly Claudia understood. Edie had been drawn to the house very much as she herself had been as a child, attracted by its air of graciousness and good living. It no longer mattered that it was now faded and shabby. Like grandfather and the rest of the family, her roots were here.

'What about that bed?' Edie was asking. 'Are you going to do it or shall I?'

'Sorry,' Claudia said, smiling and getting to her feet.

She went by the back staircase which opened off the passage just outside the kitchen and which was more convenient than using the main stairs. It led up to the narrow corridor in the nursery wing where the linen cupboard was situated on the right-hand side, large enough to walk into and fitted with slatted shelves.

Turning on the light, Claudia selected sheets and a pillowcase from the pile of linen, monogrammed with a letter A, which had formed part of her grandmother's trousseau and which she thought would please Uncle Rollo to have on his bed, before carrying them, together with two towels, across the passage to the night nursery.

She liked the room and would gladly have changed it for the blue bedroom. It was low-ceilinged and simply furnished, still equipped with its original cast-iron grate and high mantelshelf although the bars on the window and the nursery fire-guard had been removed and the child's bedstead replaced by a modern divan which she began to make up with the linen. A pillow and blankets were already in place, hidden under the flounced chintz cover.

The bed made, Claudia checked that the bedside lamp was working before crossing the room to take the towels into the adjoining bathroom which opened off the nursery. It was barer than the other bathrooms in Howlett's which, with their solid mahogany, brass and flowered porcelain fixtures, spoke of an Edwardian love of comfort and the good things of life. This one was spartan, suitable for the needs of mere children and nursery staff, fitted with a plain white bath and basin, unadorned white tiles and an indestructible cork mat which had been there as long as Claudia could remember.

To her disappointment, she found the day nursery next door was locked, possibly to save Edie the trouble of maintaining at least one room on the upper floors, which contained, counting the servants' quarters in the attics, twelve bedrooms.

Continuing on along the passage to the baize door at the far end, Claudia emerged on to the landing and descended by the main staircase to find Teddy alone in the drawing-room with Uncle Rollo – the others, Great-aunt Constance and Basil, ominously absent. Entering the room, Claudia caught the tail-end of Teddy's remarks.

Uncle Rollo was sitting forward in his armchair, still grasping his sticks and looking down disconsolately at the carpet as Teddy explained, '. . . and besides, he won't be able to understand what you're saying to him, Roland. The stroke's left him more or less comatose.'

He broke off and looked up guiltily as Claudia came into the room.

It was quite clear not only from his comments but from his expression that Teddy had been despatched by Great-aunt Constance to dissuade Uncle Rollo from seeing her grandfather, a realization that angered Claudia.

Seeing Uncle Rollo's disappointment, she came to a decision. At the risk of inviting Great-aunt Constance's disapproval, she would appeal directly either to Robert Callender or the night nurse for permission on Uncle Rollo's behalf to visit the sickroom.

The nurse arrived at half past six; a young woman, crisp and efficient-looking in the agency's blue uniform who, having introduced herself as Mary Holden and shaken hands all round, disappeared upstairs to take over the care of her patient. There was no opportunity to speak to her privately. Great-aunt Constance monopolized her attention, explaining the routine of the house and sending for Edie to show her upstairs to her room although Claudia offered her services.

'No, Claudia. Edie had better do it. She knows far more than you about the hot water and where the clean towels are kept.'

She fared no better with Robert Callender who arrived soon after the nurse. He went straight upstairs, returning after about half an hour, clearly in a hurry and pausing only long enough in the drawing-room to announce that, if there was no change in the patient, he would call again in the morning. Meanwhile, Miss Holden would telephone him if it became necessary.

He made the proviso as a kind of warning and Claudia realized that he did not expect her grandfather to live much longer.

And then he left but, before doing so, his glance sought out Claudia and he again gave her that look of surprised acknowledgement as if assuring himself that she was, after all, an adult and not a child any more.

Dinner, which was served shortly afterwards, was a gloomy meal, not enlivened by the dining-room itself which was panelled with dark oak and equipped with the type of furniture which would have better suited a gentleman's club at the turn of the century.

Edie served them in silence, placing vegetable dishes and a sauce-boat of bread sauce on the table and leaving Teddy to carve the roast chicken at the sideboard where dessert, in the form of a cold damson compote together with cheese and biscuits, had already been set out. At the door, she announced abruptly that the nurse's tray had already been taken upstairs and that coffee would be waiting for them in the drawing-room when they had finished.

During dinner, conversations spurted briefly into life

74

and died. Teddy asked Claudia about her time abroad but didn't really listen to her answers while Great-aunt Constance chatted to Uncle Rollo and Basil about the new Lloyd Webber musical she and Teddy had seen in London. Somehow the social niceties were observed but it was heavy going, even for Great-aunt Constance. Basil replied in monosyllables, his normal conversational style unless he was discussing investments and the state of the City with Teddy. As for Uncle Rollo, he appeared to have lost all appetite for either food or words. Claudia noticed that he hardly touched the main course and that half the chicken and the vegetables were left uneaten on his plate.

The final blow to any pretence at pleasantries came over the damson compote.

Great-aunt Constance had just asked Uncle Rollo in a sprightly voice, 'And how do you like Beechcroft, Roland?'

He laid down his spoon and fork.

'If you really want my honest opinion, Constance, which I very much doubt, it's an extremely expensive, half-way house for the elderly on their way to the grave.' Turning to Claudia, he continued, 'I think I'll go upstairs now.' Basil half-rose from his chair but Uncle Rollo waved him away. 'No, not you. Claudia and I will manage on our own.'

As she assisted him from the room, Claudia was aware of the consternation on the faces of the others still seated at the table.

Somehow they managed the stairs. The treads were, thank God, broad and shallow. By clinging to the banister rail on one side and to Claudia's arm on the other, Uncle Rollo hoisted himself step by step to the landing from where the going was easier to his room. Once inside, Claudia helped him to sit down on the bed, seating herself beside him and waiting while he rested. The climb had clearly tired him and it was several minutes before he recovered his breath sufficiently to announce, 'I want to see Edgar.'

It was said with the stubborn determination of a child who, having made up his mind, has no intention of being thwarted.

Claudia hesitated. She was not sure that her earlier decision to appeal over Great-aunt Constance's head to the nurse was such a good idea after all. There was still another flight of stairs to climb to her grandfather's bedroom on the main landing, shorter than the first flight, it was true, but Uncle Rollo looked in no state to attempt it.

As she hesitated, Uncle Rollo repeated more loudly, 'I want to see Edgar. I don't give a damn what Constance and Teddy say. All I want to do is apologize to him. Please, Claudia.'

He had never appealed to her in this manner before and it was hard to say no to him. Instead, she compromised.

'Not yet, Uncle Rollo. Perhaps later, when you're better, I could ask the nurse if you could see him for a few minutes. But not straight away.'

He seemed to accept her decision although his reply, 'All right, Claudia. Later, then,' warned her that he was not likely to give up easily.

While he rested, she unpacked his overnight case which someone, probably Edie, had left in the room, placing his pyjamas and dressing gown on the bed and the waterproof bag containing his toilet and shaving gear in the bathroom.

That done, she sat and talked to him for ten minutes until, at his insistence, she went downstairs for coffee although he himself refused any as, he explained, it kept him awake.

The others were in the drawing-room, Great-aunt Constance installed with her feet up on the sofa, talking to Teddy who was trying to read *The Times*, Basil seated at the small rosewood writing table, papers spread out in front of him, his briefcase open at his side. All of them looked up as she entered.

'How is Roland?' Great-aunt Constance asked in a tone of voice which implied that, if he were unwell, he had no-one to blame but himself.

'Better. Resting,' Claudia said briefly, helping herself from the coffee pot.

'I can't imagine what put it into his head to drive over here this afternoon,' Great-aunt Constance announced to the room in general.

But I can, Claudia commented silently to herself.

She took her cup and carried it over to the door.

'I'll drink this upstairs,' she said and went out.

As she closed the door, she heard Great-aunt Constance remarking, 'But he's always been a stubborn man. Remember the fuss over that annuity, Teddy, and how rude he was to Edgar?'

Which is why he's here now, Claudia thought, as she returned upstairs. To make amends. But she could not expect Great-aunt Constance, who had never in Claudia's recollection ever apologized to anyone, to understand.

She found Uncle Rollo up and pottering about.

'Nice room,' he commented. 'Comfortable. I remember your mother always slept in here when she was a little girl. Your grandfather had it redecorated for her.'

He nodded his head towards the wallpaper scattered with bunches of wild flowers, the colours faded by the sun.

'Is there anything else you want?' Claudia asked him. 'Another pillow,' he suggested. 'I have to sleep propped up these days. Can't lie flat.'

She fetched one for him from the linen cupboard, together with another of the monogrammed pillowcases and returned to the room where Uncle Rollo stood watching, leaning on his sticks, as she placed it on the bed.

'And now,' he announced, 'it's time I saw Edgar.'

The nurse had no objections and seemed sympathetic when Claudia explained the situation to her.

'I can't see it'll do any harm,' she replied. 'Dr Callender said your grandfather could have visitors, provided they didn't stay more than a few minutes.'

Coming away from the room, Claudia took the precaution of leaning over the banister rail to check that the hall below was empty. It was. Judging by the faint sound of the introductory music to the nine o'clock news coming from the morning-room where the television set was installed, the others were safely shut away for at least half an hour. It seemed an appropriate time to smuggle Uncle Rollo upstairs.

He managed the climb to the upper landing more easily than Claudia had feared. Rested and, she suspected, also invigorated by the opportunity of a reconciliation with his old friend after their quarrel of seven years' standing, he refused even the help of Claudia's arm, stumping briskly from tread to tread, a stick in one hand, his other grasping the rail.

She left him at the door where Nurse Holden was waiting to escort him inside, catching a glimpse only of Uncle Rollo's back, the nurse at his side, slowly approaching the bed where her grandfather was lying in the low light from the bedside lamp, in almost the same position as she had seen him earlier – both hands now resting side by side on the counterpane, the mouth a little open as if in surprise to find himself in such a condition.

She had no idea what took place between them. Although the door had been left ajar, she preferred not to remain even as a sympathetic eavesdropper and, moving away to the other side of the landing, she kept watch on the hall below just in case Great-aunt

Constance or one of the others should take it into their heads to leave the morning-room and come upstairs. But the hall remained empty.

A few minutes later, the door of her grandfather's bedroom swung open and Uncle Rollo came out, accompanied by the nurse, and she hurried forward to help him. But he appeared not to need her. Head lowered, stick digging into the carpet, he set off down the stairs towards his room without saying a word to her.

Once inside, he sat down on the bed, still not speaking, his stick grasped tightly in his hand.

'Are you all right, Uncle Rollo?' Claudia asked anxiously. She began to regret her part in the whole episode. Perhaps Great-aunt Constance had been right, after all, and it had been foolish of her to allow Uncle Rollo to see her grandfather. The visit had clearly distressed him. He looked so terribly old and sad.

As if he had not heard her question, he said abruptly, 'I want to speak to Edgar's doctor.'

'Robert Callender?' she asked, surprised by the request although she assumed Uncle Rollo wanted to discuss her grandfather's state of health. 'He won't be here until the morning. You'll probably see him before you leave.'

He shook his head.

'In that case, I'll talk to Constance. Ask her to come upstairs, will you, Claudia?'

She was about to say that it was unlikely that her great-aunt would know much about the medical details and then changed her mind at the sight of Uncle Rollo's face. He was wearing that stubborn look of his again which told her that nothing she said would dissuade him.

'Yes, of course,' she agreed. 'I'll get her.'

It meant that Great-aunt Constance would learn that Uncle Rollo had visited grandfather but that couldn't be helped. It was bound to come out sooner or later.

As she turned towards the door, he added, 'And while

you're downstairs, would you mind fetching me a glass of water? Sorry to be a nuisance, my dear. I forgot to ask you for it earlier.'

Great-aunt Constance was not in the morning-room when Claudia entered. There was only Teddy who informed her that Constance had just gone upstairs to have a bath, while Basil was in the study.

Claudia said good night to him and left without explaining the purpose of her visit. Teddy was absorbed in watching the television and anyway, it was none of his business.

She found Edie also alone, sitting at the big deal table in the kitchen, picking over blackcurrants which she was putting into a pie dish, presumably in readiness for lunch or dinner the following day.

'Don't get up,' Claudia told her. 'I've only come to get a glass of water for Uncle Rollo.'

Fetching a glass from one of the wall cupboards, she filled it at the cold tap and carried it upstairs to the night nursery where Uncle Rollo was waiting.

'Pity,' he said when she told him that Constance wasn't free to see him. 'But it doesn't matter. It's probably better that I speak to the doctor in the morning. Leave me now, my dear. I'm rather tired.'

Having assured herself that there was nothing else he needed, Claudia left the room, returning by the main staircase to the upper landing.

Great-aunt Constance was still occupying the principal bathroom. As she passed it, Claudia could tell by the rush of water in the antiquated plumbing system that the tank was being used.

She took her own bath in the second bathroom near her own bedroom; not nearly so well appointed as the other but adequate. Afterwards, returning to her room, she sat in the chair in her dressing-gown and read until half past ten when, before going to bed, she went quietly

along the passage to the night nursery. Turning the
handle, she opened the door a mere inch and listened.

The room was in darkness and from inside it came the
faint sound of breathing.

Reassured that Uncle Rollo was asleep, Claudia closed
the door as silently as she had opened it and returned to
her own room.

6

Claudia was awakened the next morning by a tap at her door. Opening her eyes, she was confused momentarily by the unfamiliarity of the room and the unaccustomed quality of the light seeping in round the edges of the curtains. It had the sharp, thin clarity of early morning.

For a few seconds, Edie's figure approaching the bed was also unrecognizable. Wearing a dressing-gown, her grey hair, usually wound into a neat coil at the back of her head, hanging down in a stiff little braid, she looked to Claudia, who had never seen her anything other than fully clothed, in an almost shocking state of undress. From her expression, lips tightly folded, features rigid, it was quite clear that something had happened.

'It's grandfather,' Claudia said, sitting up and pushing back her hair.

'He died about a quarter of an hour ago in his sleep,' Edie told her. 'The nurse woke me up and then Miss Constance who's with him now. Do you want to get up?'

She clearly expected Claudia to comply for, crossing to the window, she drew open the curtains so that the room was flooded by the clear, bright sunlight. For several moments, she remained at the window, looking out into the garden, her angular figure in the navy blue woollen dressing-gown very dark and still in front of the dazzling glass before she turned back towards the room.

'I'll get up,' Claudia agreed quickly. She felt she ought to say more to express her own grief or offer some expression of sorrow but was intimidated by Edie's grim, closed expression and by her own inability to find anything adequate to say.

When Edie had left, Claudia put on her own dressing-gown and crossed the landing to find Great-aunt Constance coming out of her brother's room, a silk wrapper clutched about her and looking, like Edie, almost unrecognizable without jewellery or make-up, her hair still flattened by sleep.

Grasping hold of Claudia, she kissed her but with none of the theatricality of her usual greetings.

'Oh, Claudia!' she cried, her voice shrill with a very real near-hysteria. 'Edie's told you? How dreadful it all is! What on earth are we going to do?'

Her last remark startled Claudia by its inconsequentiality. It was as if Great-aunt Constance were looking for some practical answer to a soluble problem. But, in the face of death, what possible solution could she suggest?

Before she could answer, Edie, who had gone ahead of them down the stairs, paused on the landing to announce, 'I'll serve coffee in the morning-room.'

'Yes! Yes!' Great-aunt Constance replied in sudden exasperation at the triviality of these domestic arrangements.

'Has the doctor been sent for?' Claudia asked.

'Teddy's phoned him. He's on his way. The nurse is with Edgar, of course. Did Edie tell you he died in his sleep? He was in no pain. Do you want to see him?' The disjointed sentences sounded all the more incongruous coming from Great-aunt Constance who was usually in command of any situation.

'Not now. After the doctor's been,' Claudia said, taking her gently by the arm. 'Let's go downstairs.'

There would be time later, she felt, when some of the emotion had died down, to take her own farewells of her grandfather.

Teddy was already in the morning-room, sitting disconsolately in one of the armchairs. The curtains had not yet been drawn and the room, with its lamps switched on, looked very much as it had the evening before when Claudia had called in briefly in search of her great-aunt and had found Teddy alone watching the television. The chairs were still grouped in front of the set, a copy of the *Radio Times* lying across the arm of one of them.

Reminded of that occasion, Claudia remembered that she had come downstairs on Uncle Rollo's behalf to look for Great-aunt Constance. In the sudden events of the morning, she had forgotten all about him. He would have to be told about her grandfather's death but not, she thought, looking at the others, quite yet.

Basil had just entered the room, fully dressed even to a neatly knotted black tie. After bending down to kiss Great-aunt Constance, he placed himself behind her chair, his expression suitably sombre, like someone taking part in a cenotaph service but in a minor capacity, not detracting from Great-aunt Constance's role as chief mourner. In the brief time between the first shock of her brother's death and Basil's arrival, Great-aunt Constance had recovered herself sufficiently to accept the part in which she had been cast. It was not entirely assumed; Claudia was prepared to believe that some of the tears were quite genuine. All the same, she was wringing the most out of the situation.

Lying back in the armchair, a handkerchief pressed to her lips, she clung to Teddy's hand as he repeated, with an embarrassed affection, those phrases which seem to be all that most people can summon up on such occasions.

'It's all for the best, Constance. He had a good innings and you wouldn't want him to suffer any longer, would you?'

84

Claudia caught Basil's glance and then both of them immediately looked away.

No, Claudia thought. She would wait a little longer before going upstairs to speak to Uncle Rollo. Grand-father's death would be a shock to him, as well. Better to tell him later, just before breakfast when, by offering to take the meal upstairs to him in his room, she could give him time to recover from the worst of his grief before offering to drive him back to Beechcroft.

Edie came into the room at that moment with a tray. In the interval between waking Claudia and making coffee, she, too, had dressed and was now wearing a black frock, her hair wound up into its usual neat, hard, little bun.

Claudia took the opportunity of her arrival to slip out of the door and go upstairs to her room where she also dressed although, unlike Edie in her funeral black, she had no clothes suitable for the occasion apart from a dark blue cotton skirt and a paler blue blouse. Looking at herself wryly in the glass as she tied back her hair, she realized she was making these gestures more for Edie's and Great-aunt Constance's sake, for whom such signs of mourning would be important, than for her own.

But she did mourn him; not as the old man she had seen lying in the bed the day before, nor even on her earlier visit to Howlett's after her return from Corfu, but as she remembered him years before, walking in the garden, wearing his panama hat and throwing sticks for his elderly retriever which, in those days before its own death, had been his constant companion.

The doctor arrived while she was still in her room. She heard Basil greeting him in the hall and then footsteps coming up the stairs and crossing the upper landing. A door opened and closed.

She would tell Uncle Rollo now, Claudia decided. At least there would be medical help at hand should he need it and Robert Callender's presence in the house would help calm everybody down, especially Great-aunt Constance. She did not expect Uncle Rollo to take the news badly. It was not his style. But he would grieve, perhaps more than anybody else, and he was, after all, very old himself.

As she crossed the landing, she saw that the door to grandfather's room was closed. So, too, was Uncle Rollo's. Claudia knocked and, having received no reply, knocked again before quietly opening the door and stepping inside the room.

The casement window was open and a faint breeze, stirring the drawn curtains, allowed the sunlight to enter but only intermittently. At first, in this billowing light, she thought the bed was empty and that he had already got up, perhaps to go to the bathroom, leaving the bedclothes tumbled half on to the floor. But it seemed out of character. His own clothes were lying neatly folded on the chair by the window, his shoes placed side by side under it. Then, as she moved closer, she saw that Uncle Rollo was lying among the disordered sheets and blankets, one arm flung out as if to save himself from falling further, the other resting more easily at his side.

Somehow she got across the room and, lifting one of the limp hands, tried to feel for a pulse but she already knew that he was dead. The skin on his wrist was dry and quite cool, despite the warmth in the room. She couldn't bear to look at his face. It was tilted back at an unnatural angle, the neck with its corded muscles pitifully exposed, as if in death he were still straining to look upwards at the ceiling although the closed eyes could register nothing.

Her own calmness surprised her. A doctor would have to be sent for to confirm death, she remembered thinking. Thank God Robert Callender was still in the house although, as she went back towards the passage, she realized on a less rational level that there was something wrong about the room; exactly what she couldn't define.

Robert Callender came as soon as her message was conveyed to him by Nurse Holden who answered the door. Claudia, who had no wish to go inside, remained on the landing. Within seconds, he came out to join her. As if by common consent, neither of them spoke as Claudia led the way down the stairs to the lower landing and through the baize door into the nursery wing.

'Is this how you found him?' Robert Callender asked.

He had drawn the curtains and, for the first time, Claudia was able to see the room in detail. Uncle Rollo lay on his back, the upper part of his torso slumped sideways off the bed, his body prevented from falling to the floor by bedclothes which were twisted round his legs and by the bedside table, which stood leaning at an angle, tipped back against the wall. The lamp was lying on the floor to the left of the table, its parchment shade dented, while a little further off still, the glass which she had brought upstairs for him the previous evening had rolled across the carpet and lay on its side, empty.

Robert Callender was kneeling at his side, feeling for a pulse and then, as the doctor turned away to open his medical bag which he had brought with him, Claudia realized what was wrong.

It was the pillows. One had tumbled half off the bed and was wedged between Uncle Rollo's head and the wall as if, in falling, he had dragged it with him. The other was still in place on the mattress. But it was the wrong pillow.

She remembered distinctly that, when she had made up both pillows for him, the second at his particular request, she had deliberately chosen the monogrammed cases from the pile in the linen cupboard. But the pillowcase on the bed was plain. There was no question of her having made a mistake. The monogram was a large letter A, embroidered across one corner. This pillowcase bore no such distinctive marking.

Robert Callender was saying, 'I'm sorry, Claudia. I'm afraid Mr Saxby's dead; probably of a heart attack in the night.'

She said quickly, 'No, you're wrong. I don't think he died like that.'

She saw the shocked expression in his face although he listened without interruption as she explained the reason for her unexpected outburst.

'So don't you see,' she concluded, 'if the pillow's been changed, someone must have come into the room?'

'You're sure it isn't the same one?' he asked her.

'Quite sure.'

He was silent for several seconds. Then he said, 'I can't write out a death certificate anyway; Mr Saxby wasn't one of my patients. There'll almost certainly have to be a post-mortem. I see the key's in the lock so this is what I suggest I do. I'll lock this door and take the key away with me so that the room can't be disturbed. Then I'll ring up the Inspector at Howlett police station – I know him quite well – and ask his advice. Is there a phone anywhere else in the house apart from the one in the hall?'

'There's an extension in the study.'

'I'll use that,' Robert Callender said with a decisiveness for which Claudia was profoundly grateful. Without him, what would she herself have done in the situation?

'In the meantime, I'd try avoiding the rest of the family if I were you, until I've had a chance to sort something out,' he advised her.

'I'll wait in the garden,' Claudia replied.

They parted in the passageway outside Uncle Rollo's door which Robert Callender locked before pocketing the key and going on down the corridor towards the main staircase.

Claudia turned to the left, descending by the back stairs to the kitchen wing where she let herself quietly out by the side door which led into a small cobbled yard. There was no sign of Edie, nor, thank God, of her nephew, while the others, Great-aunt Constance, Teddy and Basil, were presumably still in the morning-room.

The rose garden, when she crossed the yard and skirted behind the back of the building, was also deserted. It lay to the side of the house, overlooked by only the study and the dining-room. In her great-grandfather's time, it had been set out with lawns, backed with shrubbery, and with formal rosebeds in the centre of which steps led down to a sunken pool. But it had been neglected for years and the grass and flowerbeds were now unkempt while the pool had dried up long ago, its fountain silent and its marble basin discoloured and full of dead leaves. But it still had its stone benches on which to sit and wait although it was only after she had seated herself on one of them that Claudia remembered Uncle Rollo telling her that it was by the pool that he had proposed to Great-aunt Constance.

She wept then for the first time – for grandfather, for Uncle Rollo and a little also for herself. She felt suddenly and overwhelmingly alone with no-one she could turn to or confide in, those she had loved the best dead, and the others who should have been close to her, her parents, her former lover Ross, Great-aunt Constance, too far away or too self-absorbed or too bloody untrustworthy for her to be able to rely on their loyalty.

But as she felt the tears dry and stiffen on her face, the grief turned to anger. This was not the time for self-pity. She was confronted by a situation which was much more important – the enormities of the implications behind Uncle Rollo's death.

She went through them step by step, forcing herself to think logically and rationally. There was no room for sentiment. The facts had to be set out in cogent form.

Firstly, she was quite sure about the pillow. There was no mistake about that. It wasn't the one she had placed on Uncle Rollo's bed the day before.

That being so, there was only one inference which could be drawn – that someone else had entered Uncle Rollo's bedroom after she had left it the previous evening; not necessarily under suspicious circumstances, she realized. There could be some quite innocent explanation. Supposing the pillow had needed changing for some reason?

What reason? she asked herself.

Well, Uncle Rollo might have spilt some of the water from the glass on to the pillow. If that had happened, he might have sent for Edie or gone along the passage to the linen cupboard to fetch a clean pillow himself. After all, he was familiar with Howlett's from his boyhood.

In that case, there need not be anything suspicious about his death and Robert Callender could be right; he had died of a heart attack in the night.

The sound of footsteps coming along the gravel path which ran along the edge of the lawn caused her to break off. Getting to her feet, she saw Robert Callender approaching from the direction of the front door and looking about him. She raised her hand and he came down the steps to join her by the pool.

'I've telephoned Inspector Dwyer,' he told her, 'and explained the situation to him. He'll get in touch with Divisional Headquarters in Chelmsford. It's more than likely someone will be sent to make inquiries.'

'Oh, God!' Claudia said.

She was struck by the awfulness of the events which she had set in motion, imagining the police cars arriving and uniformed men taking over the house, questioning Great-aunt Constance and Edie, examining the bedroom where Uncle Rollo was lying dead.

She said, 'But supposing the pillow was changed quite innocently?'

'It's better to leave it to the police, Claudia,' Robert Callender told her. 'They're used to handling that sort of inquiry. There'll have to be a second medical opinion anyway so questions will have to be asked. We can't just ignore the situation, can we?'

She saw the common sense of what he was saying and was forced to agree.

He went on, 'I think it best if I, not you, tell Mrs Nugent and the others what's happened, and at this stage I'll stick to the truth as far as possible but play it down as much as I can. I'll simply say that you discovered Mr Saxby dead in his room and that you sent for me. That much at least is true. As I wasn't satisfied with the cause of death, I've informed the police and asked for a second medical opinion which, as a doctor, I'm obliged to do professionally. That will throw the onus of the inquiry on to me rather than you. I shan't say anything about the reasons for the suspicions and I advise you to do the same. Keep that kind of information for the police. I'll also tell them that I've locked the bedroom door and taken the key with me. No doubt the police will get in touch with me first and I'll be able to hand it over to them. Stay here,' he added, rising from the bench. 'Don't come back to the house until I've had a chance to talk to them. I'll make the excuse that you're distressed and want to be left alone.'

As he got to his feet and stood looking down at her, she thought how kind and reliable he was; not handsome – Robert Callender had possessed few pretensions to good looks even as a younger man. Now, in early middle age, a certain lanky awkwardness which she remembered had characterized him as a young doctor had been replaced by the more self-assured, professional manner of the country GP, although the gentleness was still there and the rather touchingly old-fashioned courtesy which she had liked in him when she had been a child.

He would make a good lover, she thought; tender and considerate of her needs; not like Ross. With Ross, she had felt most alone when they made love as if his passion had been entirely self-gratifying and she was merely the means through which it was expressed.

All the same, she was unable to voice aloud even to Robert Callender the thought which had crossed her mind earlier and which she only now was able to articulate properly for herself.

If after all Uncle Rollo had died of natural causes, had she, by agreeing to take him to see grandfather the evening before, helped to contribute to his death?

7

It was with relief that Finch received the telephone call that morning, cancelling his leave and summoning him back to Divisional Headquarters in Chelmsford. He had been wondering what the hell to do with himself for the rest of the week now that Marion had returned to Leeds. The three days off-duty, looked forward to so eagerly, had turned into an emptiness which he'd have to fill, God alone knew how. At least the case which Chief Superintendent Davies proposed turning over to him would serve as a diversion, keeping his mind off her and what might have been.

Not that the inquiry sounded all that promising when Davies filled in the details for him. They had been passed on by an Inspector Dwyer from Howlett and concerned the suspicious death of an elderly man.

Not necessarily murder. Davies, a cautious man at the best of times, was careful to stress this point.

'It could be natural causes. The doctor who was called in and who got in touch with Dwyer isn't too happy about the circumstances, it seems. And that's all I know. Dwyer couldn't tell me much more except that Callender is the local GP and isn't the type to involve the police without good reason. You'd better have a chat with him. He'll be able to put you in the picture. And keep a low profile, Jack. Take Boyce with you and have a sniff round yourselves first. We don't want to wheel in the experts if it turns out the old chap died in his sleep after all. Bad for our image.' As an afterthought, he added, as Finch walked towards the door, 'Sorry about cancelling your leave.'

Boyce wasn't nearly so off-hand when Finch rounded him up.

'Bloody lousy luck,' he sympathized. 'Bloody lousy case, too, by the sound of it. Suspicious death? What's iffy about it?'

'God knows,' Finch admitted. 'No-one else seems to. But I suppose we'll find out when we get there.'

Howlett was either a small town or a large village, depending on your point of view. Long-term residents still referred to it as a village and deplored the changes which had taken place since the war. It wasn't the same, they complained, now that the newcomers had moved in and the modern housing estate had crept out behind the cottages into the surrounding fields. But their wives welcomed the improved shops – the supermarket, the enlarged post-office, the hairdresser's. There was even a branch of Lloyds bank and the Abbey National Building Society.

The police station was new, too. It was tucked away in a side turning behind the main street and, from its car park, it was possible to see the two Howletts, the old epitomized by the flint tower of St Mary's church, the new by the white concrete and steel buildings of EAMCO, the East Anglian Manufacturing Company, makers of farm implements whose post-war expansion had been the direct cause of Howlett's mini-boom.

The police station was a compromise between the two. Contemporary but not too alarmingly so, its flat-roofed, functional shape was softened by a strip of front garden, paved and planted with conifers in round concrete containers. Inside the foyer, another round pot, white plastic this time and containing a sickly-looking rubber plant, stood on the red and grey tiled floor.

As Chief Superintendent Davies had predicted, the local Inspector, Dwyer, wasn't able to give them much more information than he had already passed on to Divisional Headquarters. They met in his office where Dwyer, a soft-bellied, easy-going man, whose accent confirmed an Essex upbringing, explained that he had received a telephone call at 8.45 a.m. from Dr Callender who had reported the death of a Mr Saxby, a guest staying with a local family, the Astons, under suspicious circumstances, and that he, in turn, had rung Davies at Headquarters to request Divisional help.

Judging by the little comments in parenthesis scattered throughout his account – old Howlett family, the Astons; used to own the local manufacturing firm until Edgar Aston sold it to EAMCO after the war; still highly respected; tricky case all round – Dwyer was clearly relieved to pass the buck of the investigation to a senior CID officer from DH and to wash his hands of the whole affair.

'Better have a chat with Callender,' Dwyer concluded. 'He was there at the time Saxby's body was found. He'll be best able to fill you in with all the facts.'

Callender's surgery was in the old part of the town, close to the church where a small enclave of original houses, a row of eighteenth-century cottages, a pair of even older timber-framed buildings, the Rectory and Callender's own Regency house, had been saved from the depredations of the developers by preservation orders of their owners' unwillingness to sell.

It was set back from the road, a gravelled drive leading round to the back where a sympathetic architect had transformed a range of stables and outbuildings into a surgery and waiting-room.

The interview took place in the house itself, in a pleasantly shabby room, part office, part sitting-room, furnished with club chairs of worn brown leather, an oak desk and glass-fronted bookcases of a period which pre-dated Dr Callender. It was nevertheless a setting in which he seemed perfectly at home. He was a tall, loose-limbed man of early middle age, a little diffident in manner, heightened, Finch suspected, by the circumstances in which he found himself involved. Listening as Callender briefly sketched in the background to the case, the Chief Inspector could understand his dilemma.

He was, he explained, the local GP and had been attending Edgar Aston, the elderly head of the family, who had suffered a major stroke earlier in the week. Staying in the house, Howlett Hall, were other members of the family – Aston's sister Constance Nugent, her husband and stepson, together with Aston's granddaughter Claudia Byrne, all of whom had travelled down from London at various times over the past two days to be present at the patient's bedside, Aston not being expected to live much longer.

More permanent members of the household were Edie Cole, Aston's housekeeper, who had been caring for Aston, and her nephew, Colin Knapp, who had been called in to help his aunt with the heavier household and nursing duties. In addition, as Aston's condition had deteriorated, Callender himself had arranged for an agency nurse to move into Howlett Hall.

Then, the previous afternoon, an unexpected visitor had arrived – Roland Saxby, a former friend of Edgar Aston.

'Former?' Finch asked.

'I gather that Aston and Saxby had quarrelled years ago,' Callender explained. 'I don't know the details. Claudia Byrne should be able to tell you more. It seems Saxby was living at Beechcroft – that's a residential home about ten miles away. Claudia called on him yesterday on her way down to Howlett's and told him her grandfather was seriously ill. Later in the afternoon, Saxby turned up in a taxi, asking to see Aston so that he could apologize for his part in the quarrel. He was exhausted by the journey and I gather he was asked to stay the night. Yesterday evening, Claudia took him to see her grandfather at Saxby's insistence. She had the nurse's permission and, tacitly, mine.'

'But not the family's, I gather,' Finch said, reading between the lines of Callender's statement. There was a lot more unspoken evidence which could also be inferred, chief amongst which was Callender's attitude to the granddaughter, Claudia Byrne. It was quite clear to Finch that Callender was attracted to her, a reaction which was implicit in Callender's increased diffidence whenever he spoke of her and in his anxiety to protect her from any criticism the Chief Inspector might choose to make of her actions, an interpretation which seemed confirmed when Callender continued:

'I gather the family weren't too keen on Saxby seeing Aston last night and wanted to put it off until this morning. But Claudia told me that Saxby – Uncle Rollo, as she calls him – was so determined to be taken to Aston's room straight away that she finally agreed. As it happened, it was probably as well that she did. Edgar Aston died early this morning. And no,' he added more sharply, as Finch seemed about to intervene again, 'there is no question that Aston's death was due to anything except natural causes, the result of the massive stroke he had three days ago. Believe me, Chief Inspector, I've been over this a hundred times since I decided to call in the police and I can assure you I can sign Aston's death certificate without the slightest hesitation. I've been attending him for the past two years, ever since I took over the practice from my father. Considering his age, Aston had been remarkably fit, apart from an attack of bronchitis two winters ago, until earlier this year when he began to get more frail. Since then I've been attending him regularly, keeping a check on his health, although after he had his stroke, I've called in to see him twice a day. Nurse Holden was with him from half past six yesterday evening until just after six-fifteen this morning when he died. But Saxby's death is another matter entirely. He's not my patient so even if the circumstances hadn't been suspicious, I couldn't have signed the death certificate.'

They had reached the heart of the matter although it would not have been possible to guess it from the Chief Inspector's expression, which remained bland and non-committal.

'Go on,' he said.

Callender's pleasant features took on a more harassed look.

'I assume you know very little about Saxby's death,' he continued. 'I deliberately gave Inspector Dwyer as few details as possible apart from telling him I thought an inquiry ought to be made. There seemed no point in stirring up a hornets' nest if after all Saxby died in his sleep from natural causes. The facts very briefly are these: Claudia discovered Saxby dead in his bedroom at about eight this morning and came immediately to fetch me. I was already in the house, having been called in earlier by Nurse Holden when Edgar Aston died. To all outward appearances, Saxby's death was perfectly straight-forward. He was an old man, in his late seventies and partially crippled. He'd also been under considerable emotional as well as physical strain the day before. It could have been more than likely that he'd died of a heart attack, brought on by stress and fatigue. Except for one factor. Claudia is quite certain that the pillow on the bed had been changed. You can see the implications?'

Finch merely nodded. He didn't need Callender to point out to him that, if Claudia Byrne was right, someone must have entered the bedroom and substituted one pillow for another. That in itself needn't be suspicious. The change could have been made quite innocently. Nevertheless, until that fact could be established, a question mark hung over Saxby's death.

It was an aspect of the case which was evidently on Callender's mind for he was saying, 'Claudia appears to be the last person to see Saxby alive last night. No-one else admits to going into his room after he went upstairs shortly after dinner yesterday evening. I made a point of finding that out this morning when I spoke to the family although, of course, I had to put it diplomatically. I merely asked them if any of them had talked to Saxby yesterday evening after he had gone to bed and if so, what was his state of health at the time. All of them, including Edie Cole, told me they hadn't seen him since dinner last night. I didn't get the chance to speak to Colin Knapp but Edie Cole assured me her nephew hadn't even met Saxby so he'd have no reason for going to Saxby's room.'

'So none of them realizes that you know about the pillow being changed?'

'Not as far as I'm aware. Neither Claudia nor I have mentioned it to anybody.'

Finch again noticed that hint of self-consciousness in Callender's voice as he spoke of himself and Claudia Byrne, as if by bracketing their names together, he was revealing an intimacy which he would have preferred not to acknowledge in front of strangers.

As if aware of it himself, Callender hurried on with his account.

'Apart from making sure Saxby was dead, I was careful not to disturb anything. You'll find the body exactly as I found it. And, judging by the skin temperature when I felt for a pulse, he'd been dead at least eight hours although your own police surgeon will probably be able to fix the time of death more accurately.'

'Thank you, Dr Callender. You've been most helpful.'

Finch got to his feet. 'My Sergeant and I'll take a look ourselves before calling in the pathologist. In the meantime, I'll leave it to you to tell the family that they can go ahead with arrangements for Aston's funeral.'

'I'll ring them and let them know,' Callender replied with obvious relief. 'I shan't be calling again at Howlett's until later this afternoon. By the way, you'll need the key to Saxby's room.' Taking it from the desk drawer, he handed it to the Chief Inspector. 'I locked the door after I left to make sure no-one else went in there.'

'Sensible precaution,' Finch said. It was clear that this was not all Callender wanted to say although it wasn't until he had escorted them into the hall that he added, 'I don't want to teach you your job, Chief Inspector, but I'd be grateful if you could make the inquiry as discreet as possible. The family's distressed enough already over Edgar Aston's death without making it worse for them. Aston's sister, Mrs Nugent, in particular has taken it badly. I've had to sedate her and I'd prefer it if you didn't question her for the time being. Claudia, too, is under a lot of strain. She was very fond of Mr Saxby and finding his body has been a great shock to her.'

'We'll do our best,' Finch assured him although, as he pointed out to Boyce as they crossed the drive to the car, carrying out even a preliminary investigation without making their presence known to the family just wasn't possible.

'At some stage we may have to interview them. All the same, Tom, we don't want to play the heavy coppers until we've had a chance to look at the body and decide whether or not it's murder. See if there's somewhere round the back of the house where we can leave the car out of sight of the main windows.'

'All right by me,' Boyce agreed off-handedly, 'although if it turns out to be natural causes after all, we could be in and out of the place like a dose of salts. I mean, we haven't got much to go on so far, have we, except for a pillow?'

'Depends why it was changed. *If* it was changed.' Finch was careful to stress the supposition. 'We'll need to check that with Miss Byrne. And, if she's right, then one good reason for replacing it could be because there was evidence on it which points to murder.'

'Like blood?'

'That's one possibility. Or saliva. Supposing Saxby was suffocated in his sleep? He was an old man. It wouldn't have taken more than a few minutes, perhaps even seconds, to snuff him out by holding a pillow over his face. And if that's what happened, there could have been traces on it which meant it had to be replaced.'

As he had been speaking, they had driven out of Howlett, taking the turning to Easeden, following the directions which Inspector Dwyer had given them for Howlett Hall. There was no time for Finch to add anything more. They had come to a brick gate-house where Boyce turned off the road, following an overgrown drive which led them past the front of Howlett Hall to a cobbled service yard at the far side of the building.

8

After she heard Robert Callender's car drive away, Claudia remained seated in the sunken garden, postponing the moment when she would have to return to the house.

What on earth would she say to them? To Great-aunt Constance? To Teddy? Even to Edie?

In the event, it was Basil who waylaid her when, having summoned up the courage, she walked across the lawn and let herself in at the front door. No sooner had she closed it behind her than he appeared in the open doorway of the study where she assumed he had been lying in wait for her.

'I'd like a word with you, Claudia, please,' he announced, ushering her inside the room where he seated himself behind the desk.

So it was to be in the nature of a formal interview, she thought, taking one of the small armchairs. Caution warned her to wait for him to speak first and not to rush headlong herself into an explanation. At the same time, she was aware of a small tremor of apprehension at the coming confrontation, not just at the necessity to lie – deceit had never come easily to her – but at Basil's capacity for scenting out falsehood.

Despite his image of the conventional business man, correct and formal in his dark suit, an outward appearance which suggested good manners and conformity, he was, she realized, a man of few passions, much more adept than she was at hiding his feelings and of manipulating the situation to his advantage.

Years of experience in handling boardroom meetings had given him a quality of watchful calculation and of estimating the strengths and weaknesses of the opposition.

He was watching her now, his face expressionless, as they sat opposite one another, each waiting for the other to begin.

It was Basil who at last opened the conversation, going straight for the heart of the matter without any introductory preamble.

'What exactly do you know, Claudia, about Dr Callender's decision to notify the police of Mr Saxby's death?'

'Only that he can't, under the circumstances, sign a death certificate,' Claudia replied, repeating almost word for word what Robert Callender had instructed her to say. Foolishly, she added, 'I believe it's usual.'

He picked it up at once.

'Is it? So you discussed the decision with Dr Callender?'

Claudia felt the colour rise in her face, partly through anger at Basil's inquisitorial manner, partly through guilt at her own involvement in the situation.

'I naturally asked him what would happen after I found Uncle Rollo dead.'

She kept her eyes fixed on his, aware of seeing him properly as an individual for the first time. Although she had never liked him much, she had tended to dismiss him as a merely peripheral member of the family, Great-aunt Constance's stepson and as such something of an outsider who played no significant part in Aston affairs.

He had a large, smooth face in which the features seemed to have been deliberately arranged to give him a reassuringly urbane appearance, the flesh well-padded but firm, the expression polite but attentive. It was a type of corporate image, dignified, temperate, trustworthy, designed to be photographed and reproduced in a company's brochure to reassure the shareholders. And yet, facing him, Claudia was aware of an acute intelligence behind that formal expression.

He seemed to relax, leaning forward across the desk to convey commiseration.

'Ah, yes. Dr Callender said you'd found Mr Saxby's body. It must have been a dreadful shock to you, Claudia.'

Wary of his sympathy, Claudia merely said, 'Yes, it was.'

'You went to his room?'

'I thought he ought to be told of grandfather's death.'

'And found him dead in bed?'

'Yes.'

It was all she was prepared to say. She had no intention of passing on to him any other information either about her discovery of Uncle Rollo's body or the reason for her suspicions.

There was another small silence. The desk was placed at right angles to the French windows and Basil glanced away across the garden, his expression inscrutable. Then he repeated, his eyes still on the view, 'A dreadful shock.' But he was referring not just to Claudia's feelings as his next comment made clear. Swinging back to face her, he continued, 'Of course, Mr Saxby was an elderly man. The drive over here yesterday from the nursing home must have been a great strain on him. In my opinion, it was unwise of him to make the journey.'

It was said in a perfectly reasonable tone of voice which contained a hint of regret at Uncle Rollo's imprudence, to which she could only respond by replying, 'Yes, I suppose it was,' implying that she agreed with his comments although she felt that, underneath his apparent solicitude, he was angling for something more than her assent.

What it was exactly, she had no idea. Was he trying to convince her that Uncle Rollo's death was from natural causes? Or was he attempting to discover, God alone knew why, exactly what she had seen when she had found Uncle Rollo's body? On the other hand, she herself could be reading far more into his remarks than they warranted.

Basil was saying, with the same reasonable air, 'Of course, we shall have to wait for the expert's opinion although I must say, Claudia,' and here he paused and regarded her closely, 'that I think it very odd that Dr Callender should have locked the door to Mr Saxby's room and taken the key away with him.'

'Did he?' she said, without thinking.

'But you were there. Didn't you see him do it?'

It was too late to withdraw the remark. All she could do was to try to cover up the mistake as best she could.

'He may have done. I wasn't really taking all that much notice. I was too upset at Uncle Rollo's death happening so soon after grandfather's.'

Although she had managed to control her feelings when speaking to Robert Callender, to her great embarrassment Claudia heard her voice tremble. It was contemptible, especially in front of Basil, to whom she would never normally have allowed herself to show such weakness. But at least her distress had the effect of bringing the inquisition to an end.

Pushing back his chair, Basil got to his feet, looking genuinely contrite.

'I apologize, Claudia. I'm afraid I've acted most thoughtlessly. I can only offer the excuse that Dr Callender's decision to call in the police has put all of us under considerable strain, Constance in particular. In fact, she's on the verge of collapse. My father has had to take her upstairs to lie down.'

'I'm sorry,' Claudia said in her turn. It seemed a

ludicrously inadequate response in view of her own guilt over the part she had played in the events but there was nothing else she could say. Seizing the opportunity to escape, she added, 'I'd better ask Edie if there's anything I can do to help.'

There was no sign of Edie when Claudia entered the kitchen. The nephew was there, however, elbows propped up on the table, drinking a mug of coffee and talking to Nancy Fuller, both of them too absorbed in the conversation to notice Claudia's presence in the doorway.

Nancy, who came in two mornings a week from the village to help Edie with the housework, had evidently only just arrived for she was still in the act of taking off her headscarf as she listened to what the nephew was saying.

Claudia caught the tail end of his remarks.

'. . . so it seems both of them snuffed it in the night or early this morning.'

It was said with an amused and callous indifference which angered her. Both deaths, her grandfather's as well as Uncle Rollo's, seemed to mean nothing more to him than a piece of titillating gossip.

At the same time, she was aware of an intimacy between the pair of them which was something more than the ordinary, everyday familiarity of two people who happened to share the same place of work. The nephew was grinning up at Nancy Fuller, eyes glittering, head set at a jaunty angle, not merely enjoying the pleasure of being the one in the know but flaunting that easy, swaggering masculinity of his. And Nancy Fuller was responding to it. Headscarf in hand, she was running her fingers through her hair to loosen it, half-turned towards him so that her small breasts were shown to advantage under the thin nylon blouse she was wearing.

She was in her thirties, divorced with two young children; a thin, narrow-featured woman but, under the blonde hair-do and the make-up, already showing signs of that withering of the skin and hardening of expression that in ten years' time would leave her prematurely old and embittered.

They were suddenly as conscious of Claudia's presence as she was of theirs and, to give Nancy Fuller credit, she at least had the grace to look embarrassed. Backing away towards the door, she tried to dissociate herself from the situation.

The nephew seemed prepared to brazen it out. Lolling back in his chair, he said with an insolent assurance that was probably intended to be disarming, 'I was just telling Nancy here about your grandad's death and then Mr Saxby's so soon after.'

'So I heard,' Claudia said coldly.

Nancy, her voice rising defensively, put in, 'I didn't know nothing about it. I only just got here.'

'Then you can turn round and go straight home again,' Edie said from the door. She had entered noiselessly, carrying a tray on which were the remains of breakfast – Great-aunt Constance's and Teddy's, Claudia assumed. Grim-faced, she put it down on the table. 'I'll manage what needs doing today. And you,' she went on, addressing the nephew, 'can make yourself useful by fetching in the coke.'

It was a measure of her control over the household that they obeyed her without protest, the nephew picking up the coke-hods and slouching out of the kitchen, Nancy Fuller retying the headscarf over her hair and going to the door where she paused to ask, 'When do you want me back?'

'Tomorrow,' Edie told her. 'There'll be washing that'll want doing.'

After Nancy had left, Claudia still lingered.

'Is there anything I can do to help?' she offered.

Edie had carried the used china over to the sink where she stacked it up on the draining-board, returning to the tray to remove a vase of roses, past their best but still beautiful. Foot on the pedal of the waste-bin, she snapped the stems in two and dropped the flowers inside before emptying the stale water down the sink.

Claudia watched her, unsure if Edie had heard her or not. There was a steely efficiency about all her actions as if it was only by keeping busy that she was able to maintain control. Her face was as rigid as the hard little bun of hair at the nape of her neck. Claudia wondered if she had ever wept but doubted it. She looked too dried up for tears.

And then, just when she was about to repeat the question, Edie said, 'You can make your own bed. I'll see to the others when I get the chance.'

'About the linen,' Claudia began, forgetting momentarily Robert Callender's advice to say nothing to anybody about the circumstances surrounding Uncle Rollo's death. She spoke on an impulse with no clear idea how she was going to finish the sentence except that she was looking for reassurance from Edie that she was, after all, right about the monogrammed pillowcases being kept in a separate pile from the others.

It was a mistake. Edie turned away from the sink to face her.

'What about the linen?' she asked.

'Nothing, really,' Claudia replied, feeling foolish.

'If you want clean, you know where the sheets are kept although your bed was made up fresh only yesterday.'

'It doesn't matter.' Claudia tried to sound off-hand. 'I only wondered . . .'

She was spared the effort of trying to think up a plausible excuse by the reappearance of the nephew who, dumping the two full coke-hods down by the Aga, announced, 'The police are here. I've just seen a car turning into the yard.'

'I'll let them in,' Claudia said quickly and was out of the kitchen before Edie could assume that duty herself.

9

To her relief, there was only one car on the point of drawing up in the side yard, containing a tall, bulky man and his shorter, stockier companion who was wearing a shabby linen jacket and whom she took to be the other's assistant.

She saw her mistake when he came towards her where she stood waiting by the door which led into the yard.

'Miss Byrne?' he asked pleasantly. 'I'm Detective Chief Inspector Finch.'

Quickly adjusting her reaction to him, Claudia saw that he was a fresh-faced man with the open, bluff geniality of a countryman. But there was more to him than that. She was aware of a subtle alertness about him which missed nothing. Even as he was speaking to her, he was taking in every detail of her appearance. He had, she felt, stamped her on his memory.

His knowledge of her name suggested that he had already spoken to Robert Callender about her and must therefore be acquainted with the circumstances of Uncle Rollo's death and her suspicions regarding it, a supposition which was confirmed when he continued:

'If you'll show us to Mr Saxby's room, we'll take a look round.'

'Of course,' she replied and led the way into the house and up a narrow staircase which opened out on to an upstairs corridor where, half-way down, she stopped outside a closed door.

'This is Uncle Rollo's room,' she said. 'I assume Robert Callender gave you the key? If you want to ask me any questions, I'll be in the garden at the far side of the house. There's a path which leads to it from the yard where you parked the car.'

And smiling at them briefly, she left them, walking quickly to the stairs down which she disappeared.

After she had gone, Finch unlocked the door and entered the room, followed by Boyce although, once inside, he remained standing just inside the doorway, hands in pockets, familiarizing himself with the body and its setting.

The room had a faded prettiness and, with its sprigged wallpaper and white painted furniture, looked as if it had been designed for a young girl. Against such a charming and virginal setting, the body of the old man looked totally out of place.

It was lying half out of the bed, the legs still caught up in the bedclothes which had prevented the body from falling completely to the floor, the head and upper part of the torso resting against a bedside table which had been tipped back against the wall. A little to the left of the table, a lamp, its parchment shade dented and the bulb shattered, lay on the floor while two feet away, an unbroken drinking glass was lying in a patch of dampness which showed up as a dark stain on the shabby green surface of the carpet.

Finch let his gaze pass over the dead man's face, registering briefly the fine, white hair and thin, high-nosed features. A distinguished-looking face, he noted; lean; fastidious; with the weather-beaten skin of a man who has spent much of his life in the open air. No trace of blood anywhere that he could see and no mucus round the mouth and nostrils, the obvious sign of suffocation.

To the casual observer, the man might have suffered a heart attack and collapsed sideways as he was attempting to get out of bed, the right arm, which was extended, knocking over the lamp and the glass as he did so. A natural death in other words except for Miss Byrne's evidence about the pillow.

There were two pillows, one lying neat and plump on the bed, foursquare to the headboard, the other, which seemed to have been dragged down as the body fell, crushed against the wall behind the dead man's head. Even from the doorway, a distance of several feet, it was possible to see that, while both pillowcases were white, the one pinned against the wall was monogrammed, a large letter A clearly visible in one corner to the right of Saxby's head, while the one that was still lying on the bed was plain. It was a small point of difference about which Claudia Byrne could easily have been mistaken. So, too, could a murderer if Saxby had not died of natural causes and it was necessary, for whatever reason, for that one pillow to be replaced.

Except she hadn't been mistaken. The evidence was there, even if it wasn't immediately apparent.

Turning to Boyce, he said, 'Get on the car radio, Tom. I want Pardoe over here straight away and the Scene of Crime officers to give this room a going over.'

'But what's up?' Boyce asked. 'I can't see anything wrong about the set-up. The old bloke feels ill, starts to climb out of bed and collapses. Probably with a heart attack. Seems straightforward enough to me.'

'Then why is the pillow on the bed so damned tidy? Look at it. There's no sign that Saxby's head so much as touched it and yet he must have been using both the pillows. And why when he fell didn't he pull that second pillow down with him like the first? The undersheet's been dragged to one side. You can see where it's rucked up. You'd expect the pillow to have shifted if only a little out of true and not be left lying as neatly as that up against the headboard. Well, I'm not buying it. I'm convinced Miss Byrne's right and someone went to the trouble of changing the pillow on the bed at some time after Saxby collapsed and I want to know why.'

'Right,' Boyce said. 'I'll get on to D.H.'

After he had left, Finch took the opportunity of examining the room in more detail. Looking about him, it was possible to reconstruct at least some of the dead man's movements the previous evening. He had undressed, leaving his clothes folded on the chair by the window before propping up his sticks against its arm and presumably climbing into bed.

A door in the wall nearest to the chair led, he discovered when he pushed it open, into a small, bleak bathroom which evidently Saxby had made use of at some point during his stay. A towel hanging over the edge of the bath felt damp and a cake of soap on the basin was still sticky from use. Apart from shaving-gear on the shelf above the basin and a dressing-gown hanging behind the door, the room was empty of any personal possessions.

Finch was feeling in the pockets of the dressing-gown when Boyce returned.

'They're on their way; should be here in about half an hour,' he announced, adding, as if to voice objections which he hadn't liked to raise before, 'There's not much to go on.'

He meant not just the bathroom with its spartan fittings but the whole case and Finch was inclined to agree with him. Indeed, there wasn't much to go on. An old man had died but, apart from a pillow placed too tidily on a bed, the evidence was minimal.

He grunted and moved back into the bedroom where he said, 'While we're waiting for them, we'll have a chat with Miss Byrne. Make sure this room's locked and sealed, Tom. I don't want anyone snooping round here while we're gone.'

When Boyce had carried out these instructions, turning

the key in the lock and pocketing it before fixing a strip of adhesive paper over the crack between the jamb and the door which he then initialled, they returned downstairs to the yard and, having followed a narrow path round by the back of the house, found her in what had evidently been a formal rose-garden in the centre of which steps led down to a sunken pool, empty now of water. She was seated in the low coping which surrounded the pool, hands clasped in her lap, and appeared to be doing nothing except staring out across the lawn to a bank of shrubbery on the far side.

In those few seconds before she was aware of their presence, Finch was able to study her. On first meeting her, he had been struck by her unusual beauty which he supposed most men would notice first about her without bothering to look any further.

Now, observing her as he and Boyce approached across a strip of shaggy lawn, he was aware of an air of solitariness about her. She was seated alone, against the backdrop of the ruined garden, an oddly symbolic figure although of what Finch himself was unsure. But she reminded him absurd though the comparison was, of that last glimpse he had caught of Marion Greave walking away alone towards the gates of the British Museum. The similarity ended there. There was no physical resemblance between the two women nor their surroundings. All the same, he was touched by an unexpected compassion and, taking his place beside her, he motioned to Boyce to sit on the far side so that, while he remained in earshot, the Sergeant was out of her direct line of vision.

Finch began easily, taking her through her account of the previous day's events, a broad outline of which he had already learned from Dr Callender, and only stopping her to clarify certain details.

It seemed she had called on Roland Saxby – Uncle

114

Rollo, as she called him – the previous afternoon to tell him of her grandfather's illness and had been surprised when he had arrived unexpectedly by taxi about an hour later.

'Who suggested he should stay the night?' Finch put in.

'Great-aunt Constance. Uncle Rollo had intended putting up at the George in Howlett but he was so obviously exhausted, she said he should stay here and someone could take him back to the residential home in the morning. It was Edie who suggested he used the old night nursery.'

'Why?'

Claudia Byrne seemed taken aback by the question.

'For several reasons. There were fewer steps to climb, for one thing. For another, it has its own bathroom next door. Most of the main bedrooms were already occupied anyway, although I'd've quite happily swapped with Uncle Rollo and slept in the night nursery myself.'

'And who made up the bed?'

'I did, to help Edie. The blankets and a pillow were already on the bed. I took clean sheets and a pillowcase from the linen cupboard on the landing . . .'

'Monogrammed?' Finch broke in to ask.

'Oh, yes.'

'You're quite sure of that?'

'Positive. They were part of my grandmother's trousseau and I remember thinking that Uncle Rollo would like having them on the bed. He used to stay at Howlett's quite often when my grandmother was still alive.'

She continued with her account, speaking calmly and coherently although Finch noticed that her voice grew more tense as she drew closer to the events which had taken place later in the evening.

'After dinner, I helped Uncle Rollo upstairs to the night

115

nursery where I asked him if he had everything he wanted. He said he'd like another pillow. I fetched one from the linen cupboard and put a pillowcase on it. And yes,' she said, anticipating Finch's question, 'that was monogrammed as well. I'm absolutely sure about it.' She turned to look at Finch, her eyes very clear and candid. 'There aren't many of the monogrammed sets left and I know I didn't make a mistake and take one of the others.'

Finch merely nodded, as if in agreement, although the question of whether she was right was now only corroborative evidence to the fact that, monogrammed or not, the pillow on Saxby's bed had been changed.

'And then,' he continued cheerfully, as Claudia Byrne seemed reluctant to continue, 'you took Mr Saxby to see your grandfather?'

'Perhaps I shouldn't!' she exclaimed. 'But he wanted to so much. He'd come all this way to make up the quarrel and I hated to disappoint him. I spoke to the nurse first and she said it would be all right, providing he stayed only a few minutes. And Uncle Rollo himself insisted he was rested and could manage the stairs. But I blame myself. Perhaps he'd still be alive if I hadn't taken him to see grandfather.'

Finch let that one pass. Until he knew the cause of Saxby's death, it wasn't his place to make any comment.

Instead, he asked, partly to distract her, for she was close to tears, 'Tell me about the quarrel between Mr Saxby and your grandfather.'

It had its effect. Straightening up, she continued.

'It was over money. When Uncle Rollo sold the farm at Easeden about seven years ago, grandfather wanted him to invest the money in some financial scheme or other that Basil, Great-aunt Constance's stepson, was involved with. Uncle Rollo refused and the quarrel developed from there. They could both be very stubborn and grandfather seemed to think Uncle Rollo had acted out of pique. You see, Uncle Rollo had once proposed to Great-aunt Constance but she turned him down and married Teddy, Basil's father, instead.'

'I see.' Finch sounded deliberately off-hand although it crossed his mind that, if Saxby had been murdered, the motive might lie in the past, in these old quarrels and resentments which, in the case of Saxby and Aston, had apparently gone on festering for years. 'Go on, Miss Byrne. After Mr Saxby had seen your grandfather, what happened next?'

She took up the account once more but in a low, hurried voice as if anxious to get to the end of the ordeal.

'I helped him downstairs to his bedroom. He didn't say much. He seemed too upset about grandfather which was understandable. I don't think Uncle Rollo realized how ill he was. When we got back to the night nursery, he asked to speak to Robert Callender.'

'Did he say why?'

'No; but I had the impression he wanted to discuss grandfather's illness with him. When I told him that the doctor wouldn't call again until this morning, he asked to speak to Great-aunt Constance instead. I went downstairs to find her but Teddy told me she was having a bath. Uncle Rollo had also asked me for a glass of water which I got from the kitchen.'

'Just a moment,' Finch put in, interrupting her account. 'I'd like to get one or two facts sorted out. What time was this?'

'About quarter to ten.'

'And Teddy – Mr Nugent – was downstairs. Whereabouts exactly?'

'In the morning-room, watching television.'

'Alone?'

'Yes.'

'And the others?'

'As I said, Great-aunt Constance was upstairs, having

117

a bath. I gathered Basil was in the study, going over some papers.'

'What about the housekeeper, Miss Cole, and her nephew?'

'Edie was in the kitchen when I went to get the glass of water. She was alone, too, preparing the pudding for today's lunch. I don't know where her nephew was. I hadn't seen him since much earlier yesterday afternoon.'

'Go on,' Finch told her. 'You were saying you got a glass of water for Mr Saxby. What did you do then?'

'I went upstairs again. Uncle Rollo was sitting in the chair. I told him about Great-aunt Constance and he said: Never mind. He'd speak to Robert Callender in the morning. I put the glass of water down on the bedside table and left the room. A little later, I went back to the night nursery to make sure that he really was all right. The lights were out and I could hear him breathing.'

'Regular breathing, was it?' Finch asked casually. It occurred to him that in checking up on Saxby, Claudia Byrne might have been feeling guilty over the part she'd played in the previous evening's events and that she was assuring herself that Saxby hadn't after all suffered any ill effects.

'Oh, yes. There was nothing to suggest he was ill. In fact, I assumed he'd gone to sleep.'

'And when was this?'

'I'm not exactly sure. About half past ten or quarter to eleven, I think.'

Which meant that Saxby was still alive at that time.

The next question couldn't be avoided, although he asked it as gently as he could.

'And I believe it was you who found him this morning?'

'Yes. Edie came to tell me that grandfather had died. Later, at about eight o'clock, I went to Uncle Rollo's room to let him know. I was worried he'd hear us moving about and the doctor's car arriving and would guess what had happened. I wanted to be there with him when he found out. He and grandfather had been so close, I knew Uncle Rollo would be distressed.'

'Did you touch anything?'

If she had, it might mess up the evidence of prints in the room.

'No. At first, I thought he'd got up and left the bedclothes in a heap on the floor. It was only when I was half-way across the room that I noticed anything was wrong. I didn't try to move him. Instead, I felt for a pulse and, when I couldn't find one, I went straight upstairs to grandfather's room to fetch Robert Callender who'd already been sent for. It was while he was examining Uncle Rollo that I noticed the pillow on the bed had been changed. I told Robert and he agreed it looked suspicious. It was he who suggested the room should be locked up and the police told.'

Finch stood up, indicating that the interview was over. At the same time, Boyce quietly slipped his notebook away into his inside pocket.

'Thank you, Miss Byrne,' Finch said. 'I may have to ask you for a written statement at some later time. I'll also need to have your fingerprints taken, merely for elimination, of course. We'll be checking on everybody's in the house.'

'Yes, of course, I understand,' Claudia Byrne said quietly.

'I'd like to speak to the housekeeper next. Could you tell me where she's likely to be?'

'Edie? She's most probably in the kitchen. That's on the right of the back door where you came in.'

'I'll find it,' Finch assured her.

As soon as he and Boyce were out of earshot, the Chief Inspector remarked, 'If Claudia Byrne heard Saxby breathing normally at about quarter to eleven last night, it means he collapsed and died some time later which was when the pillow must have been changed. In that case, we're going to have to check on everyone's movements from ten forty-five onwards.'

'Seems like it,' Boyce agreed, adding gloomily, 'What's the betting that all of them claim they were tucked up in bed?'

They had walked round by the back of the house, past a neglected kitchen garden, the beds overgrown although someone had cleared a path through to a small orchard and a patch of soft-fruit bushes over to their right. The rest of it had been allowed to revert to nature.

Boyce commented on it.

'Seems a shame to let a place like this go to pot.'

'It'd cost a small fortune to keep it up these days,' Finch replied, thinking that, if Saxby had been murdered, it wasn't on account of the Aston money. Judging by the state of the house and its grounds, that was in short supply. But a motive might lie in Saxby's wealth, if he had any. He wondered who might benefit from Saxby's will. Constance Nugent? It was a possibility, especially if, as Claudia Byrne had said, Saxby had once been in love with her.

They paused to contemplate the rear façade of Howlett Hall where more neglect was apparent in the peeling paint and stained brickwork where water from a broken gutter had cascaded down the wall. A little further along, a woman's face could be seen watching them from a downstairs window – the housekeeper, Miss Cole, Finch suspected – and touching Boyce on the elbow to draw his attention to her, the two men walked on towards the yard where they found the woman already waiting for them at the side door.

'Were you looking for someone?' she asked suspiciously.

She was in her late sixties, dressed entirely in black with nothing not even a brooch or a necklace, to relieve its drabness. There was no frivolity here; no concessions either to the advancing years. It was evident in the strong, bony hands, in the hard little knob of hair and in her stance as she guarded the doorway, allowing no-one to enter her domain without her permission. Finch half-expected her to demand that they wipe their feet first before she let them cross the threshold.

As it was, she showed them reluctantly into her kitchen once Finch had introduced himself and Boyce, making it quite clear to them that she was in no mood to waste time.

'I've got lunch to get,' she informed them.

The evidence for such preparation was laid out on the big deal table which occupied the centre of the room. Tomatoes were in the process of being sliced up and a pie containing blackcurrants, judging by the juice which had oozed through the little cuts made in the pastry lid, stood ready to be glazed with milk before being put into the oven; presumably the pudding which Claudia Byrne had said Miss Cole had been preparing the previous evening.

'I won't keep you long,' he assured her. 'There's just a few questions I'd like to ask. When was the last time you saw Mr Saxby yesterday?'

'At half-past seven, when I served dinner.'

'And I believe it was you who suggested he slept in the night nursery?'

'Yes, I did. All the other rooms were occupied.'

'But Miss Byrne made up the bed?'

'That's right.'

'She'd've got the clean sheets and pillowcases from the linen cupboard?'

'I suppose so. That's where they're kept.'

'Where exactly is it?'

'Upstairs; a bit further down the passage from the night nursery.'

'And who's responsible for putting the linen away?'

'I am.'

She replied to all the questions with an off-hand air, barely deigning to look up at him as she continued slicing up the tomatoes and placing them in a large cut-glass bowl together with lettuce leaves, slices of cucumber and cold new potatoes, a typically English salad arranged like a still life but with no benefit of any accompanying dressing that Finch could see although a pair of heavy silver servers lay on the table beside the dish.

'No-one else?'

For the first time, Edie Cole glanced across at him.

'Nancy might.'

'Nancy?'

'Mrs Fuller. She comes in twice a week to help with the cleaning. She sometimes does the ironing as well. She could have taken the clean linen upstairs.'

'What's this about Nancy?'

Turning, Finch saw a man standing in the kitchen doorway, the housekeeper's nephew, Finch suspected, of whom Dr Callender had spoken. A family likeness to Edie Cole was apparent in the bony structure of the face, especially round the cheekbones and above the eyes where the skull seemed to be too close to the surface. It was evident, too, in his casual air, as if he didn't give a damn about other people's opinions although in his case it was more irreverent and nonchalant. Hers was much more tightly buttoned up.

Edie Cole said, 'He's asking about who puts the linen away.'

'Oh?' The man came forward into the room and looked the Chief Inspector up and down. 'Why?'

'Something to do with who made up Mr Saxby's bed

122

yesterday,' Edie Cole said, shrugging as if the matter were of no importance.

It was time, Finch decided, that he reasserted his authority.

'Colin Knapp?' he asked and was gratified to see the cocky smile turn to a much warier expression.

'What if I am?'

Finch recognized the look. He had seen it many times before on the faces of men brought into Divisional Headquarters for questioning – that closing over of the features and the shift of focus in the eyes. He was willing to bet that it wasn't the first time that Colin Knapp had brushed up against the law.

It gave him an advantage which he was quick to use.

'What were you doing yesterday evening after Mr Saxby went upstairs to bed?'

It was Edie Cole who answered. Without so much as pausing in the act of slicing, she replied, 'He was here with me in the kitchen.'

'All evening?' Finch demanded, deliberately addressing Colin Knapp.

He saw the man hesitate and glance across at Edie Cole as if appealing to her for help.

Again it was the housekeeper who spoke.

'Most of it.'

'But he wasn't here when Miss Byrne came into the kitchen for a glass of water.'

Colin Knapp answered this time. He seemed to have recovered his assurance. The self-satisfied smile was back, quirking up the corners of his lips.

'Wasn't I? Then I must have nipped out for a fag. Aunt Edie doesn't like me smoking in the kitchen. Do you?'

'Not where there's food,' she replied calmly.

Finch stood watching the pair of them. He was conscious of a strange alliance between them, close and intimate and yet at the same time edgy as if the relationship wasn't without its tensions.

At that moment, in the brief silence, the sound of cars drawing up in the yard could be heard, announcing the arrival of Pardoe, the police pathologist, and the Scene of Crime officers.

The rest of the interview would have to be postponed but it would be better, he decided, to question them separately next time. Colin Knapp in particular would be more vulnerable without his aunt's presence, especially if in the meantime he had checked up on Knapp's background and found something to the man's disadvantage.

He said, 'I'd like Mrs Fuller's address.'

'She lives on the council estate,' Edie Cole told him. 'Number five, Woodbank Road.'

As Boyce noted it down, Finch continued, addressing them both, 'And I'll need your fingerprints. We'll have to check on who's been in Mr Saxby's room.'

It was a good point at which to leave, while he still had the upper hand and, as he and Boyce walked to the door, the Chief Inspector glanced back.

Edie Cole, with the same imperturbable expression, was arranging a final layer of tomato slices fanwise in the glass bowl but Colin Knapp was staring after them, shoulders hunched, the smile wiped clean off his face, much to the Chief Inspector's secret satisfaction.

10

There were two cars already parked in the yard when Finch and Boyce came out of the side door, one containing McCullum, the photographer, the other the Scene of Crime officers, including Wylie, the fingerprint expert.

As the men began unpacking their equipment and carrying it across to the house, Pardoe's Rover arrived with a flourish, the pathologist flinging open the driver's door and climbing out, medical bag in hand, almost before the car had come to a halt, eager to take a look at the body, like a small, sandy terrier let loose in a barn.

'Well, where is it?' he demanded.

Boyce led the way, tramping ahead of them up the service stairs to break the seal on the door and turn the key in the lock.

Finch hung back, letting the experts go ahead. They didn't need him to tell them their job although, when McCullum had finished photographing the body, the Chief Inspector checked that he had taken some close-up shots of the bed with its rucked up bottom sheet and the pillow lying so neatly on top of it.

If murder should be proved, this photographic evidence would be vital.

As McCullum moved away to take some more general views of the room, Pardoe came bustling forward, bending down over Saxby's body to roll back the eyelids with his thumbs and peering at the eyes with the aid of a powerful torch.

'No obvious signs of suffocation,' he announced, addressing Finch over his shoulder. 'No petechiae and no mucus round the nose and mouth. How old was he?'

'Seventy-eight.'

Pardoe clicked his tongue with annoyance as if, by choosing to die at this age, Saxby had deliberately set out to be provoking.

'As old as that? I've known cases of elderly people being smothered in a matter of seconds with little or no immediate evidence of asphyxia. I'll need to open him up and take a look at the internal organs for petechial haemorrhages before I can be sure one way or the other.'

He bent lower, holding the head by the chin and turning it a little to the left and then to the right to examine the neck, so that the long line of Saxby's nose was seen in both profiles, like a mug shot, before he turned his attention to the hands, picking up each in turn to scrutinize them carefully.

'No bruising on the throat so it's unlikely it was manual strangulation and, as the hands look unmarked, it wouldn't appear he tried to fight off an attacker although I'll take some scrapings from under the nails to be on the safe side.'

'Time of death?' Finch asked.

Pardoe gave him a sardonic, sideways grin.

'Always keen, aren't you, Jack, to have the time of death established? I'd say dead keen, if it wasn't so damned appropriate. Rigor's fully developed so he's been dead for about twelve hours.'

He beckoned to Marsh and Johnson, the two SOCOs, who, dressed in white coveralls and boots, were waiting to make their own examination of the corpse and its setting.

'Help me get him up on the bed and turn him over. I'll take the rectal temperature. If it's asphyxia, it should be above normal, not below. At the same time, I'll have a look at the lividity stains on his back. They should tell us if the body's been moved after death although, by the look of him, he collapsed and died as we found him.'

As he was speaking, he was briskly unbuttoning the pyjama jacket, exposing the chest with its arched rib-cage straining against the thin flesh.

It seemed a good point at which to leave and, jerking his head at Boyce to follow, Finch went off down the passage, opening doors in search of the linen cupboard and at the same time establishing the layout of this part of the house.

There were five more doors along the corridor, not counting Saxby's; one adjoining it which was locked and another on the far right-hand side at the top of the service stairs which opened into a small, old-fashioned lavatory with a mahogany seat and an iron cistern. Facing it, another set of stairs led upwards, presumably to the attics. Next to it was a bathroom, as bleak and as functional in its fittings as the one in the nursery, intended originally for the servants, and, judging by the toilet articles strewn about it, shared by Miss Cole and her nephew. Next door to it was Miss Cole's bedroom.

Keeping his head round the door for longer than was strictly necessary merely to establish whom it belonged to, Finch took in with a few rapid glances a high bedstead with a blue candlewick counterpane, dark oak furniture polished to a high gloss and a square of plain brown carpet. The room looked cheerless. It faced north, towards the back of the house with its ruined kitchen garden, and contained little in the way of knick-knacks or ornaments apart from a serviceable-looking hairbrush lying on the dressing-table together with a jar of zinc and castor oil cream and an alarm clock busily ticking away on the bedside table. A few pictures, mostly Edwardian oleographs, hung on the walls but they looked less like Miss

Cole's personal choice than household rejects which, rather than being thrown away, had been banished upstairs to this back room.

The linen cupboard was at the far end of the passage, next to a door covered with green baize which closed off the corridor from the rest of the house. As soon as Wylie had dusted the cupboard door for fingerprints and McCullum had photographed both that and the interior, Finch himself took a look inside.

It was a large, walk-in cupboard, windowless but well lit by a hanging overhead light, and was fitted with slatted shelves which held an assortment of bedding – pillows and blankets on the upper levels, sheets, pillow-cases and towels on the lower. With Boyce watching a little sceptically from the doorway, Finch went swiftly through the bed linen which had been arranged neatly in piles, the monogrammed sheets on a separate shelf, the accompanying pillowcases stacked up beside them. There were only three, all embroidered with the letter A, some carefully darned. A larger pile beside them and immediately on the right as they entered bore no mono-gram. But, as he pointed out to Boyce as he switched off the light and closed the door, anyone entering the linen cupboard in a hurry might reach for the pile of plain pillowcases which was nearer to hand.

Boyce merely shrugged as if these domestic arrange-ments were no concern of his before following the Chief Inspector back along the passage to the night nursery where Wylie was still at work, dusting the room for prints, while the SOCOs, now that Saxby's body had been lifted on to the bed, were bagging up the bedding. The broken lamp and the drinking-glass were already sealed and labelled inside their own containers ready for forensic examination together with the dead man's clothes.

Saxby lay on his back, the beaky profile turned

up towards the ceiling. Somebody, probably Johnson who cared about such niceties, had folded the two halves of the pyjama jacket together so that the old man's thin, bony chest was now decently covered.

'You can move him whenever you want to,' Pardoe announced as Finch entered. 'I've finished with him for the time being. I'll perform the PM at three o'clock tomorrow afternoon, if that's all right with you, Jack. Can't make it sooner. I've already got three bodies to deal with from that warehouse fire. No sign that he was moved after death, by the way; not according to the lividity stains anyway. And judging by the rectal temperature, he's been dead between twelve and fourteen hours.'

Which would place the time of death between ten o'clock and midnight the previous night, Finch calculated, glancing at his watch.

'If in the meantime, you could find out when he ate his last meal . . .'

'Half past seven last night,' Finch put in quickly.

Pardoe gave him an appreciative nod.

'Good. In that case, that'll help to establish the time of death more accurately when the stomach contents are analysed which you'll probably want to have done once you've seen this.'

He pointed towards the bedside table, now set upright on its feet and bagged up, on which a small pill bottle was standing, also enclosed in its own clear plastic envelope. As Finch picked it up to examine it, Pardoe continued:

'If the label's correct, the prescription's made out for Mr R. Saxby and the tablets are Angipol, a brand name for Propranolol Hydrochloride, used in the treatment of atheromatous disease. Or a dodgy heart condition to you, Jack, in which the coronary arteries get bunged up with cholesterol deposits. For your further information, the symptoms – pains in the chest usually – can be triggered off by physical exertion as well as emotional stress and quite often occur when the patient is asleep or lying down. And that would tie in with the other signs, or rather lack of them, which I'd expect to find in a case of asphyxia – no petechiae in the eyes or scalp, no mucus or bleeding from the ears, and a rise in the rectal temperature. All of which suggests to me that your *corpus delicti* wasn't suffocated but died of a heart attack. But it's up to you what you make of it. I'm just a simple medical man, passing on a few bits and pieces of scientific fact.'

And with another unrepentant grin at Finch, he picked up his bag and marched briskly out of the room.

'Where was the bottle found?' Finch demanded as soon as Pardoe had gone.

'On the floor behind the table,' Johnson explained with an apologetic air as if its concealment were in some obscure way his fault. 'We found it after the body had been moved. I suppose it could have been knocked off the table with the lamp.'

Finch ignored this piece of speculation, turning instead to Boyce who was wearing his formal, on-duty expression from which the Chief Inspector knew damn well that the Sergeant was thinking 'I told you so'.

It took a great deal of self-control on Finch's part to speak to him normally.

'Get off downstairs, Tom. See if the mortuary van's arrived. If it has, we'll get the body moved.'

It evidently had for Boyce was back within minutes, accompanied by the two attendants.

Finch stood watching as Saxby's body was lifted, wrapped in plastic sheeting and placed inside the canvas container which, with its strong handles, put Finch in mind of a monstrous golf bag. It was then carried from the room, the Sergeant going ahead to make sure that

130

the downstairs doors were closed and its removal was completed in reasonable privacy.

There was a moment's silence after the body had gone. Then, with a glance at the Chief Inspector, Marsh and Johnson resumed their task of examining the bedding, folding back the sheets before placing them inside the waiting bags. Time was short.

Finch left them to it, going out into the passage where he met Boyce as the Detective Sergeant came up the back stairs.

'OK,' the Sergeant said briefly, meaning that the body had been driven away without any undue fuss. 'What now?'

Finch nodded towards the door at the far end of the passage.

'I want to see where that leads,' he said.

It led on to a large half-landing from which a broad oak staircase opened out, one flight going to an upper gallery, the other descending to a hall. Doors were visible in both the gallery and the hall but all of them were closed and the house seemed unnaturally silent as if deserted by its occupants.

Finch took a few steps forward, looking about him at the layout. Claudia Byrne had said that when she had taken Roland Saxby to see her grandfather, she had waited for him on the landing outside the room. It would therefore be one of the doors which opened directly on to the gallery at the head of the stairs, which one was impossible to tell. She must also have come down the stairs and through the baize door to listen outside Saxby's room at about quarter to eleven the previous evening, at which time he must have still been alive because she had said she had heard him breathing.

So, if he had been murdered, and at the moment, according to Pardoe's findings, a hell of a large question mark hung over that supposition, then whoever had

131

killed him could have approached his room either by using the main staircase or the back stairs which led up from the kitchen wing.

He was leaning over the banisters, trying to look down obliquely into the hall, when one of the doors opened and a man emerged. Catching sight of the Chief Inspector peering down from the half-landing, he paused.

'Are you the police?' he demanded.

There was nothing Finch could do except put a good face on it and walk down the stairs with Boyce in tow to meet the man.

He was Basil Nugent, Finch discovered once the introductions had been completed, and therefore, as Dr Callender had made clear, not a member of the family except through marriage although, from his manner, he might have been the head of the household.

'We'll talk in the study,' he told the Chief Inspector, ushering Boyce and Finch into the room from which he had just emerged and where, judging by the files and papers laid out on the desk, he had been working. Taking his seat behind the desk, he waved the Chief Inspector and the Sergeant towards two upright chairs.

He was a large, smooth man, very much on his dignity and, from the way in which he settled himself back in the leather chair, fully intending to take charge of the interview from its outset, a position which his opening remarks made quite clear.

'I must point out to you, Chief Inspector, that I object most strongly to the police being involved in Mr Saxby's death. In my opinion, Dr Callender has overreached his responsibilities by calling you in. Mr Saxby was an old man. The drive over here yesterday obviously exhausted him. There's no doubt in my mind that he suffered some kind of collapse, most probably a heart attack.'

Finch had heard enough. It was not often that he chose to play the heavy policeman. When it was necessary for official weight to be thrown about, he preferred to leave it to Boyce who was better built for the part, reserving for himself the role of the listening copper, nice to narks and with plenty of time for anyone with a tale to tell. On such occasions, he could assume an avuncular expression, head cocked attentively, by his very silence encouraging witnesses or suspects to pour out all they knew.

But Nugent exasperated him. It was bad enough that Pardoe had voiced much the same opinion regarding Saxby's death. He didn't need anyone else, and certainly not Nugent, to tell him his business. It was time that the man was put firmly in his place and he gave an ostentatious nod in Boyce's direction who, picking up the cue, made a great show of taking out his notebook and opening it at a clean page.

'My Detective Sergeant will make a note of your objections, Mr Nugent,' he said in his official voice. 'In the meantime, while you're not obliged to answer my questions, it would assist our inquiries if you co-operated.'

Nugent climbed down; not far and with bad grace but, after staring across the desk for several seconds at the Chief Inspector, he made an abrupt movement with his shoulders, indicating that the interview could continue.

Finch plunged in at once. Seeing there was no chance of a gossipy, heart to heart approach, the only alternative was a brisk question and answer session, establishing the facts.

The facts seemed straightforward enough and, up to the latter part of the previous evening, corroborated Claudia Byrne's account. Roland Saxby had arrived unexpectedly, had been invited to stay the night by Constance Nugent, Nugent's stepmother, and, after dinner, had been escorted upstairs to his room by Claudia Byrne.

At this point, the two statements diverged. Nugent had

spent part of the evening watching the nine o'clock news on television with his father and stepmother. After it was over, he had left them to come to the study where he had worked on a client's accounts. He had therefore not been present when Claudia Byrne had come downstairs looking for Mrs Nugent.

He himself had remained in the study until a quarter past eleven when he had gone upstairs to his room. The lights were still on in the hall and on the landing so he had assumed that the housekeeper, Miss Cole, had not yet gone to bed. Anyway, it was not his responsibility to see that the lights were turned off or the house secured for the night.

And no, he had not gone to Mr Saxby's room that evening nor at any time during the day. He himself had only arrived at Howlett's the previous day, having driven down from London at his father's request.

'I hadn't even met the man until he turned up here yesterday afternoon!'

'But you knew which room Mr Saxby was sleeping in?'

'Yes; my stepmother and the housekeeper discussed it in my hearing. Personally, I thought it most unwise that Saxby was asked to stay the night.'

'Why was that?'

'I should have thought that was obvious, Chief Inspector. Mr Aston was very ill indeed; dying in fact. Miss Cole had more than enough to cope with without asking an elderly man as an overnight guest. If I'd had my way, he'd've been driven back to the nursing home last night after he'd had time to recover. I understand that he wanted to speak to Mr Aston but that, of course, was out of the question although I'd've had no objections to his seeing Mr Aston this morning when Dr Callender was present. Of course, Mr Aston's death as well as Mr Saxby's made such a visit impossible.'

Finch let it pass. As Dr Callender had made clear, no-one apart from Claudia Byrne and the nurse knew of Saxby's visit the previous evening to the sick man's bedroom and it was better that the rest of the family remained in ignorance of that fact, at least for the time being.

Instead, he remarked, 'I'd like to speak to your father and stepmother.'

Nugent, his account finished, had half-risen to his feet, expecting the interview was over. He sat down again abruptly.

'You can certainly speak to my father. I can't imagine he'll raise any objections. But I really must insist that my stepmother is spared any cross-examination. She's under sedation. The double shock of her brother's death followed by Mr Saxby's has caused her a great deal of distress.'

'Very well,' Finch agreed with apparent equanimity although he added his own silent rider that at some stage in the inquiry Mrs Nugent would have to be questioned, even if it meant carrying out the questioning in Dr Callender's presence.

At the same time, he couldn't resist waiting until Nugent was half-way to the door before adding in the same pleasant manner, 'By the way, Mr Nugent, we'll need to have everyone's fingerprints taken, yours included.'

'Mine?' Nugent sounded outraged at the idea. 'But I've already told you I haven't been inside Saxby's room.'

'Then in that case, you'll have no reason for refusing, will you?'

As the door slammed smartly behind Nugent, Finch exchanged a quick grin with Boyce and then, leaning forward casually across the desk, turned the topmost sheet of paper a little towards him so that it was possible for him to read its contents. It was a letter from a firm of property developers in Birmingham, requesting an appointment with Nugent in order to discuss the possibility of buying into a similar London-based business. He barely had time to replace it and resume his seat when Nugent reappeared, accompanied by his father whom he introduced briefly to the Chief Inspector and the Sergeant before, giving Finch a suspicious look, he gathered up his papers and left the room.

Finch took the opportunity of his departure to take Nugent's place behind the desk from which vantage point he observed the new witness.

Nugent senior was in his seventies, Finch estimated, a small, dapper-looking man and much more willing than his son to be co-operative, which made the interview easier going. All the same, Finch sensed a certain reticence about the man, whether out of wariness or a quite natural concern that the police were involved in a family tragedy it was impossible to say.

Yes, he agreed, he, too, had been surprised when Saxby had turned up the previous afternoon and, like his son, had thought the decision to invite him to stay the night had not been a wise one.

As for Saxby himself, Nugent had met him several times in the past after his own marriage to Constance; Saxby had been an old family friend. But he understood there had been some quarrel with Edgar Aston and Saxby had ceased to come to the house.

'Over an annuity, wasn't it?' Finch asked.

Nugent looked embarrassed.

'I suppose Claudia told you about it?' he replied. 'It was a most unfortunate situation which I'm afraid I got drawn into. As I understood it, Saxby was thinking of retiring and selling up his farm. Edgar, Constance's brother, happened to mention this fact to me and I suggested Saxby consulted my son before coming to any decision. Basil's a financial consultant and it seemed to me that, with the right kind of investment advice, Saxby could get more return on his capital than the annuity he was proposing to buy. It was said casually, in the course of conversation, you understand, Chief Inspector. I had no intention of concerning myself in Saxby's affairs. But it seems Edgar passed on my advice to Saxby who took great exception to what he called my interference in his private affairs. The quarrel developed from there. They could both be very stubborn and neither was prepared to apologize.'

Head cocked, Finch listened attentively as if it were the first time he had heard such a detailed account of the dispute. On the face of it, Nugent's statement seemed frank enough. But it had been suitably censored, he realized. There was no suggestion, for example, that Saxby had once proposed marriage to Constance Nugent and that the quarrel might have been fuelled by Saxby's resentment that the man who had eventually married her had been trying to meddle in his affairs. Nor was there any reference to the purpose of Saxby's visit to Howlett Hall, a point which Finch himself raised.

'Didn't Mr Saxby come here in the hope of making up the quarrel?'

'So I understand.'

Finch picked up the equivocation. Nugent's statement so far had been punctuated by similar phrases as if he were reluctant to admit to any first-hand knowledge of any family disputes or decisions.

'Weren't you there when Mr Saxby arrived?'

'Yes, I was. But I wasn't present all the time. My wife asked me to telephone the nursing home where Saxby was staying to let the matron know he was here with us and to cancel his booking at the George. Later on, Constance mentioned that Saxby wanted to speak to Edgar but we thought it better that he waited until this morning. Unfortunately, events overtook that decision.'

It was spoken with what appeared to be genuine regret at the deaths of both Aston and Saxby which, as far as Nugent seemed aware, had made that meeting impossible and, preferring to skirt round this issue for Claudia Byrne's sake, Finch led him through the rest of his statement.

He and his wife had arrived at Howlett Hall, Nugent said, the previous morning, Edie Cole having telephoned them in London to tell them that Edgar Aston had been taken ill and that she had sent for Dr Callender. As Aston's condition had deteriorated, they had got in touch with Claudia, Aston's granddaughter, and also with Basil, Nugent's son.

At this point Finch interrupted.

'Why was your son sent for? As I understand it, he had no close connection with the Aston family.'

For the first time during the interview, Nugent showed some of his son's characteristics by objecting to this line of questioning but more in sorrow than in anger.

'I really don't see that my son's presence has anything to do with your inquiry into Saxby's death, Chief Inspector. But if you insist. Basil and Edgar were, in fact, quite close. Basil had helped him over the years with advice over several transactions – the sale of part of the land, for example, and with such matters as his income tax returns, especially as Edgar grew older and tended to become rather muddled and forgetful. I thought that, as Basil was much more informed about Edgar's affairs than either Constance or myself, he ought to be here to advise us, especially when we realized that Edgar was seriously ill.'

It sounded plausible and, as Nugent had quite properly pointed out, the Chief Inspector's concern was with Saxby's death, not Aston's. Under the circumstances, there was nothing Finch could do except continue with the interview although it occurred to him that both the

Nugents, father and son, had been damned quick off the mark in moving in to take control of Aston's affairs even before Aston himself was dead.

Nugent's account of his movements the previous day was quickly covered. After dinner, when Claudia Byrne had taken Saxby upstairs, Nugent, together with his wife and son, had retired to the small morning-room to watch television, Basil leaving them to work in the study at half past nine when the BBC One news programme had finished. Shortly afterwards, at about twenty to ten, Constance had said good night and had gone upstairs to take a bath. Nugent had therefore been alone when Claudia had come into the room, looking for her great-aunt.

No, he answered in reply to Finch's question, Claudia had not said why she wanted to speak to Constance. On learning where she was, Claudia had left. Nugent himself had gone to bed at half past ten. He hadn't spoken to his wife although he had looked into her bedroom. As she wasn't there, he had assumed she was still in the bathroom. He himself had gone to his own room and had heard nothing until Edie Cole woke him up the following morning to tell him that Edgar Aston had died.

As Finch raised an eyebrow at the reference to separate rooms, Nugent added a little defensively, 'My wife is a very light sleeper. The smallest sound wakes her up.' He added, 'And I really must insist that she isn't questioned yet, Chief Inspector. She's still recovering from the shock.'

As Finch nodded his agreement, Nugent went on to explain that he had first heard of Saxby's death when Dr Callender had asked to speak to all of them that morning. He, Nugent, like the others, had been extremely distressed to hear that the police were to be informed.

Finch got to his feet, signalling the end of the interview and, having thanked Nugent, asked him to send Nurse Holden to the study.

She arrived shortly afterwards, a sensible, cheerful woman who answered Finch's questions briskly and to the point.

She had been sent for by Dr Callender the previous afternoon and had arrived at Howlett Hall early that same evening. Dr Callender had taken her straight upstairs to the patient's bedroom.

At about nine o'clock, Miss Byrne, who had introduced herself as Mr Aston's granddaughter, had asked if Mr Saxby, an old family friend, could visit the patient. As Dr Callender had instructed her that visitors, provided they stayed no more than five minutes, were allowed, she had agreed. Shortly afterwards, Miss Byrne had returned accompanied by an elderly man whom she had introduced as Mr Saxby. While Miss Byrne had remained outside on the landing, she, the nurse, had helped Mr Saxby to a chair by the patient's bed. Mr Aston was then in a coma and she doubted if he was aware of what Mr Saxby had said.

'And what did Mr Saxby say?' Finch inquired.

'Not a great deal. What can anyone say to someone who's unconscious and is clearly dying? I went to the other side of the room and tried to look busy. It can be very embarrassing when you can't leave and yet you don't want to look as if you're listening in to a private conversation. Mr Saxby said, "It's me, Edgar. Roland. I've come to say I'm sorry." He then asked me if I thought Mr Aston could hear him. Well, what could I do? I could hardly tell him he was wasting his time. Besides, he looked so upset; close to tears, as a matter of fact. So I told him, "Go on talking. He may be able to take in what you're saying even if he can't answer." I couldn't hear much of what he said after that; he spoke in such a low voice and anyway I wasn't trying to listen. He seemed to be reminiscing about the time when they were boys – about going skating one Christmas and a tree-house they'd built and how angry Mr Aston's father had been about something or other they'd done although at that point I had to interrupt. The five minutes were up so I went across to the bed to ask Mr Saxby to leave. To tell you the truth, it was rather moving. Mr Saxby bent over the bed and took both Mr Aston's hands in his and said, "Good bye, old chap. Sleep well. And let bygones be bygones." And then he gave a funny little cry as if he was choking back the tears. I don't mind admitting I was touched myself. I mean, poor old man! When I helped him out of the room, I could feel his arm shaking under mine. Then Miss Byrne took charge of him and I went back to my patient.'

'And Mr Aston died early this morning?' Finch asked.

'Yes; soon after quarter past six; quite peacefully, in his sleep. I'd been told by Dr Callender that if anything happened to him, I was to go straight to Miss Cole and leave it to her to tell the family. Her room had been pointed out to me by Dr Callender when I first arrived. It was at the far end of the passageway which opens off the landing.'

'So you passed Mr Saxby's room?'

'Did I? Well, if I did, I wasn't aware of it. I wasn't told which room he was sleeping in, nor any other members of the family, come to that. Anyway, I didn't notice anything unusual. All the doors were closed. I simply knocked at Miss Cole's door, told her that Mr Aston had just died and went straight back to his room. I assume she let the others know what had happened because they started coming shortly afterwards, Mr Nugent senior first. He wanted to make sure everything was ready.'

'Ready?' Finch asked.

She laughed a little awkwardly.

'Well, you know – tidy. Relatives don't like it if the body isn't lying nicely and the room looks as if someone's just died in it. So I straightened up the bed, moved the medicines to my room next door and put a vase of flowers on the bedside table. Mr Nugent went to fetch his wife. Poor thing. She was so upset. I felt really sorry for her. Then shortly afterwards, Dr Callender arrived to write out the death certificate. I gathered the young Mr Nugent had sent for him. While the doctor was still in the room, Miss Byrne asked to speak to him. He was away for quite a long time. When he came back, he said that Mr Saxby had been found dead and I was to say nothing to the others about him visiting Mr Aston last night; not that I would have told them anyway. It's none of my business.'

The next question had to be asked although Finch put it as casually as he could.

'I suppose there's no question that Mr Aston died of anything other than natural causes?'

She was too experienced to show surprise.

'Oh, no, Chief Inspector. I've nursed many stroke patients, both in NHS hospitals and privately. There was nothing suspicious about Mr Aston's death. In fact, when I took over the case yesterday, I didn't think he had long to live.' She paused before asking, 'When will the body be removed?'

'This afternoon, I imagine. Dr Callender said he'd let the family know. He'll call at the house later.'

'So there won't be a PM?'

'There's no need.'

'I'd better stay on then until Dr Callender gets back.' She glanced at her watch. 'It'll be lunch soon anyway. Miss Cole said it was always served at half past twelve.'

She was right. When Nurse Holden had left, Finch and Boyce emerged from the study to find the housekeeper on her way upstairs with a tray and the door opposite set open, revealing a dining-room with the table laid for a meal.

It seemed a good moment to break for lunch themselves and, having made arrangements with Wylie to fingerprint the occupants of the house later that afternoon when the examination of Saxby's room was finished, the Chief Inspector and his Sergeant drove into Howlett in search of a quiet pub.

11

Claudia was spared the strain of lunching tête-à-tête with
Basil by the presence of Nurse Holden who joined them
in the dining-room, Teddy having decided to keep Great-
aunt Constance company by taking his meal upstairs on
a tray.

Even so, it was a sombre occasion. Basil was almost
totally silent apart from a small conversational exchange
addressed specifically to the nurse.

'Dr Callender has telephoned to say that we may go
ahead with Mr Aston's funeral arrangements. I assume
everything's in order as far as you're concerned? Good.
I've already spoken to my stepmother and she wants the
matter put in hand straightaway.'

He pointedly ignored Claudia and, as soon as the meal
was over, took his cup of coffee and retired to the study
to telephone the firm of funeral directors in Howlett,
Claudia assumed.

His departure gave her the opportunity to put a
question to the nurse which she had hesitated to do in
Basil's hearing.

'May I see grandfather this afternoon?'

To her relief, the nurse treated the request with a brisk
matter-of-factness and later, when Claudia went upstairs
and knocked at the door, Miss Holden, having shown
her in, retired to her own room, leaving Claudia alone.

And it was not so much an ordeal as she had feared.
Although the blinds had been drawn, the sunlight,
filtered through the cream-coloured fabric, cast a subdued
yellowish glow into the room and across the high

bed where the body of her grandfather lay quietly as if asleep.

Claudia sat down on the chair beside it. She had never seen a dead person before and had assumed that some lingering vibration of the trauma of dying would have remained to disturb the atmosphere. But it was not so. The room was tidy and smelt of roses, a vase of which had been placed on the bedside table. The clutter of medicines had gone, together with his dressing-gown and the battered leather slippers which had stood by the chest of drawers.

All that was left of him was a shape under the bedclothes which were drawn up to his chin, and a face which she recognized as if from a photograph, supported by the pillows, and which seemed to represent not any one she had known personally but some symbolic portrayal for which the Victorians, so inventive where death was concerned, might have found a suitable title such as 'Home at Last' or 'Eternal Rest'.

She remained there for five minutes, the length of time permitted for a visit when he had been alive, and then, getting to her feet, she walked a little further down the corridor to Great-aunt Constance's room where she knocked on the door.

Teddy let her in, placing one finger conspiratorially against his lips although Great-aunt Constance was not asleep. She was propped up like grandfather against the pillows in a big double bed in a similar subdued, creamy light cast by the drawn blinds and might herself have been dead except for the intense brilliance of her eyes as she watched Claudia cross the room.

She was still wearing her nightdress although the dressing-gown had been replaced by a satin bed-jacket, extravagantly ruffled round the neck, the lacy folds seeming to accentuate the puckered skin.

Claudia was shocked at the sight of her. She looked so

dreadfully old as if she had aged ten years overnight, the face finely netted with tiny lines which not even the make-up she was wearing could disguise and the flesh fallen away from round the eyes and mouth so that the family resemblance to grandfather was even more apparent.

Claudia approached the bed, wondering what on earth to say.

It was Great-aunt Constance who spoke first.

In a voice so low that Claudia had to lean forward to catch the words, she asked, 'Have the police gone yet?'

'Yes, I believe they have,' Claudia replied, omitting to add that they would almost certainly be back.

'And what's happened about Roland? Have they taken away his body?'

Claudia looked at Teddy in appeal, wondering whether to tell the truth or not. But Teddy had dissociated himself from the conversation and was standing, head lowered, hands behind his back and an expression of such deep distress on his own face that she was forced to come to her own decision about how to reply.

'Yes, they have.'

To her consternation, Great-aunt Constance began to cry; not histrionically as Claudia had sometimes seen her weep in the past but quietly as if out of a great and overwhelming despair. The tears seemed to pour out of her, running down over her cheeks, the words tumbling out in the same uncontrolled flood.

'Poor, poor Roland! He was so charming, Claudia, so very attentive. A darling man. But he shouldn't have come. It was too much for him, you see. Too great a strain.'

'Yes, of course,' Claudia said and was relieved when Teddy came bustling forward to sit beside Great-aunt Constance on the bed, putting an arm about her shoulders and rocking her to and fro as one might a child, at the same time catching Claudia's glance and looking towards the door to indicate that she should leave.

As she started down the stairs, a door above her opened and closed and Robert Callender called her name, hurrying down after her to join her on the half-landing.

'Are you all right, Claudia?' he asked in a low voice.

She shrugged and smiled, touched by his obvious concern but trying to make light of the situation.

'Basil's not at all pleased that the police have been called in. As for Teddy, he's too involved with looking after Great-aunt Constance to bother much with me.'

'It's one of the reasons I'm here – to check on Mrs Nugent. And also to tell the nurse she can leave. She won't be needed any longer. I saw Basil Nugent briefly when I first arrived. I gather the arrangements for your grand-father's funeral are going ahead. His body should be taken away this afternoon. Would you like me to speak to Basil while I'm here? Ask him to leave you alone? You've been under a lot of stress yourself, Claudia.'

'I think I can cope with Basil,' she assured him.

'If it gets too much, come over to the surgery.'

'Thank you,' she said with genuine gratitude. 'But I'd rather stay on here and see it out to the end. Edie may need help and besides, I don't think the police have finished here yet. Finch said we'd have to have our fingerprints checked on.'

'I'm sorry.' He sounded as if it were all his fault.

'If anyone should be sorry, it's me,' she replied. 'I started the whole thing off.' Turning away towards the baize door, she added, 'I'll see if there's anything I can do for Edie.'

She had gone before he could say any more, conscious that his kindness and concern might break her resolve and that what she needed more than anything else at that moment was a stiff dose of Edie's brisk practicality to give her the courage to face the rest of the afternoon.

Finch and Boyce lunched well on ham salad and draught bitter in the Cock, a small pub in Howlett's main shopping street, from the front door of which it was possible to glimpse not only both ends of the small town but also some of its surrounding suburbs, including the private development of exclusive housing at the smart end, near the church, and the roofs of the council estate at the other.

Having collected the car from behind the public-house, they drove into the estate which began and ended abruptly, its new-looking roads and lampposts contrasting oddly with the surrounding wheatfields where a combine harvester was at work, cutting wide swathes into the standing corn.

The semi-detached houses were alike, apparently constructed from grey oblong blocks like those in a child's building set, and all conformed to the same basic design with four windows and a door to which a perfectly straight concrete path led, neatly bisecting a rectangular front garden, surrounded with chain-link fencing.

To cheer the place up, the developers had painted the doors in bright, primary colours, red, yellow and blue, an attempt at individuality which had failed in its object for the coloured doors followed each other in strict succession and the crude paintbox shades only made the grey walls appear more drab and unfinished. Nor had the planners taken into account the various tastes and idiosyncrasies of the tenants and, as they drove slowly down Woodbank Road, looking for number five, Finch was heartened to see a motorbike in process of being dismantled here on a front lawn or a home-made rockery there, lovingly constructed out of some of the broken concrete blocks. Even a collection of garden gnomes was a visual pleasure.

Nancy Fuller's garden showed no such imaginative

endeavour. It was laid entirely with grass, roughly cut, with no benefit of even a shrub or a climbing rose to disguise the metal fencing.

Her attitude, when she opened the front door to them, was as unwelcoming as her garden, a reaction which changed to hostility when Finch introduced himself and his Sergeant and explained the object of their visit.

'I don't know nothing,' she told them and seemed about to close the door in their faces. It was with considerable reluctance that she was finally persuaded to let them inside the house.

In the event, she had little to tell them. Boyce questioned her, Finch sitting back and listening, at the same time observing her and her surroundings.

The room was shabby but clean, furnished with cheap stuff that was already showing signs of wear. She was of a piece with it, a once attractive girl, now in her thirties, but, like the armchairs and the sideboard, had lost her original showroom gloss. She looked tired and frayed.

And pregnant. The small, incipient bulge could be seen under the thin cotton dress she was wearing. She sat, too, as pregnant women tend to do, with her knees slightly apart.

Her statement seemed straightforward enough. She had been working at Howlett Hall for two mornings a week for the past three years, ever since Miss Cole had found the place getting too much for her. In fact, she had been due to work there that morning but Miss Cole had sent her away on account of the two old blokes dying.

Yes, she did do the ironing and had at times put it away in the linen cupboard but not often. Miss Cole usually took it upstairs. But she didn't know anything about separate piles of monogrammed sheets and pillow-cases. She simply ironed the bloody things and left Miss Cole to sort them out.

She knew old Mr Aston, of course. When she'd first

149

gone to work at Howlett's, she'd seen him pottering about in the garden on occasions but he'd been ill with bronchitis a couple of winters before and since then he'd had to take things easy. He'd come downstairs some mornings when she was there and read the newspaper in the big sitting-room but quite often he'd stay upstairs resting in his room.

No, she didn't know the other old man, Mr Saxby. She'd never heard anyone even mention him. But she was asked to clean out what Miss Cole called the night nursery from time to time, mostly dusting as the room was hardly ever used. In fact, most of the bedrooms except for Mr Aston's and Miss Cole's were closed off, except when Mr and Mrs Nugent came to stay, and Miss Cole always saw to the cleaning of them and made up the beds.

Listening to her, Finch was aware of other impressions which underlay this mere catalogue of facts. Largely it was a sense of deep resentment – against Miss Cole, who was clearly a hard taskmistress; against the Nugents who arrived quite often to see old Mr Aston and made extra work; and against the house itself which, according to Nancy Fuller, needed half a dozen servants to run and which should have been pulled down years ago.

This resentment was also directed against her children who, because it was the school summer holiday, were at home, playing in the back garden, and at whom Nancy Fuller shouted at regular intervals, breaking off the interview with Boyce to bang on the window with orders to 'Stop that!' or 'Pack it in!' else they'd cop it from her.

'Bloody kids!' she announced, returning to her chair after one such excursion.

'Who looks after them while you're working at Howlett Hall?' Finch asked.

She took exception to this show of concern as well, shooting him a glance full of suspicion.

150

'They go round to my sister's,' she told him in a grudging voice which suggested it was none of his business.

'Can't be easy for you.'

Finch offered the remark as a small sop to her better nature and saw her expression soften a little.

'No, it's not,' she agreed. 'But I need the money, now I'm on my own.'

'On her own?' Finch repeated when, the interview over, he and Boyce walked back to the car. 'Since when? And who's the father of the child she's expecting?'

'God knows,' Boyce said, slamming the driver's door viciously. He was in a bad mood, having caught the rough edge of Nancy Fuller's tongue himself on informing her that, as she sometimes cleaned the night nursery at Howlett Hall, she would have to have her fingerprints taken. It was small consolation that Wylie, when he was sent round to take them later that afternoon, would cop it in the neck even more.

'Colin Knapp?' Finch suggested. 'He was damned quick off the mark picking up her name this morning.'

'Could be, I suppose.' Boyce sounded indifferent as he started the car. 'Where to now?'

'Back to the Hall. I want another chat with the house-keeper; alone this time.'

There was no sign of the nephew on this occasion although Finch made a point of introducing his name into the interview with Miss Cole which again took place in the kitchen but more formally this time, with the three of them seated at the big deal table, Boyce taking notes.

Finch began with Miss Cole's own movements on the previous evening. She had, it seemed, served dinner at half past seven and then had taken coffee through to the drawing-room about three quarters of an hour later. Colin had been with her most of that time;

they always ate together in the kitchen once the family had been served. Shortly after she returned from the drawing-room, he went out into the garden for a cigarette.

'Gone for long, was he?' Finch asked.

'I didn't notice,' she said. 'I was busy doing the washing-up.'

'Which took how long?'

'I couldn't say. I didn't look at the clock.'

'But you were alone when Miss Byrne came into the kitchen at a quarter to ten for a glass of water.'

'Yes.'

'When did your nephew return?'

'Not long afterwards.' She anticipated his next question by adding, 'And he was here with me until we both went to bed.'

'What time was that?'

'About quarter past eleven.'

Which meant they gave one another an alibi for the earlier part of the evening, supposing that Pardoe's estimate that the time of death was between ten and midnight was correct.

'Where's your bedroom, Miss Cole?' Finch continued innocently, as if he had not already looked inside it for himself.

'Near the top of the back stairs.'

'Next to Mr Saxby's?'

'No. It's on the other side of the passage.'

'Did you hear anything in the night?'

'I heard nothing until the nurse came to wake me this morning to say that Mr Aston had passed on.'

'I see. And where does your nephew sleep?'

'On the top floor.'

'And I assume he heard nothing either?'

The irony was wasted on her. She said impassively, 'I couldn't say. You'll have to ask him, won't you?'

'I intend to,' Finch told her.

Her retort came quickly and with an odd little air of triumph.

'Well, you won't be able to until this evening. It's his afternoon off. He's gone into Chelmsford on the bus.'

'In that case,' Finch replied, 'perhaps you could answer a few questions about him.'

If he had hoped to disconcert her, he was disappointed. She merely said in the same even, unemotional voice, 'If I can. But I don't know all his business. What do you want to know?'

'How long has he been working here?'

'Since February.'

'And before that?'

'He had a job in London until he was made redundant.'

'Doing what?'

It was like getting blood out of a stone, Finch thought disgustedly. Each little drop of information had to be squeezed out of her.

'As a hospital porter.'

'Where?'

'Saint Margaret's.'

Her answer came as a small shock to him. It was the hospital where Marion Greave had told him she was applying for a post and he was jolted out of the present reality of the question and answer session, a routine in which he felt comfortable and at home, knowing the rules, into the much less familiar territory of personal loss where he was still fumbling to find a way. Signalling to Boyce to take over the questioning, much to the Sergeant's surprise, he sat back, arms folded, a mere observer of the rest of the interview.

Boyce began tentatively by asking her about Nancy Fuller's duties, facts which had already been established. Listening to him, Finch allowed his mood to change to one of exasperation – at himself and his own vulnerability, at the Sergeant's handling of the situation and at Miss Cole's infuriating impassivity.

Several moments passed before Boyce had the sense to move on to a more personal aspect of Nancy Fuller's background.

'How long has she been divorced?'

'A couple of years.'

'You realize she's pregnant?'

Miss Cole folded her lips, indicating both her knowledge of this fact and her disapproval.

'Who's the father?'

But between them they had lost the initiative although the question had stung her into a more positive reaction.

'How should I know?' she demanded. 'It's not my business who she goes trolloping off with as long as she does her work here.'

Finch stood up, indicating the interview was over and, having thanked her, tramped off ahead of Boyce who caught up with him in the yard where the car was parked.

'You all right?' the Sergeant asked. It was evident that the Chief Inspector was in a foul mood and Boyce assumed he was the cause of it, which prompted him to add, 'Sorry about the interview. I didn't realize you'd want me to take over the questioning.'

'It can't be helped, Tom. Even if she knew who's the father of Nancy Fuller's child, she wasn't going to let on to us. And I can't see that it's relevant to the case anyway.'

He was standing in the yard, hands stuffed deep in his pockets, shoulders humped, a sure sign of low spirits.

Boyce asked brightly, 'So what happens now?'

'Back to headquarters. Wylie can cope here with the fingerprinting without our help. Besides, I want to check up on the hospital where Knapp used to work and run him through the police computer; see if we can come up with anything on him.'

He supposed he ought to call in at Beechcroft, the

residential home where Saxby had been living, and make inquiries there. But, like Nancy Fuller's pregnancy, that line of investigation seemed peripheral to the case and could be dealt with at another time.

'OK by me,' Boyce replied.

He seemed disposed to chat on the drive back, one of his more exasperating habits, as if by keeping up a flow of conversation he could talk the Chief Inspector out of whatever mood he happened to be in.

But to Finch's relief, about half a mile along the Easeden road on a particularly sharp bend, they encountered a large black hearse, on its way, he assumed, to Howlett Hall to collect Aston's body, and in the flurry of braking and changing gear, Boyce lost the thread of what he wanted to say and remained relatively silent for the rest of the journey.

12

There was a message waiting for Finch when he and Boyce returned to Divisional Headquarters. Mills, on desk duty, waved the piece of paper at him as he entered through the swing doors.

'Someone phoned for you, sir. Personal, the lady said.'

For an absurd moment, Finch thought it was from Marion and he tried to appear casual and unhurried as he crossed to the desk to take it from Mills although he was aware of the sudden release of adrenalin which raised his pulse rate, making it difficult to keep his hands steady as he unfolded the message slip. He was aware, too, of Boyce's curiosity and, turning aside so that the Sergeant could see neither his face nor the contents of the piece of paper, he scanned it eagerly.

It was from Kitty Laud. Had he had any luck with his inquiries, it read, and would he call to see her?

Mills was saying, unnecessarily as the time the message had been received was written on the top, 'She rang in at about half past eleven. Seemed anxious to get hold of you. I said you were out on a case and there was no knowing what time you'd be back.'

'Thanks,' Finch said, his face expressionless.

He refolded the message carefully along its original creases and put it in his pocket.

'She?' Boyce asked as he and Finch passed through the security door into the corridor beyond.

'Mrs Laud; the old lady who was here the other day about her brother.'

'Oh, her,' Boyce said dismissively to Finch's relief. It

saved him a lot of explanation about his involvement with Kitty Laud and of his trip to London the previous morning to make inquiries on her behalf about her missing brother, which in turn reminded him too painfully of how the rest of the day had been spent with Marion.

He had managed to blank it off most of the time, shoving it to the back of his mind behind the convenient protection of his professional duties; a sort of fall-out shelter for the emotions, he supposed wryly, as he tramped up the stairs behind Boyce. Suddenly he felt very tired.

All the same, it was a cruel trick that Kitty's message should have come at that particular moment, raising in him all kinds of false hopes and desires even though he had only himself to blame for being such a bloody fool as to believe that Marion might get in touch with him.

It was over. Finished. Kaput. And the sooner he came to terms with that the better.

Even so, he'd have to do something about Kitty Laud. He still had her brother's suitcase in the boot of his car. He'd go and see her that evening, he decided. Get rid of the blasted luggage and her, too, at the same time.

Boyce was saying, 'It's not much to hang a case on, is it?'

He had installed himself in the baggy armchair in Finch's office, the one in which the Chief Inspector sometimes slept when he was kept late on an investigation, and looked settled in for the rest of the evening.

'Case?' Finch asked, bemused, his mind still on Hal Dixon's luggage.

He realized that Boyce had been speaking for several minutes, about what he had no idea.

'The evidence about the pillow. Miss Byrne could have got it wrong . . .'

'But even if she did, Tom, it doesn't make any difference. You saw the evidence yourself. Someone had straightened that pillow on the bed after Saxby died.'

'I still don't think it's enough to go on. Pardoe seemed convinced Saxby wasn't suffocated and, if he's right, why the hell should anyone want to muck about with the pillow?'

'I've no idea,' Finch admitted. He knew Boyce in this mood and was in no state of mind himself to spend the next hour or so arguing with him about the rights and wrongs of the inquiry. 'Anyway, we're committed now. We can hardly back out at this stage. Let's wait for the results of the PM before we decide to chuck it in.'

He had gone to stand by the window, hump-shouldered, hands stuffed in pockets, running his right thumb along the folded edge of Kitty Laud's message.

The view was the same as he had seen on the afternoon before his trip to London – slated roofs, television aerials, the top branches of a tree. No plane though today. Only a slow procession of creamy-white clouds, like sailing ships, moving majestically behind the chimneys, their undersides stained a cindery-red by the setting sun.

Behind him, Boyce was saying, 'So what's our next move now?'

Finch turned back from the window. The only way to shut Boyce up was to give him something to do.

He said, 'Check with the national computer; see if you can turn up anything on Colin Knapp. I've got a feeling you might. And ask Kyle to phone that hospital where he used to work and make a few inquiries there.'

He deliberately avoided using its name which would have reminded him too painfully of Marion. But trust Boyce to stick his bloody great foot in it.

'St Margaret's, wasn't it?' he asked, heaving himself out of the chair. 'OK. Will do.'

He was back in the office within ten minutes in a better

frame of mind, announcing jubilantly, 'You were right about Knapp. He's got form – for nicking. He was fined fifty quid as it was a first offence and put on probation. And there's something dodgy about his hospital record as well. Kyle was told he wasn't a porter; he was a mortuary attendant. And that's not all. He was sacked, not made redundant, although whoever Kyle spoke to wouldn't come clean over the phone exactly why he got the push. Interesting, isn't it? Worth checking on, wouldn't you say?'

Finch, who had been sitting at his desk during Boyce's absence, staring gloomily down at a file which he had merely labelled with Saxby's name but which he could not bring himself to do anything more positive with for the time being, felt his own spirits stir.

'Right,' he said. 'I want Kyle round at the hospital tomorrow morning to get a statement. And while you're at it, Tom, round up Barney and get him in here. He can call in at that residential home where Saxby was living – Beechcroft – and have a chat with the matron.' Glancing at his watch, he came to another decision. It was six o'clock. If he left soon, he could call on Kitty Laud and, by dropping off her brother's suitcase, get the pair of them off his back and leave the way clear for him to concentrate on the Saxby inquiry.

Even so, it was another half an hour before he had briefed Barney on what questions to ask at Beechcroft and could drive the short distance to Kitty Laud's house.

Parking the car outside, he lifted the suitcase out of the boot and lugged it across the pavement to her door where he rang the bell.

Judging by the alacrity with which she answered it, she must have been expecting him to call, an impression which was confirmed by the tray already set with cups in the hot little back room and by Kitty's appearance.

She had spruced herself up for the occasion in a red

silk frock of the type which used to be known as a 'cocktail dress',.with a full skirt and *diamanté* clasps in the corners of a heart-shaped neckline. More rhinestones glittered on the buckle of the belt, so wide and stiff that she had difficulty in bending over to examine the suitcase which Finch dumped down on the one clear area of worn carpet in front of the gas fire.

'You've brought Hal's luggage!' she exclaimed delightedly, adding, her voice full of a half-pleased, half-regretful nostalgia, 'Oh, God, I remember this case! It's been in and out of half the variety theatres in the country. Hal used it for the evening clothes he wore on stage – tails, topper, white tie. He looked a proper West End gent when he was dressed up.'

As she was speaking, she had opened it and was sorting quickly through its contents, patting some of the articles of clothing as if recalling them as old friends, particularly the dressing-gown with the quilted lapels, running her hands over the burgundy-coloured silk.

Finch said, 'His landlady said it's all there.'

He spoke stiffly, unable to match her mood or to re-establish the easy camaraderie of the first occasion he had been with her in this room, only two days earlier. Then, he had felt at home among its shabby, theatrical mementoes. Now, even though she had evidently made an effort to tidy the place up, in honour of his visit, he suspected, he found the crowded photographs and ornaments claustrophobic. He longed to escape.

'All?' Kitty was asking in disbelief. 'But didn't he take anything with him when he went?'

'Only a small attaché case.'

Kitty scrambled to her feet and stood over him, holding in her hand the little leather jeweller's box which she had found under the clothes. Ridiculous though she was in her red dress, it was Finch, seated on the sofa with that daft pierrot doll propped up on the cushions beside him, who felt at a disadvantage.

Snapping open the box, she flourished it under his nose.

'He didn't take his cuff-links.'

It was said in a tone of accusatory triumph as if she were producing in court a piece of unexpected evidence which would establish his guilt without any further question.

Finch retorted, 'I don't know what he took or what he left behind. I've simply delivered the suitcase for you.'

He regretted the words as soon as they were out of his mouth, realizing that he was expressing his anger, not just at her, but at Boyce and at the investigation they were involved with. And at Marion Greave as well. Taken all round, the situation was a bloody shambles.

But he had not bargained for Kitty Laud's reaction. Skinny little legs trembling, she fumbled backwards for the armchair into which she lowered herself, her features, under the grotesque mask of powder and lipstick, falling to pieces under his gaze into the face of an old woman.

'I'm sorry, dear,' she whispered. 'I didn't mean to blame you. It's his cuff-links, you see. I gave them to him for his twenty-first and he'd never go anywhere without them; said they brought him good luck.'

Guilt-stricken, Finch leaned forward to pat her hand.

'My fault,' he said gruffly. 'And don't feel too worried about your brother.'

'But where is he?' she asked.

She was sitting with the leather box open on her lap, the cuff-links exposed like a reproach.

'I'll go and put the kettle on,' Finch announced. 'Then I'll tell you what I know while we have a cup of tea.'

The few minutes' separation gave them both time to recover. In the kitchen, Finch rattled about with a forced

161

cheerfulness, filling the kettle and lighting the gas ring under it, at the same time trying not to look too closely at the squalor about him, not all of it of Kitty's making. The wall above the window was stained with damp which had lifted the plaster off in great, scabrous patches while the lino on the concrete floor was cracked and discoloured. And damned dangerous, too. Finch caught his heel in it as he turned away from the stove.

Emptying the stale contents of the teapot into the plastic sink-tidy, already full of other elderly tea-leaves, crusts of bread and eggshells, he let his anger spend itself on more rational causes.

It was a bloody disgrace that an old woman of over eighty was expected to live in such conditions. Her landlord ought to have a rocket shoved under him. He'd write to the council. No, he'd go one better. He knew several councillors personally. He'd have a word with one or two of them on the quiet. Even if nothing could be done to rehouse her, which Kitty herself might not welcome, at least he'd do his best to make sure that the place was repaired to some decent standard.

As the thought crossed his mind, he knew he was committed. And it wouldn't simply be a matter of chatting to a couple of council members over a pint of beer about dodgy electric wiring and how he'd hate it if anything happened to the old girl and it got into the local papers. There'd be more to it than that.

Even as he sniffed cautiously at the half-empty bottle of milk which was standing on the window-sill in the sun, before scalding out the teapot with boiling water, trying to convince himself that, as far as he knew, you couldn't get food-poisoning simply from drinking a cup of tea, he knew it wouldn't end there. He'd start dropping in on his way home from headquarters to make sure she was all right. And that was only a beginning. Stepping carefully over the rent in the lino, he knew the next time he called it'd be with a box of floor tiles and a tin of adhesive.

Oh bloody hell! he thought, but smiling this time with an amused exasperation.

She had perked up in his absence, applied fresh lipstick and repowdered her face. There were grains of the stuff still floating in the air and clinging to the red silk bodice of her dress.

'Tea!' Finch announced with a flourish, as if he'd just conjured up the teapot and the milk jug out of thin air.

While Kitty poured, he gave her an account, suitably censored, of his visit to Clapham the previous day and what he had been able to find out about her brother, making no reference to the landlady's belief that Hal Dixon had come into money nor to his own suspicion that Dixon had found himself a mistress with whom he was now living.

'But he doesn't know anybody on the south coast!' Kitty protested when Finch had finished.

'Couldn't he have met someone he didn't tell you about?' Finch asked, not unreasonably considering that Hal Dixon seemed to have kept a large part of his private life a secret from his sister.

'I suppose he could,' she admitted. 'He's always been good at making friends; not that they usually lasted, mind you. It was a case of off with the old and on with the new with Hal. But it still doesn't explain why he didn't write for my birthday. Nor why, when he went, he didn't take the rest of his clothes with him.'

It was a point which had already occurred to Finch but one which he was inclined to play down in order not to arouse her fears.

'Perhaps he intended going away for only a few days and then changed his mind,' he suggested.

'I still can't see why he left his cuff-links behind. He never went anywhere without them.' She looked across

163

at him, her eyes wide with anxiety. 'I've got a feeling something's happened to him.'

Finch had come to the same conclusion himself – that Hal Dixon was lying seriously ill somewhere or possibly was even dead – but he said, trying to sound unconcerned, 'Not necessarily. He may have written and the letter got lost in the post. It's been known to happen. As for the cuff-links, he may not have bothered to take them if he thought he'd only be gone for a few days. I expect he'll turn up again any day now or get in touch with you.'

'You could be right,' Kitty said although she didn't sound all that convinced.

This time, when he rose to go, she didn't offer to read his tea-leaves, to Finch's relief, but remained seated in the armchair, bolt upright as he had first seen her in the entrance at headquarters, her head held stiffly on its thin neck, her hands still grasping the little leather box.

Not liking to leave without giving her some reason for hope, he said, 'I'll ask around again; see if I can come up with any more information about your brother.'

Not that he really believed it himself and God alone knew when or how he'd make the inquiries.

Kitty took him at his word. Brightening up, she said, 'You'll need a photo of Hal then, won't you, dear? You can choose any one you like.'

To please her, he took one of the smaller, framed photographs standing on the mantelpiece of Hal Dixon on his own, smiling dreamily into the camera, chin resting on his cupped hand. Judging by the inscription, dashed across one corner in elaborate handwriting, 'Good luck. Yours ever, Hal Dixon', it was a left-over hand-out, intended for some long-ago fan but never sent. Or perhaps never asked for. Finch slipped it into his pocket.

'I'll call round again another time,' he assured her.

On the way home, he stopped at an Indian take-away

and bought himself a chicken tikka, a portion of pilau rice and an onion raita which he ate on a tray straight from the foil dishes in front of the television.

The meal finished, he wasn't quite sure what to do for the rest of the evening. He ought, he supposed, to make a start on writing up his notes on the Howlett case, not that he felt much enthusiasm for the task or for anything else, come to that.

All the same, he settled himself down at the dining-room table in front of a pad of A4 paper and wrote out the heading which he carefully underlined twice. That done, he sat and looked at it.

The house was very quiet. With the door left open, he could hear the refrigerator in the kitchen suddenly start up its low, humming vibration and the faint sound of next door's television through the party wall.

The silence, broken only by these background noises, was almost palpable. So, too, was a sense of isolation which he had rarely experienced before. Being alone had never bothered him to any large extent. He generally preferred his own company. Now he was aware of other people's lives taking place around him; not just next door but in all the other houses in the road; indeed, in the whole city itself. Lights were being switched on, meals eaten, conversations exchanged.

He wondered what Marion Greave was doing at that moment. She had intended returning to Leeds some time that day but, knowing nothing of her life there, apart from her address, he had not even the smallest detail with which to begin imagining her actions – whether she walked home from the station, for instance, or took a taxi; the type of flat she lived in; her day-to-day routine at the hospital.

Picking up his pen, he wrote 'Evidence of Claudia Byrne' under the heading. And then, without intending to do anything of the sort, he found himself writing: 'My

165

dear Marion, Although you said you wished to be left alone to come to a decision, I felt I couldn't . . .'

At this point, the telephone in the hall rang.

It was his sister, Dorothy.

'So you're home, Jack,' she said in that reproachful tone of voice which he had always found exasperating. 'I tried ringing you several times earlier but there was no reply.'

'I've been out on a case,' he replied.

'I thought you might be. Frank and I wondered if you'd like to come round for a meal one evening.'

He was silent for several seconds. In his present mood, he was far from eager to visit his sister and her second husband and act as witness to the married happiness which he so ardently desired for himself.

On the other hand, he couldn't keep turning down her invitations.

Dorothy was saying, 'Are you there, Jack? What about tomorrow evening? Could you manage to be free for seven o'clock?'

He supposed he'd have to make the effort.

'Fine,' he said. 'I'll look forward to it.'

Hanging up, he went back to the dining-room where, seeing the piece of paper still lying on the table with that ridiculous attempt at a letter to Marion, he screwed it up into a ball and chucked it into the wastepaper basket before taking himself off upstairs for a bath.

13

Claudia slept badly that night. Even if her mind had not been full of the recent events and guilt over the part she had played in them, the air was stifling, making sleep difficult. There was not enough breeze even to stir the curtains at the open window.

In the early hours, she woke again, disturbed by a succession of small sounds outside in the garden. Someone was crossing the gravel path immediately below her room. Instantly alert, she sat up in bed. The footsteps had stopped and, by the time she reached the window, whoever had made them had gone, too.

The garden lay deserted under the clear morning sunlight and curiously still as if whoever had walked there so quietly and cautiously only a few seconds earlier had been absorbed into the surrounding trees.

It was futile to go back to bed. She was now thoroughly awake and what was more inimical to sleep, curious as well to know who in the household was up and about so early. Putting on a dressing-gown, she let herself out of her room and, crossing the landing, started down the stairs.

The house was silent, all the doors closed, even those opening off the hall downstairs, while the front door was not only locked but bolted as well. So also would be the side door leading into the yard and it was too close to the back stairs and Edie's bedroom to make it a sensible means by which to leave the house.

But there was a pair of french windows in the study which led out on to the gravel path and, having unbolted them, she stepped out into the garden, conscious of the sound her own footsteps made on the gravel although there was small chance that anyone could hear her. Edie and her nephew slept in the far wing, while Great-aunt Constance, Teddy and Basil occupied rooms overlooking the front of the house.

Reaching the edge of the lawn, Claudia hesitated. Whoever had crossed the path could have come from either the front or the back of the house. There was no way of knowing which. But it was perfectly obvious the direction which that person had taken afterwards. The side lawn was uncut and in the long grass, heavy with dew, it was possible to see the dark track where feet had brushed the moisture from the stems and to follow it as it led past the formal rose garden and the ruined pool to the edge of the shrubbery. Here it ended at a narrow opening between the overgrown rhododendron bushes which marked the beginning of what had once been a broad path. This in turn had led into a semicircular clearing in which stood a mock Chinese summerhouse with a narrow veranda which had been a feature of this part of the garden. Now that the shrubs had closed over the path, it was completely hidden from sight apart from the wooden finial which crowned the top of its octagonal roof.

Claudia hesitated, reluctant to follow the track any further. Even in the early morning sunlight, the place had a sinister air. The leathery leaves of the rhododendrons hung closely together, exuding a bitter, pungent scent and she was aware of a strange silence about the place. No birds sang although the rest of the garden was loud with their chorus. It was as if the shrubbery were lying in wait for her, holding its breath while she decided whether or not to go forward.

It was absurd, of course. The solid bulk of Howlett's was behind her, less than fifty yards away, looking safe and inviolate. Turning her head, she glanced back at it and, as she did so, something came crashing through the branches on her left. She had a momentary, oblique impression of a figure looming over her, arm upraised and holding what in those few seconds of terrified awareness she thought was a large rock or stone. The next moment, there was only a vivid, red pain before she went spinning sideways and downwards into a black vortex.

She emerged from it slowly, conscious of the smell of earth and warm grass. Opening her eyes, she could see the blades criss-crossing her vision, so immense that they looked like swords, each outlined with light so that their edges shone as if newly sharpened. Beyond them were two darker shapes which she could not distinguish at first until they moved and she realized they were the legs of someone standing over her.

She heard herself cry out. Listening to it with a distanced objectivity, she thought how stupid it sounded; not a full-blooded scream which might have brought people running from the house to her rescue, but a low-pitched whimpering sound like that injured dog she had once seen at the side of the road.

Then Basil's voice said, 'Are you all right, Claudia? Can you get up?'

He was trying to help her to her feet but in a panic of nausea and genuine fear she struck out at him.

Finding her voice at last, she shouted at him, 'Leave me alone! Oh, God, don't hit me!'

He came swooping down over her, his voice sounding cold and distant despite the proximity of his face which seemed to hang directly over her, blotting out everything else.

'I'm going to take you back to the house. Let me help you up.'

She struggled to her knees, feeling his arm under hers.

Nausea swept over her again and with it the black sensation of toppling forwards into a void but she managed to force herself upright, shaking off his hand as Uncle Rollo had pushed aside the taxi driver. For some reason, the recollection strengthened her. Walking slowly, for each step seemed to jolt the pain loose again, she crossed the lawn, conscious of Basil beside her, guiding her round to the front of the house where the door was now set open and into the hall where Teddy met them.

She had a blurred impression of their voices, Teddy's high and anxious, asking what had happened, Basil's giving some explanation which she was too sick to listen to, and then of being helped upstairs to her room and on to the bed which seemed to rise up and absorb her.

When she regained consciousness, she found Robert Callender sitting beside the bed on one of the upright chairs.

He said, seeing her eyes were open, 'Don't talk, Claudia, unless you want to. Someone attacked you in the garden.'

'Who?' she whispered. 'Was it Basil?'

Instead of replying, he got to his feet and went to the window, drawing the curtains so that the room was darkened. Returning to her side, he said, 'I'm going to give you something to make you sleep. You should feel better when you wake up.'

She took the two tablets he offered her, swallowing them with a sip of water from the glass he held out to her. As he rearranged the light blanket which someone had put over her, she had an idiotic urge to smile. It was like being a child again, tucked up in bed by her father when she had been unwell. Rowena had never bothered with such maternal concerns. He was wearing the same expression as her father had done on such occasions, a little self-conscious and yet absorbed and serious, as if all

170

that mattered was making sure the blanket covered her feet.

Whatever was in the tablets, was fast-acting. She remembered him walking away to the door and closing it gently behind him before sleep came flooding in to claim her.

Finch said, 'It looks like some kind of bolt-hole.'

He and Boyce were standing just inside the doorway of an octagonal summerhouse, vaguely Chinese in design, its sides covered with panels of trellis which had once been painted white and which were now stained green with mould. A veranda fronted the construction, behind which a small room opened off, containing some mildewed deck-chairs, a couple of croquet mallets and the remnants of a tennis net bundled up in a corner. More recently someone had installed a canvas chair, set open beside a plastic picnic table of the type that can be folded up to go into the boot of a car, its top littered with empty beer cans. More lay on the floor together with a quantity of crushed cigarette ends, suggesting that the place had been used for some considerable time.

'We'll get Wylie to go over it for prints,' Finch continued, 'but my bet is all he'll find is Colin Knapp's. I reckon Knapp came here for a quiet cigarette, and a drink, too, by the look of it, when his aunt wouldn't let him smoke in the kitchen.'

The Chief Inspector and the Sergeant had arrived about half an hour earlier, having been informed by the local Inspector, Dwyer, of the attack on Miss Byrne in the garden of Howlett Hall. So far he had only had the time to confer with the uniformed Constable, the first to arrive on the scene, and with a harassed-looking Teddy Nugent who had come hurrying out of the house as soon as their car had drawn up to tell them that Colin Knapp was missing.

Finch had greeted the news non-committally, merely thanking Nugent and requesting that he remain in the house with the others for questioning, before walking away across the lawn to the place near the shrubbery where the attack had taken place and where the SOCOs were already at work, making a preliminary examination while they waited for Sergeant Henty and the dog-handlers to arrive.

Noticing the summerhouse, Finch had wandered off, accompanied by Boyce.

'Makes sense that Knapp used the place,' Boyce agreed. 'So what's the theory? That Knapp attacked Miss Byrne? But why the hell should he want to do that?'

'God knows unless it's connected in some way with Saxby's death although I can't see why Knapp should want to murder Saxby, if that's what happened. As far as I can make out, Knapp didn't know Saxby; didn't even see him after he arrived at Howlett Hall. And what was Knapp doing out in the garden at half past six in the morning anyway?'

As he had been speaking, he had taken a couple of steps inside the room where he paused, hands in pockets, looking down at the rough boards which formed the floor. Then, stepping carefully backwards, he said, 'Get Johnson and McCullum here, Tom. It looks as if some-one's had part of this floor up recently.'

Boyce peered over his shoulder. The boards were dirty, covered with a scattering of dead leaves and bird drop-pings as well as old dust which had fallen from the roof timbers. But to one side of the canvas chair, close to the wooden wall on the left, a patch had been cleared. It was possible to see where the leaves had been brushed roughly to one side to reveal a short length of board, its edges free of the compressed dirt which filled the chinks in the rest of the flooring.

He stood back watching when, Boyce having fetched

Johnson and McCullum, the interior of the summerhouse was photographed and then Johnson bent down to prise up the floorboard with the blade of a penknife. It came up easily, revealing a section of packed earth below in the centre of which an oblong impression had been clearly stamped into the loose dust and leaf mould which covered the bottom of the cavity.

Finch looked down at it. Something had been standing there – a small hold-all or suitcase of some kind, he suspected, and heavy enough to have left its mark in the dirt.

Leaving Johnson and McCullum to their tasks, he jerked his head at Boyce and tramped out on the veranda where he paused to look about him.

As a bolt-hole, the summerhouse was ideal. It was surrounded by a shrubbery of rhododendron bushes left to go wild and so dense that it was impossible to see anything of Howlett Hall, not even its roof, although it couldn't have been much more than fifty or sixty yards away across the lawn which lay beyond the shrubbery.

A rough path led from the summerhouse towards this lawn and the formal rose-beds which, with the pool, formed the garden at the side of the house. As he followed it, he saw that there were signs here, too, that the path had been regularly used. Broken twigs and leaves, some of them hanging withered on their stems, suggested that someone, Colin Knapp presumably, had cleared a way through.

Marsh met them on the edge of the shrubbery close to the scene of the attack.

'No sign of the weapon yet, sir,' he informed the Chief Inspector.

'Then keep looking,' Finch replied. 'And when the handlers arrive, see if the dogs can pick up a scent from the summerhouse. I'll be in the house, interviewing, if you want me.'

In the event, the interviews were not to take place until later. As he and Boyce crossed the lawn towards the front of the house, Dr Callender came out on to the steps to inform them that Detective Chief Inspector Finch was wanted on the telephone.

Finch took the call in the study, leaving Boyce and Callender to wait outside. He emerged shortly afterwards, his expression inscrutable. Jerking his head towards the front door, he went outside where the two men joined him on the drive.

'That was Inspector Dwyer from Howlett,' he told them. 'A body's just been found – Colin Knapp's by the sound of it. The description fits.'

'Where?' Boyce asked.

'Somewhere in the fields behind the village – a place called Pondend. Do you know it?' He turned to Callender who nodded in agreement. 'Then, if you don't mind, you can come with us and show us where it is although Dwyer said he'd post a PC on the road to direct us. And while you're there, you can certify death at the same time.'

'I'll get my bag,' Dr Callender replied.

The Constable had been posted at a lay-by about a quarter of a mile from the gates of Howlett Hall. They left the cars there and walked, following the edge of a cornfield before joining a footpath which ran roughly at right angles to it. Here Callender turned to the right in the general direction of the village and Finch paused for a few moments to get his bearings.

They were quite close to the outskirts of Howlett. In fact, he could see, across the width of the cornfield they had just skirted, the roofs of the council estate where Nancy Fuller lived. To his left stood Howlett Hall, hidden behind the clumps of trees which marked its position. But when Boyce, who had halted with him, raised his eyebrows inquiringly, Finch merely humped his shoulders and moved on.

Their destination lay a couple of hundred yards ahead. It was a pond, roughly circular in shape, situated close to the edge of the path in a broad declivity in the ground, its perimeter ringed by willow trees, their narrow leaves showering down to touch the water. A picturesque place; the sort of setting that Constable might have painted, cool and green and leafy, although he would probably have chosen to omit the sagging remains of a post and barbed wire fence which enclosed the side of the pond nearest to the footpath and which was no doubt intented to prevent passers-by from falling down the shallow bank into it. He would also have dispensed with the figures of the two uniformed police officers, rather muddy about the feet and trouser legs who, together with Inspector Dwyer, were waiting on the path.

And the body itself.

It was lying face downwards on the bank, arms bent at the elbow and extended parallel to the torso and the head turned to one side to reveal a patch behind the left ear, wet with something more than just pond water. A red trickle had oozed down the neck to darken the collar of his shirt.

'My men tried to resuscitate him,' Dwyer was saying, 'but it was too late. He'd gone.' As Callender bent over the body to examine it, Dwyer continued, 'A farm worker found him. He takes a short cut along the footpath to Dacre's place.' He waved a hand to indicate a farm somewhere over to their right. 'Didn't touch him but cycled into Howlett to report it. Said he thought the man was already dead. Could have been, I suppose. When we arrived, he was lying face down in the water close to where he is now. My men simply pulled him up on to the bank.' Unexpectedly he added, 'It's Knapp, isn't it?'

'You know him?' Finch asked.

'Seen him in the Crown a couple of times,' Dwyer said.

'I like to make it my business to know who's moved into the area. Got chatting to him, not that he had much to say for himself but he told me he was working up at the Hall; relative of the housekeeper, he said.' As Callender with the help of one of the uniformed men turned the body over on its back, he added in the same laconic manner, 'Somebody cropped him one. Saw the back of his head, did you?' When Finch nodded, Dwyer continued, 'Judging by the position he was in when we found him, he was clobbered as he stood on the path. He was close in by the edge, feet almost on the bank. The water's too shallow there for him to have floated out to the middle.' As he was speaking, he led the way a few yards back along the footpath and pointed. 'That's where he was found. I got my men to wade in after him from further up so that they wouldn't go trampling the place about.'

'Thanks,' said Finch.

Despite Dwyer's care, he doubted if the SOCOs would find much at the scene of the crime. The bank was narrow, a mere few feet of worn grass which was too dry to carry any recognizable footprints, only scuff marks on the soil and a bruising of the grass stems where Knapp had toppled down it, while the surface of the footpath itself, composed of flints and compacted earth, was too hard-packed.

A length of two by two, one of the fence supports by the look of it, lay in the water close by the edge.

Seeing Finch had noticed it, Dwyer said, 'I reckon that's the weapon. I told my men to leave it there.'

'Thanks,' Finch said again, adding silently to himself that Dwyer needn't have bothered about that either. The post was old and weatherworn, not a good surface for prints, while its immersion in the water would have effectively ruined any chances of the dogs picking up a scent from it.

He'd go through the motions, of course; get Johnson and the others to examine the scene and photograph it; even ask Henty to let the dogs have a nose about the place but he'd be surprised if they came up with anything worthwhile.

He could see Callender waiting to speak to him and, before walking back to join him, he asked Dwyer, 'Any sign of a bag or suitcase?'

'Not that we've found so far but we haven't searched the area.'

So whatever Knapp had kept hidden under the floor of the summerhouse had either been concealed somewhere else, possibly by Knapp himself, or had been taken by whoever had killed him, Finch thought. And looking for it could be a damned sight more difficult than examining the scene of the murder. It could be anywhere between there and Howlett Hall, stuffed into a hedge or chucked into a ditch. Or even thrown into the pond itself and searching that would mean calling out the team of frogmen.

The case would have to be found, though. Whatever it contained could supply a motive for Knapp's murder although what it had to do with Saxby's death was anybody's guess.

From his earlier appraisal of the scene, he could himself have supplied Dwyer's answer to his next question.

'Where does the footpath lead to?'

'Into Howlett in that direction,' Dwyer said, pointing to the right. 'It comes out into Stag's Lane by the Crown. The other way, it leads towards Howlett Hall but finishes up eventually about a mile along the Easeden road.'

Finch nodded. Dwyer's reply had confirmed what he had already suspected – that the footpath was probably familiar to Knapp who could have used it to walk into the village where Dwyer had seen him drinking at the Crown. It was also a short cut to Nancy Fuller's place.

He moved off to speak to Callender who was waiting on the footpath, his stethoscope still round his neck.

'He's dead,' he announced, 'but you probably won't need me to tell you that. And although I'm no pathologist, I'm fairly certain he died by drowning. The injury to the back of the head isn't serious enough to kill him but it could have knocked him out. After that . . .'

He broke off, anxious not to commit himself too far.

Finch left it there. Pardoe would confirm the facts after he'd examined the body and the PM would no doubt establish an approximate time of death. As for the murder itself, the Chief Inspector had already seen enough to draw his own conclusions.

Someone had met Knapp on the footpath; someone known to him, Finch suspected, who had either followed him there or had met him by prearrangement. That person had then struck Knapp with one of the fence posts, almost certainly from behind and most probably unexpectedly. Apart from the crushed grass where Knapp had fallen or rolled down the bank, there was no sign of a struggle.

And the murder had not been premeditated. Whoever had killed him had picked up the nearest weapon to hand, not brought it with him. Or her.

Callender was saying, 'If there's nothing else, Chief Inspector.'

'Yes; thanks for your help,' Finch replied, rousing himself.

He could see from the doctor's expression that this was not all the man wanted to say.

He was right. Callender continued a little diffidently, 'I think I ought to tell you that when I was called in to treat Claudia, she seemed to be under the impression that it was Basil Nugent who attacked her. Of course, she was still very confused; suffering from mild concussion, in fact. So I don't think you ought to put too much store on what she said. And she certainly isn't in any fit state yet to be interviewed. I really must insist on that. I won't have Claudia – Miss Byrne – questioned without my permission and without my being present at the time.'

'Of course,' Finch agreed quickly to save the man any further embarrassment. He had coloured up and, in the eyes of the two policemen, cut something of an absurd figure standing there on the footpath, clutching his medical bag in one hand, as if about to do battle there and then on Claudia Byrne's behalf, his stethoscope still hanging round his neck and the body of Colin Knapp lying at his feet.

Beside him, Finch heard Boyce clear his throat, a sure sign of suppressed amusement on the Sergeant's part.

So love can make fools of us all, the Chief Inspector thought bleakly.

'I'll be at Howlett's if you want me,' Callender concluded and began to walk away with as much dignity as he could muster, stuffing his stethoscope into his pocket as he went.

As soon as he was out of earshot, Boyce remarked with a grin, 'He's got it bad, hasn't he? Love, I mean.' When Finch didn't reply, he changed tactics, adding in a more businesslike tone, 'So what do you make of Claudia Byrne thinking Nugent had attacked her? It's not likely, is it?'

'We'll discuss it later, Tom,' Finch replied.

Dwyer was approaching them along the path and Finch, moving forward to meet him, arranged for one of the local PCs to remain on duty at the scene before turning back to Boyce.

'I'm going to walk back to Howlett Hall by the footpath. I want to check how long it takes. You take the car and warn McCullum and the others that they're going to be needed over here. And get in touch with

179

Pardoe,' he added as Boyce, having acknowledged these instructions with a nod, began to turn away.

As Boyce struck off along the edge of the cornfield towards the lay-by where the car was parked, Finch, having first checked his watch, continued on along the footpath.

It was easy going. The path was broad and relatively flat, running between the fields behind high hedges and confirming his earlier suspicion that it was probably an old drovers' way, one of the green tracks which can still be found criss-crossing the countryside and possibly date back to pre-Roman times, the 'rolling English road' which he remembered reading about as a schoolboy in Chesterton's poem.

But although on one level he was aware of his surroundings – the hedgerows deep in grass and wild flowers, and the smell of the place, the scent of meadowsweet overlaid with the farmyard odour of warm cow dung, patches of which spattered the path – on another level he was back on the steps of the British Museum, watching Marion walk away from him towards the gates.

Damn Callender, he thought, for reminding him of that occasion and for arousing in him that old, absurd longing which, like a fool, he had imagined that he was at last beginning to forget.

At the far end of the second field, the footpath swung away to the right, skirting the edge of the grounds of Howlett Hall. Here, a rough gap in the hedge indicated the place where Colin Knapp, and possibly also his murderer, had gained access to the lane.

Finch clambered through further down, pushing a way through the tangle of twigs and branches with his arms over his face as a protection.

Once through, he found himself in the shrubbery at the side of Howlett Hall and, after a few more minutes of scrambling and ducking under the branches of the rhododendron bushes, he emerged at last, out of breath and covered with pieces of torn leaf and twig, at the edge of the lawn, where he checked his watch.

Howlett Hall was in front of him; the summerhouse somewhere over to his left, hidden behind the closely-growing shrubs.

It had taken him just over nine minutes, a good enough estimate allowing for the fact that he had lost two or three minutes breaking through the hedge and avoiding a direct route through the shrubbery. But that would be cancelled out by the time it would have taken the murderer, if it was someone from Howlett Hall, to leave the house and cross the lawn.

The other possibility, that Knapp's murderer had come from the direction of Howlett village, would have to be checked on later.

At that moment, Boyce came into sight round the side of Howlett Hall and, raising his arm to catch his attention, Finch set off across the grass towards him.

14

Because of what Callender had told them about Claudia Byrne's suspicions concerning the identity of her attacker, they interviewed Basil Nugent first. He was hanging about the hall anyway, clearly anxious to know what was going on and, as soon as the study door had closed on the three of them, he demanded to be told the facts.

Finch gave them to him in his flat, official voice at the same time watching the man closely to observe his reactions.

Almost before the Chief Inspector had finished speaking, Nugent burst in.

'Claudia's quite mistaken, Chief Inspector! Why should I want to attack her? The whole idea's absurd. The truth is I heard someone go downstairs early this morning and I thought I ought to investigate. By the time I'd put on a dressing-gown and let myself out by the front door, the attack was over. I found her lying on the lawn by the shrubbery. I'm aware that she seemed to think I'd struck her which I suppose was understandable under the circumstances. She'd been knocked unconscious and came round to find me standing over her. But I can assure you she's wrong. As for Knapp's murder . . .'

It was the first time that he had referred to it although Finch, in his brief account, had given Nugent this information.

Interesting, he thought, that Nugent should choose to ignore it and concentrate instead on protesting his innocence of the attack on Claudia Byrne.

'Yes?' he said and waited, head cocked.

'It's dreadful! Quite dreadful!' Nugent replied. But these expressions of shock were mere words. Nugent didn't give a damn about Knapp.

There was a silence and, as Nugent seemed unwilling to add any more, Finch glanced across at Boyce who took up the questioning.

'We'd like an account of your movements after you found Miss Byrne, sir.'

'Certainly, Sergeant. I've got nothing to hide. I took Claudia back to the house where I met my father in the hall. He'd also heard someone moving about and had come downstairs to see what was going on. Between us, we helped Claudia upstairs to her bedroom. While my father telephoned Dr Callender and the local police, I went along to my stepmother's bedroom to make sure she was all right. She's a light sleeper and I was anxious she might have been disturbed. I then went to find Edie.'

'What time was this?'

'God knows,' Nugent admitted. 'I didn't look at my watch, Sergeant. I had other things on my mind besides the time. But it must have been soon after seven o'clock when I knocked on Edie's door. She called out that she was getting dressed and I know she's usually up by seven. I told her what had happened and she went to Claudia's bedroom to take care of her until the doctor arrived. I then went back to my room to get dressed. Dr Callender arrived shortly afterwards. In fact, I was still in my room when his car drove up. I believe my father let him in and took him upstairs.'

Teddy Nugent, who was interviewed afterwards, corroborated part, at least, of his son's statement. He had, he agreed, been wakened by the sound of someone unbolting the front door which, on going downstairs, he had found set open. He had barely reached the hall, when Basil had come in with Claudia. Basil had explained that someone had attacked Claudia in the garden but at that point, he, Teddy, had been more concerned with getting Claudia upstairs to her room and sending for the doctor than hearing a full account of what had happened. He had then come downstairs to phone the doctor while Basil had gone to fetch Edie.

'I understand he went to speak to Mrs Nugent first,' Finch pointed out.

'That was at my suggestion,' Teddy Nugent explained quickly. A little too quickly? Finch wondered. 'I was worried about Constance. The slightest sound disturbs her. I wanted Basil to reassure her. She's been under so much stress recently.'

'And then Miss Cole went to Miss Byrne's bedroom?' Finch continued, cutting short what was evidently going to be a reiteration of the state of Mrs Nugent's emotional and physical health. 'How soon was this after you'd helped Miss Byrne upstairs?'

'Oh, less than five minutes,' Teddy Nugent assured him. 'As soon as I'd put the phone down, I went back to Claudia's room to see if there was anything I could do to help. Edie was already there. She'd taken off Claudia's slippers and had put a blanket over her. She was wringing out a towel in cold water to lay across her head when I came in. Basil meanwhile had gone to his room to dress and, as soon as the doctor arrived and I'd let him in, I did the same and then went to sit with my wife. About ten minutes later, Edie knocked on the door to ask if we'd like tea. She brought a tray upstairs for Constance and myself.' He added with a disarming air, 'Is there anything else you want to know, Chief Inspector?'

'Not for the moment,' Finch replied.

Nugent got to his feet.

'Basil told me about Colin Knapp. It's quite dreadful. I can't think why anyone should want to kill him. Edie's going to be very shocked by it.'

184

If she was, there was little sign of it by the time she was interviewed.

At Finch's suggestion, Boyce carried out the questioning, leaving the Chief Inspector free to observe her as she sat at the far end of the kitchen table, her hands, as worn and as scrubbed as the wood itself, resting on its surface. It was impossible to gauge her feelings. Her face bore the polite, non-committal expression of an elderly servant, well trained in minding her manners and keeping her thoughts to herself. She was, he decided, almost entirely without imagination. And probably without initiative either. She would carry out her duties but would never dream of stepping outside the boundaries of her role.

As he watched and listened, Finch also mused over the question of timing, crucial to the investigation of Knapp's murder, a factor which he had pointed out to Boyce as they had walked from the study to the kitchen.

All three of them, the Nugents, father and son, as well as Edie Cole, appeared to supply alibis for one another and, unless there was a conspiracy between them, he couldn't see how any of them could have found the twenty minutes or so needed from the time Claudia Byrne was attacked, presumably by Colin Knapp, to follow Knapp to the scene of his murder and return to the house.

Basil's time had been spent helping Claudia Byrne back to the house, speaking to his stepmother as well as fetching Edie from her bedroom, which seemed to give him no opportunity to commit the murder. The same could be said of Teddy Nugent who, in addition to assisting Claudia Byrne upstairs, had telephoned the doctor and been on hand to let him in. As for Edie Cole, she had been in her bedroom, getting dressed, when Basil Nugent had gone to fetch her and from that moment had been fully occupied in caring for Claudia Byrne and making tea for the family.

Mrs Nugent, too, seemed out of the running as a suspect. Basil had spoken to her shortly after the attack and, as soon as the doctor had arrived, Teddy had sat with her in her room.

Which left the members of the family in the clear as far as Knapp's murder was concerned and threw the suspicion on to someone outside Howlett Hall.

Like Nancy Fuller? he wondered.

Boyce had taken Edie Cole through a brief account of her movements. Her alarm clock had gone off as usual at seven o'clock. She had got up and was in the middle of dressing when Mr Nugent, the son, had knocked on her door to tell her that Miss Claudia had been attacked. She had gone straight to Miss Claudia's room and had remained there until Dr Callender arrived, when she had gone downstairs to make tea for everybody. It was then about ten to eight.

At this point, Finch interrupted.

'Just a minute, Miss Cole, I'd like to take you back to an earlier part of your statement. You said that when you went downstairs, you found the side door unbolted which suggests your nephew left the house by that way. Now, I remember you saying the last time we talked that he slept in one of the attic bedrooms. In that case, he'd have had to come down the stairs which are close to your bedroom before unbolting the back door. Did you hear him leave the house?'

She turned to look at him, her face still wearing that calm, inscrutable expression.

'Yes, I heard him. But I didn't realize he'd left otherwise I'd've gone after him to find out what he was up to.' For the first time, she showed any emotion. Tightening her lips, she continued, her reluctance to talk about such matters apparent in her voice and the two little ugly patches of colour which appeared in her thin cheeks, 'He went to the toilet. There isn't one on the top floor so he

186

has to use the lavatory in the nursery wing. It's almost opposite my door. I heard him go in there and then pull the chain. I couldn't hear anything more after that because of the noise of the cistern filling up. I thought he'd gone back to his room.'

Which was perfectly feasible as Finch and Boyce discovered when, shortly afterwards, they tried it out for themselves. While Finch waited inside Edie Cole's bedroom, Boyce flushed the lavatory and then went as quickly as he could down the service stairs to the side door where he drew the bolts. The noise of the water running into the old-fashioned iron cistern effectively covered up any sound he made.

'Satisfied?' Edie Cole asked them when Finch rejoined her and Boyce in the kitchen. There was a pleased note in her voice at having been proved right which the Chief Inspector supposed was understandable. All the same, he couldn't resist getting a little of his own back.

'One last question, Miss Cole. You told us your nephew worked as a porter at St Margaret's. We checked with the hospital yesterday. He was employed there as a mortuary attendant and was dismissed, not made redundant. Did you know that?'

Her reaction couldn't have been feigned. Finch, who was watching her closely, saw the two patches of red reappear in her face but this time with indignation and, he thought, an angry shame.

'No, I didn't! He told me he worked on the wards but lost his job because of staff cuts. I wouldn't have suggested he came here to help with Mr Aston if I'd known he'd lied to me. He said he was used to lifting patients.'

'Yes, but dead ones,' Boyce remarked wryly as he and Finch emerged into the yard. 'Where now?'

'We'll interview Nancy Fuller,' Finch replied. 'Miss

Byrne and Mrs Nugent can wait till later. Besides, I want another look at that footpath.'

The SOCOs had begun examining the scene of Colin Knapp's murder when, having parked in the lay-by behind the waiting mortuary van, he and Boyce walked back to it along the side of the cornfield. The body still lay there, covered with a plastic sheet, awaiting removal. Pardoe, who had already examined it, had left, leaving a message that he would submit his preliminary report later that afternoon at the PM on Saxby. While Boyce went back to the lay-by to summon the mortuary attendants, Finch stood conferring with Johnson.

As he had suspected, the search had revealed very little apart from the usual rubbish which tends to accumulate even in the remotest rural areas and, in this case, the spot was well-used, particularly by children, judging by the quantity of soft-drink cans and ice-lolly sticks which had been found.

Henty and the dog team had come up with nothing much either. Both the body and the suspected murder weapon were too wet to give the dogs a scent and the trail had been further confused by the cow droppings along the footpath. Henty had meanwhile called off his team and returned to headquarters. Like Pardoe, he'd be putting in a report later. There had been no sign either of a suitcase or holdall although the search had so far covered only the immediate area surrounding the pond.

As Johnson finished his account, Finch thanked him and moved off, this time following the footpath towards the village. There was no point in waiting for the body to be removed although as he walked away, he could see the men coming from the direction of the lay-by, carrying a coffin-shell between them, an incongruous intimation of mortality amongst all that rich summer foliage but an appropriate end in the case of Colin Knapp, who must have performed the same service for others on many occasions.

In the opposite direction, the footpath led past another cornfield, the same one, Finch realized, as he had seen the combine harvester at work in when he and Boyce had called on Nancy Fuller the previous day. The harvester was no longer there and the standing corn had been reduced to stubble, giving him an uninterrupted view across the field to the back of the council houses although at that distance it was impossible to tell which one was Nancy Fuller's.

All the same, he checked his watch. It had taken him five minutes to reach this point along the path, about half the time it had taken him to reach Howlett Hall in the opposite direction. There was no direct access that he could see from the council estate into the field and he followed the path on until it finally emerged by means of a stile into a narrow cul-de-sac, Stag's Lane, where the Crown was situated, the public house where Inspector Dwyer had seen Colin Knapp drinking.

Stag's Lane led into the High Street and from there he walked the fifty yards or so to the next turning, which took him into the council estate.

As arranged, Boyce was waiting for him in the car outside Nancy Fuller's house, with a WPC from Howlett police station, whom Boyce had also been instructed to collect on his way, seated beside him.

'She's in,' he informed Finch as the Chief Inspector leaned in at the driver's window. 'I saw the net curtains move at the window when I drove up.'

'Then let's see what she's got to say for herself,' Finch replied.

She had quite a lot to say for herself – about the police in general and Finch and Boyce in particular for coming to interview her again.

'I told you all I knew yesterday,' she protested angrily.

'Bloody coppers! Why can't you leave me alone?'

'Mind if I take a look at your back garden?' Finch asked. They were standing just inside the front door and, before she had time to object, he eased himself past her and went through the kitchen to the back door which he opened, leaving Boyce and the WPC in the hall.

It led out into a small oblong garden, mainly rough grass like the one in the front, containing nothing more than two dustbins and a washing-line on which a row of children's clothes were hung out to dry.

The children in question, two young boys, who were playing on the grass with some toy cars, looked up in surprise at the sudden appearance of this stranger.

Nodding affably to them, Finch took a few steps down the concrete path.

The garden was enclosed, like an exercise yard, by chain-link fencing, undamaged except for the section which ran along the far end where the cornfield adjoined the estate. Here the fence had been trampled down low enough to allow someone to step over it into Nancy Fuller's garden.

'Now I wonder who did that?' Finch enquired of the children in an avuncular voice.

But before either of them could reply, Nancy Fuller came hurrying out of the house, Boyce behind her.

'It's the kids' fault,' she said shrilly. 'If I've told them once I've told them a hundred times – leave the bloody fence alone else I'll have the council round after me. They keep climbing over it into the field.'

'No-one else uses it?' Finch asked in the same pleasant manner.

'Like who?' she demanded.

'Like Colin Knapp. Or yourself, Mrs Fuller.'

'I don't know what you're on about,' Nancy Fuller retorted and stalked back inside the house. Behind her back, Finch nodded quickly to Boyce to assume the questioning, which took place in the living-room where Nancy Fuller sat huddled up in one of the shabby armchairs.

Boyce began in his reasonable, more-in-sorrow-than-in-anger voice.

'Now come on, Mrs Fuller. We know Colin Knapp uses that footpath that runs across the fields behind your house. We also know he goes drinking in the Crown. He's been seen in there. All we want to find out from you is how many times a week does he drop by here?'

Someone quicker on the uptake or less angry than Nancy Fuller would have realized that he had no evidence on which to base his last remark and might have challenged him.

Instead, she said furiously, 'Somebody's bloody told on him, haven't they? Well, it's none of their frigging business if he calls round here.'

'How often?' Boyce repeated.

'A couple of times a week, on his way back from the pub. He comes in through the back way 'cos it's quicker and . . .' What else she might have been about to add – that he was less likely to be seen by the neighbours, perhaps – was cut short. Suddenly recovering control, she demanded, 'What the hell's it got to do with you anyway? I thought you was asking about that old boy who died up at the Hall.'

'Colin Knapp's dead,' Finch told her.

She turned on him a face which was difficult to read from its expression. The angry resentment was still in it, tightening up the features, but it was overlaid by some other emotion that Finch couldn't quite assess. Bewilderment, was it? Or perhaps fear?

'When?' she demanded. 'What happened?' And then, incongruously, 'I don't believe it.'

'What were you doing at about seven o'clock this morning?' Boyce asked her.

Her head swivelled round in his direction.

'I was in bed.'

'You didn't happen to walk along the footpath towards the pond?'

'No, I bloody didn't!'

'Or arrange to meet Colin Knapp?'

'Why should I? It's Friday. He always went to the pub of a Friday evening. I was expecting him to call in here later tonight.'

And that's not all she's expecting, Finch added to himself.

She was close to tears and, in consideration of her state – in the club, as Boyce would have put it – he got to his feet signalling the end of the interview.

They left shortly afterwards, conferring briefly with the WPC in the hall.

'Her sister must live near by,' Finch told her. 'She looks after Mrs Fuller's children while she's at work.'

'Mrs Dowsett – yes, I know her,' the WPC replied. 'One of her kids is up on a shop-lifting charge. I'll send for her if I think she's needed.'

'Christ, what a mess!' the Chief Inspector commented as he and Boyce left the house. He meant all of it – Nancy Fuller and her sister as well as the deaths of Knapp and Saxby.

Boyce shrugged his shoulders philosophically, taking the remark to refer only to Nancy Fuller.

'It happens. So what do you reckon? Could she have done it?'

'It's possible.'

'So we have her up again for questioning?'

'I suppose so.' The prospect seemed to plunge the Chief Inspector into gloom. 'Although there isn't much to go on except supposition.'

'Oh, I don't know.' Boyce sounded deliberately cheerful as he started the car. 'She had opportunity. It wouldn't have taken her more than a few minutes to nip over the fence and across the field to meet him. She'd have motive as well. If the kid she's expecting is his and he was thinking of running out on her, she might very well have lost her temper and clobbered him with the nearest thing that came to hand. No-one else seems to have had the time; not if we accept the statements we took up at the Hall this morning as true.' When Finch failed to respond, Boyce went on, 'So what about a spot of lunch? Where do you fancy? A pub in Howlett?'

Finch roused himself.

'Not for me, Tom. I've got the PM on Saxby to attend this afternoon. I'd rather do it on an empty stomach.'

Infuriatingly, Boyce still insisted on looking on the bright side.

'Perhaps Pardoe'll come up with something useful on the Saxby case.'

Under the circumstances, it was an unfortunate choice of words although, later that afternoon, Finch managed, by concentrating on what Pardoe was saying rather than on what he was doing, to keep a tight control over his stomach muscles. It was an aspect of his professional duties with which he had never fully come to terms. Necessary though it was, a post-mortem always seemed to him a further violation of the dead. He was used to death and he could face most murder scenes, however violent, without experiencing that sickening lurch under the diaphragm. But he had never been able to face with equanimity the sight of sharp steel cutting into human flesh, although he supposed that Marion, herself a pathologist, must have learned to accept her role with the same brisk matter-of-factness as Pardoe.

Finch stood well back, trying not to watch too closely as Pardoe cut and probed, occasionally breaking off to make comments into the tape recorder which stood beside him, verbal notes which he would use afterwards as a basis for his written report.

For Finch's benefit, he made a quick summary in layman's language as he washed up afterwards in the sluice-room next door.

'There's no sign of petechiae in any of the internal organs which means he wasn't suffocated. Strangulation's out as well. In fact, all the medical evidence suggests he died from a heart attack. I'll give you the details later in my report.'

'So it could be natural causes?'

'Not could be; almost certainly was.'

'Then why was the pillow changed?' Finch asked the question more of himself than Pardoe.

'That's your problem, laddie.' Pardoe sounded jauntily self-satisfied that it wasn't his. 'I merely cut 'em up and look inside them. It's not my business to theorize about how they get on my slab.' He peered at Finch over the half-moon glasses he always wore when he was performing a PM. 'But I'll give you this for nothing. Someone could have frightened him to death although how you prove it is your affair.'

'With a pillow?' Finch asked, still thinking out loud. 'It's possible, I suppose. If someone tried to suffocate him, he might have had a heart attack trying to defend himself.'

'No sign of a struggle on the hands,' Pardoe pointed out. 'Not a scratch; not even a torn finger-nail and nothing under them either. If you're hoping for fibres off the pillow then you're out of luck.' Smiling sardonically at Finch's discomfiture, he went on, 'You'll do better with that other corpse you landed me with – the one that was fished out of the pond. That's got to be murder unless he managed to whack himself across the back of the head although my guess is he died from drowning. I'll know better when I've had time to open him up.'

'Could a woman have done it?'

'Possible,' Pardoe conceded. 'The blow was hard enough to knock him out but it hasn't broken the skull as far as I could see when I examined him this afternoon. So, yes, a woman could have done it.'

'Thanks,' Finch said and began to walk away, turning to grin briefly over his shoulder as Pardoe called out after him, 'And, Jack, no more corpses, eh? I'd like to get a couple of rounds of golf in over the weekend if you'll let me.'

15

It was half past five, Finch saw, checking on his watch
as he walked to the carpark; time enough to stop off at
an off-licence on his way home to buy wine; plenty of
time, too, to shower and change before driving round to
his sister's for seven o'clock.

There was even time to read his mail which was
waiting for him on the door-mat as he let himself into
the house and which he sorted through eagerly on his
way to the kitchen to put the kettle on for tea. But none
of the envelopes bore Marion's neat, decisive handwriting.

It had been too much to hope for and he tried not to
think of her although, as he put on his best suit and
fastened his tie in front of the wardrobe mirror, he was
reminded of the last time he had worn both.

He thought instead of Kitty Laud. He hadn't yet had
the opportunity to get in touch with anyone he knew on
the Council but he'd do that over the weekend, he
promised himself. He would also, if he could find a spare
half hour or so, stop off at a DIY shop and pick up a
couple of boxes of lino tiles for her kitchen floor. He'd
never forgive himself if she fell and injured herself.

Laying lino tiles might, in fact, form a topic of conversation with his new brother-in-law, Frank Goodall, to
whom at times Finch found himself embarrassingly short
of things to say. Goodall fancied himself as a bit of an
expert on household repairs and maintenance.

His sister and her husband lived in a bungalow, built
in the 'sixties, on the outskirts of the town; rather too

overdecorated for Finch's taste but it was Goodall's choice, not his. All the same, he couldn't help looking with some disfavour as he parked the car at the leaded lights in the windows and the oak name plate, Rosmersholm, fixed to the liver-coloured brickwork by the porch, the letters apparently burnt into the wood with a hot poker.

God knows what Ibsen would have made of the place. As for himself, he was in no position to carp, considering the obvious efforts both Goodall and his sister had made to welcome him.

And it wasn't so bad to be there after all; to stroll about the garden with his brother-in-law and admire the dahlias and to assure his sister that, yes, he was getting enough to eat and, no, he didn't need to bring his shirts round for her to iron.

'Don't fuss, Dot,' he told her with amused exasperation, using her pet family name.

'But I do worry about you sometimes,' she replied. 'I wish . . .'

She had the sense not to finish the remark although he could guess what it would have been. I wish you'd find yourself some nice young woman and get married.

He went on smiling and chatting pleasantly, making a point of asking about church affairs: both Goodall and his sister were active members of St Saviour's, Goodall as a sidesman, Dorothy on the ladies' committee and very much involved with organizing bazaars and sales of work to raise money for charities.

It crossed his mind later, as he listened to Goodall explaining at length the correct method of laying lino tiles, that he might ask his sister and her husband to take an interest in Kitty Laud, and then decided against it. Kitty might not welcome their attentions, however well-meant. She was too much of a pagan to find much to entertain her in St Saviour's Old Folks' socials with their emphasis on bingo and cups of strong tea. She'd be more at home in the local pub with a gin and orange and an impromptu sing-song round the piano.

And there was too much of the pagan in himself as well, he realized, to appreciate properly Goodall's and his sister's happiness even though, on one level, he might envy them a little. Dorothy had certainly blossomed out. She had lost that angular look and had become almost matronly while Goodall seemed at times exasperatingly complacent.

No, Finch decided, continuing to smile, such married bliss was not for him. He'd want more cutting edge to his happiness, a dash of vinegar along with the cream.

Dinner was clearly meant to be an occasion. Dorothy had laid the table with the Wedgwood service which had been his wedding present to them. There were even candles in cut-glass holders shaped like water-lilies which Goodall made a great to-do about lighting.

It was half-way through the meal that the accident happened; one of those trivial domestic incidents which on any other occasion might have been nothing more than a minor embarrassment, quickly forgotten. Refilling their glasses from the bottle of burgundy which had been his contribution to the dinner, Finch inadvertently let a little of it trickle down the stem of his own. As he picked it up, a red circle from the base of the glass stared back at him, neatly stamped on to the white linen tablecloth.

'Oh, Dorothy, I'm sorry,' he exclaimed. 'Look what I've done.'

'Don't worry. It'll wash out,' his sister assured him while Goodall, an authority, it seemed, on stain removal as well as kitchen floors, leaned across the table to sprinkle salt on it.

'The best remedy for spilt wine,' he told them and then went on a little too obviously to change the subject.

Finch hardly listened. As Goodall talked, the Chief Inspector's attention was fixed on that red ring, slowly turning pink as the salt absorbed the burgundy.

What a fool he'd been not to realize it before! Right from the start, he'd assumed that the pillow had been changed because of some evidence on it which pointed to Saxby's murder. It hadn't occurred to him that there could be a quite different explanation.

The main course was over and his sister had begun collecting up the used plates and cutlery to take through to the kitchen. Getting up abruptly from the table, much to the surprise of Goodall who was in mid-sentence, something to do with the rising cost of car insurance, Finch grabbed up a vegetable dish and followed his sister from the room.

'There's no need for you to help, Jack,' she told him as he put the dish down on the draining-board. 'Go back and talk to Frank.'

'It's you I want to talk to,' he replied. 'About that stain . . .'

'Oh, for heaven's sake!' She spoke with a sisterly impatience. 'I've told you, it'll wash out.'

'That's not quite what I meant. What else could leave stains on linen apart from wine?'

She looked him up and down shrewdly, guessing the reason behind the question.

'It's something to do with a case you're working on, isn't it? Well, then, let's think. There's blood. Or ink. Or coal.'

It could be coal, Finch thought. Or rather coke dust. Which would suggest Colin Knapp, who was responsible for keeping the Aga supplied with fuel. Supposing he had gone to Saxby's bedroom with his hands still dirty from filling up the hods? But that didn't make sense. As far as he knew, Knapp had no motive for wanting Saxby dead. He hadn't even met the man. Unless there was some connection between them which he, Finch, hadn't yet discovered.

'Tea. Grass,' Dorothy was continuing, getting a strawberry mousse out of the refrigerator. 'Grass stains can be awful to get rid of. I remember I got some once on a tennis dress and they took ages to wash out. Then there's egg. That can be a nuisance as well. Or fruit juice. Or coffee . . .'

He had gone, calling out as he went, 'Mind if I use your phone?' but picking up the receiver in the hall before she had time to give her consent.

Boyce was out, damn him! His wife, in the voice of one long resigned to her husband's habits, said he had gone down to the pub and she wasn't expecting him back until closing time.

Finch left a message, asking the Sergeant to ring him as soon as he came in and, having given his sister's phone number, put down the receiver.

There was nothing he could do in the meantime except wait, fretting all the time with impatience and, although he ate and talked, he wasn't aware of doing either. To give Goodall his due, he didn't force him to join in the conversation, probably because Dorothy had warned him not to, and for several minutes at a stretch, Finch was able to concentrate on his own thoughts.

Bit by bit, the pieces began to drop into place and form a pattern but there were still some unexplained gaps. The timing of Colin Knapp's murder now made sense and again he cursed himself for not having seen it before. It was so damned obvious. But the motive behind both deaths, Knapp's and Saxby's, still eluded him.

If only he could talk to Boyce! Between them, they might be able to thresh out an answer.

The phone rang while they were drinking coffee in the sitting-room. Finch almost knocked over his cup in his eagerness to get to it and, when he returned to the room, his sister greeted him with the same resigned tone as Boyce's wife when she had answered his call.

'I suppose you'll be leaving, Jack?'

'Sorry.' He tried to sound penitent but couldn't keep the jubilation out of his voice. 'Got to have a chat with Tom. Delicious meal, Dot. Thanks. Don't bother to see me out.'

And stopping only to kiss his sister hurriedly and shake hands with Goodall, he left.

They talked in Boyce's kitchen, squashed in round the breakfast table; hardly the best place for a conference but, as the Sergeant pointed out, it was handy for the spare cans of beer in the fridge and besides, they were less likely to disturb Mrs Boyce who, having let Finch in, had decided there was small chance of seeing her husband alone that evening and had taken herself off to bed.

'First things first,' Finch said. 'What did Kyle find out at the hospital?'

He still couldn't bring himself to name it.

'Knapp was dismissed for bad time-keeping; always turning up late, it seemed, although that wasn't all. Quite a few articles of jewellery went missing off the bodies brought into the mortuary – rings, mainly. Nothing could be proved against Knapp so no charges were brought. But the thefts stopped once he'd been given the boot. Fits in, doesn't it, with what we turned up about him on the computer? He was a tea-leaf who wasn't too choosy about who he nicked from.'

'And Barney?'

'He gave me a quick verbal report just before I knocked off this evening. The matron at Beechcroft already knew about Saxby's death. Nugent, the son, had phoned her. According to Barney, she wouldn't have been at all surprised if it was a heart attack. He'd had a heart condition for the past two years. In fact, he was having

201

medical treatment for it and was prescribed Angipol so it'd seem the bottle of tablets found on the floor was almost certainly his. He was supposed to rest as much as possible but he wouldn't. According to her, he was a stubborn old man, and, if she'd known, she'd've certainly stopped him from driving over to Howlett's. So it looks like natural causes, after all.'

'That's what Pardoe thinks as well,' Finch replied and gave the Sergeant a brief resume of the pathologist's report. 'But that doesn't alter the fact, Tom, that someone must have been in the room with Saxby when he died. He didn't change that pillow himself.'

'I'll give you that,' Boyce conceded. 'But I still think it's damn all evidence to base a case on.'

'It's enough.' Finch sounded quite positive. 'It has to be. The two deaths have to be linked, otherwise Knapp's murder doesn't make sense. Now, whoever changed that pillow had a reason. Right? But not the one we've been working on. All along, we assumed it was something like blood or saliva which would have proved Saxby had been suffocated. But supposing it was the other way round?'

'I don't get you,' Boyce said.

'Supposing the pillow was changed not because of any evidence that was left on it from Saxby but from whoever was with him in the room when he died? I'm thinking of marks or stains of some kind that got on to the pillow when it was handled. The point is, who was that person? Now, Pardoe fixed the time of death between ten p.m. and midnight.'

'Hang on a minute!' Boyce protested. 'Miss Byrne said she heard Saxby breathing when she went to his room at about quarter to eleven.'

'She heard someone breathing. It didn't have to be Saxby. In fact, if my theory's right, I'm fairly certain it wasn't. But for the sake of argument, let's say Saxby died between half past ten and eleven. Who could have been with him when it happened?'

'Well, any one of them, I suppose. None of them have an alibi to cover that time. Teddy Nugent was alone watching television. His son was working in the study while the housekeeper was in the kitchen, also alone, according to Claudia Byrne. As for Knapp, I suppose he was in that bolt-hole of his, drinking beer.'

'And Mrs Nugent?'

'We haven't interviewed her yet but, if we accept Nugent's evidence, she was upstairs somewhere, either in the bathroom or her bedroom. And if Saxby died later, after eleven o'clock, all of them were in bed so they still haven't got an alibi. Any one of them could have slipped along to Saxby's room.'

'Agreed. But I'm convinced it happened earlier. Think, Tom! Someone took evidence into that bedroom and left it on the pillow. That's why it had to be changed. And the answer was there in front of us.'

'Was it?' Boyce sounded unconvinced. 'Well, I for one didn't see anything and unless the SOCOs came up with it . . .'

'No, it was something we both saw; at least, I noticed it but didn't give it a second thought. It was also referred to in one of the witnesses' statements.'

'I give up,' Boyce said.

Finch told him.

For a few seconds, the Sergeant looked at him in disbelief.

Then he said, 'You're joking!'

'I'm not, Tom. I'm quite serious. It's the only explanation that makes any sense.'

'But why do nothing about Saxby's death? For God's sake, there was a bloody nurse in the house! Why not send for her? And where does all this fit in with Knapp's murder? We agreed it couldn't have been anyone at the

Hall. You said yourself it took you ten minutes to walk from the pond where Knapp's body was found to the house, twenty minutes there and back. It's just not possible. Every single person in the place was alibied by someone else after the attack on Miss Byrne.'

'Yes, afterwards. But not before.'

Finch was silent for several moments, giving Boyce time to digest this particular piece of information and watching with amusement as the Sergeant's expression turned from one of incredulity to an exasperated realization that he could have come to the same conclusion himself.

Then he said, picking up his account, 'As for not sending for help when Saxby collapsed, that was out of the question for some reason which I haven't yet worked out. That's why I wanted to talk to you. I thought, if we went back together over the evidence, we might come up with the answer between us, because something must have happened after Saxby arrived at Howlett Hall which made his death so damned important that no-one, apart from the person or persons with him when it occurred, had to know about it, not even the nurse. It was left to Miss Byrne to discover his body the following morning and, if she hadn't noticed the pillow had been changed, everyone would have assumed he died of a heart attack in his sleep.'

'Without apparent witnesses.'

'Exactly. But witnesses to what?'

'To something he could have said?' Boyce suggested.

'That crossed my mind, too.'

'Then could it have been something he heard or saw after he arrived at Howlett Hall?'

'Not necessarily, Tom. Don't forget he'd known the Aston family for years, especially Edgar Aston and his sister, Mrs Nugent, as well as the housekeeper, Edie Cole. In fact, that's why he turned up at Howlett's. He wanted to see Aston before he died.'

'So what's the theory? That he knew something about the Astons which for some reason had to be kept secret?' Boyce asked. 'Some skeleton in their cupboard, is that what you're thinking? If so, why didn't he come out with it years ago? Why wait until Aston was about to kick the bucket?'

'Perhaps it was because he was about to die.'

'You could be right,' Boyce conceded. 'In which case it could be to do with Aston's will – money, inheritance, that sort of thing. And that could be the reason Saxby was so keen to see Aston. He wanted to apologize to him, not just about the quarrel but about some action he was going to take after Aston's death.'

'I'll buy it,' Finch said. 'What have you got in mind?'

Boyce looked abashed.

'I haven't worked it out in detail. I thought the idea was we kicked a few theories around; see where they led us. Supposing Saxby knew that one of the heirs wasn't entitled to inherit . . .'

'Just a minute, Tom. That argument would apply to only two people who were in the house at the time, Miss Byrne, the granddaughter, and Mrs Nugent, his sister.'

'Right. But don't forget Saxby wanted to speak to Mrs Nugent immediately after he'd seen Aston only Miss Byrne couldn't get her because she was having a bath at the time.'

'So what are you suggesting? That Saxby knew some family secret which he was going to divulge and wanted to warn Constance Nugent that he intended blowing the whistle? He could have done, I suppose. It might have fitted in with some gentlemanly code of conduct of throwing down the gauntlet first. But where does Knapp's murder fit in? I can't see him knowing about any skeletons in the family cupboard. Miss Cole could have known, of course, but she's not the type to go yapping her mouth off about it, even to her own nephew.

And why, if it was so secret, did Saxby ask to speak to Dr Callender first? It's hardly the sort of thing he'd want to discuss even with the family doctor.'

Boyce helped himself to a can of beer from the fridge, offering one to Finch who shook his head at it before continuing.

'We've got to start again, Tom, and take another look at the sequence of events. Saxby goes to see Aston who's dying. He then asks to speak to Callender or, failing him, Mrs Nugent. Later that same evening, Saxby himself dies, presumably of a heart attack although there's evidence that someone was with him when it happened who took care to change the pillow on the bed. But if we go back over those events, where does that take us? Saxby asked to see Dr Callender *immediately after* seeing Aston. Couldn't that be significant?'

'What of?' Boyce demanded.

'That he'd seen or heard something in Aston's room which he wanted to discuss preferably with the doctor but, at second best, with Aston's sister; something that was connected with Aston's death.'

'It couldn't have been anything he heard. Aston was unconscious.'

'But supposing he regained consciousness if only for a few moments? The nurse admitted she was on the other side of the room and only heard part of what Saxby was saying. She mentioned something else as well. At the end of Saxby's visit, just after she told him he'd have to leave, Saxby bent down over the bed and then gave a little cry. Remember? If Aston did regain consciousness at that point, he might have whispered something to Saxby, which caused him to make that exclamation.'

'What?' Boyce asked suspiciously.

'I don't know.' Finch tried not to sound impatient. 'I'm simply chucking ideas around. It couldn't have been more than a couple of words. There wasn't time for a long conversation. So let's use our imaginations. Let's suppose he said something like "Poison" or "Wrong tablets" which suggested to Saxby that Aston's illness wasn't as straightforward as it seemed. That would explain why Saxby cried out, why he was so quiet when Claudia Byrne took him back to his bedroom and why he asked to see Dr Callender or, when he realized that Callender wouldn't be calling again that night, Aston's sister, Constance Nugent.'

'You're suggesting Aston was murdered? But Callender was positive he died from natural causes.'

'I'm suggesting that Aston's death might have been suspicious, that Saxby knew of it and admitted that knowledge to whoever was with him when he had his heart attack. That's why the nurse wasn't sent for. It was essential that Saxby should die without passing on that information to anyone else. It could also give a motive for Knapp's death. Knapp helped nurse Aston so he could have been in on the secret and when he threatened to expose it, he, too, had to die.'

'Makes sense,' Boyce agreed. 'So what are we going to do about it?'

'I haven't worked that out yet,' Finch admitted. 'So far, it's all supposition. There isn't a scrap of hard evidence. But if we go along with the theory, it's going to mean a post-mortem on Aston.'

'The family's not going to like that.'

'No, they're not.' Finch was silent for several seconds, thinking of Basil Nugent's reaction. Then he said, 'We'll have to risk it, Tom. But we'll take it step by step. For a start, we'll have a talk with Callender and get him to make a formal identification so that, if need be, the PM can go ahead. I'll arrange for that to be done first thing tomorrow morning, without involving the family. After that, God knows. We'll have to cross that particular bridge when we come to it.'

16

Robert Callender said, 'Is all this necessary? I'm still convinced Aston died of natural causes.'

He was waiting for them, at Finch's request, outside the premises of Fairchild and Son, the undertakers in Howlett, which evidently served a double duty as a car hire firm, according to a discreet printed notice in the window below a large vase of plastic lilies, suitable for either weddings or funerals.

'All I want is a formal identification at this stage,' Finch replied.

There was no time to repeat the lengthier explanation he had already given to Callender over the phone. Mr Fairchild senior was drawing the bolts and letting them through the door, out of the gaze of an elderly woman with a dog, two men on bikes and the local vicar who, although it was only a quarter to eight in the morning, had turned up from God knows where to observe their arrival.

Once inside, Mr Fairchild announced severely, 'Everything is ready for you, as requested.'

He clearly disapproved of their visit – of its timing, of the nature of Finch's request, even of the warrant, which he examined in detail as if looking for some minor discrepancy which might make it possible for him to refuse permission even at this last moment.

But it seemed in order and he reluctantly led the way through a curtained-off doorway into a small chapel of rest, furnished entirely in light oak and blue velvet, where Aston's opened coffin was waiting for them on a carpeted dais, flanked by two more vases of plastic lilies.

Finch hung back, letting Callender go forward alone. He had no great hope that Callender would be able to assist him, apart from identifying the body.

And once that formality was over, the Lord alone knew what would be his next move. A post-mortem examination? An analysis of the stomach contents? All of it seemed extreme when he had nothing more positive on which to base his suspicions except a theory.

Callender was saying, as he stepped back from the coffin, 'Yes, Chief Inspector. That's Edgar Aston.'

Afterwards Finch was to ask himself why he took the trouble to look for himself. After all, he had never known Edgar Aston either dead or alive. There was no reason why, apart from sheer curiosity, he should have mounted the two steps up to the dais and taken Callender's place beside the open coffin.

But he did and found himself gazing down at a face which he had seen many times before only under totally different circumstances.

The body lay surrounded by the ruched white satin which lined the interior of the coffin, the eyes closed, the expression faintly amused, the hands decently folded across the front of the formal dark suit in which it was dressed and which lacked only a white carnation to supply the finishing touch.

They conferred in the car which Boyce had parked in a nearby side street, Dr Callender seated in the back, Finch and Boyce in the front, the Chief Inspector doing most of the talking.

At the end of his account, Boyce asked the obvious question with the truculent air of someone who, despite incontrovertible proof, nevertheless refuses, out of sheer bloody-mindedness, to be convinced.

'Why?'

'I don't know yet, Tom,' Finch replied, trying to hide

his exasperation. Trust Boyce to put his finger on the one weak point. 'But it's got to have something to do with money. There isn't any other possible motive.'

It was Dr Callender, sensible and down-to-earth, who acted as peacemaker.

'I suggest we drive over to Howlett Hall and ask the family. But I want to be there when you do. If Mrs Nugent is involved, then, as her doctor, I ought to be present.'

Finch agreed. If, as he suspected, he was dealing with a conspiracy, then Mrs Nugent had to be part of it.

They drove in convoy, Callender, who had walked back to the surgery to collect his car, leading the way, the police vehicles following, Finch and Boyce in the first, the back-up team of WPCs and uniformed men who had arrived from Divisional Headquarters at the Chief Inspector's request completing the procession.

They drew up this time at the front of the house, where Teddy Nugent's elegant, silver Rolls Royce was already parked. Its presence and the suitcases lined up by the front door suggested that their arrival had been well timed. The Nugents were about to leave.

Teddy Nugent himself met them in the hall, greeting them with an odd mixture of consternation and relief and cutting short Finch's explanation with the words, 'Yes, yes, Chief Inspector. My wife and I are quite willing to tell you all about Dixon. In fact, we were on the point of leaving for London where we were going to consult our solicitor first. Basil's already gone. We fully intended to issue a joint statement later today.'

As he turned towards the drawing-room door, he added with a glance of quick appeal over his shoulder at Finch, 'I'd be grateful if you treated Constance with great care. It's her idea that we admit the truth. Saxby's death affected her so deeply that she felt she couldn't keep up the pretence any longer.'

Finch and Boyce followed him inside the room,

accompanied by one of the WPCs, the others remaining in the hall, while Robert Callender, as had already been agreed, went upstairs to tell Claudia Byrne what had happened and to be on hand should he be needed.

But Constance Nugent appeared to be in no immediate need of medical help. She was sitting bolt upright on the sofa, very much in command of herself and putting Finch in mind of Kitty Laud on the first occasion he had seen her at Headquarters, her face wearing a similar indomitable expression although, under the skilful make-up, the Chief Inspector could detect the lines of fatigue round the mouth and eyes.

After Boyce had finished pronouncing the words of official caution, Teddy Nugent, who had stood to attention throughout its recital, as if for the playing of the national anthem, seated himself beside his wife and plunged straight into his statement, relieved, it seemed, to unburden himself.

'I expect you'll want to know how we came to be involved with Hal Dixon, Chief Inspector. We first met him by chance about three years ago. Constance and I had gone to the theatre one evening. In the interval, we were having a drink in the circle bar when suddenly she said, "Good Lord, there's Edgar over there!"'

'Only it wasn't Edgar,' Constance Nugent broke in, anxious not to be excluded, 'although the resemblance was uncanny. I realized my mistake as soon as I went over to speak to him. I was in the middle of saying, "You might have let us know you were going to be in town . . ." when I saw it wasn't Edgar. He was slightly shorter than my brother and there were certain mannerisms and expressions which weren't at all like his. After we'd apologized, Teddy bought him a drink and we chatted with him until the bell went for the second act. He seemed amused by the situation and, before we left, he insisted on giving us his name and telephone number. The next evening, we dined with Basil and happened to mention meeting this Mr Dixon. I think, Teddy, you ought to tell the Chief Inspector what was said.'

She looked across at her husband as if, as Basil's father, the next part of the account was entirely his responsibility. Teddy Nugent took it up reluctantly.

'I ought to explain first something that happened just over six years ago, Chief Inspector. Edgar came to me for financial advice. He was desperately short of money. Although the Astons had been quite wealthy before the war, his father had spent quite a lot of the capital having this place built. It cost him a small fortune and another on its upkeep. Even so, when Edgar inherited, there should have been enough of the Aston money left to keep him in comfort for the rest of his life, taking into account the capital he'd raised by selling the business after the war. It wasn't the first time either that he'd asked for my advice. He'd come to see me in the 'fifties when he was forced to put the gate-house and some of the land on the market. The three of us, Basil, Constance and I, discussed then where the money had gone and assumed Edgar had spent it on running this place and entertaining. Like his father, he liked to make a bit of a splash socially. But the second time he consulted me, as I said about six years ago, it was quite clear he was in a bad way financially; so bad, in fact, that he was thinking of selling off Howlett's, something he couldn't do without Constance's permission as, according to the terms of her father's will, they were co-beneficiaries.

'The only alternative, he said, was to sell a life insurance policy which he'd taken out in the early 'thirties when he came of age, although I gathered old Philip Aston, Edgar's father, had insisted on the investment and had in fact, up to his own death, provided Edgar with the money to pay the premiums. It was the first time I'd heard about the policy although Constance remembered there'd been some family discussion about it when she'd been a girl.'

'Not the details,' Constance Nugent explained. 'Don't forget I was only in my teens and my father would never have dreamt of consulting me about anything. I can understand though why my father insisted on Edgar taking the policy out. He hoped Edgar would marry and have sons to carry on the family business but he didn't have much faith in Edgar's skill as a business man. The policy was intended to inject more capital into the firm on Edgar's death. As it happened, he himself died during the war and Edgar sold up the business in the late 'forties.'

'How much was the policy for?' Finch asked.

Constance Nugent leaned back against the sofa cushions, dissociating herself from this part of the affair and leaving her husband to name the amount which he did in a voice that was carefully non-committal.

'A million pounds, Chief Inspector.'

In the small silence that followed, Constance Nugent closed her eyes.

'A lot of money,' Finch remarked.

'Absurd, of course,' Constance Nugent murmured, 'but Daddy had this dream that one day the Astons would be millionaires.'

Teddy Nugent cleared his throat, bringing them back to the present realities.

'The policy explained where the money had gone. Edgar had been using capital to service the premiums. Foolish, of course. He should have let the policy go years before when he sold up the business.'

'And why didn't he?' Finch asked.

'Pride, partly. He didn't like to admit that he could no longer afford the premiums. Guilt, as well. It was bad enough selling off the family firm without letting his

213

father down a second time by giving up the policy and with it his father's dream of the Aston descendants inheriting a million pounds . . .'

'And sheer pigheadedness,' Constance Nugent put in. 'Edgar would never admit he was in the wrong. He only came to ask for Teddy's advice when he was desperate.'

'Yes. Well.' Nugent was careful not to join in this sisterly condemnation and hurried on with his explanation. 'I in turn consulted Basil and together we worked out a financial package which would serve everyone's best interests. Unfortunately at the time, neither Basil nor I was in the position to buy the policy from Edgar but all of us, including Edgar, were anxious that it shouldn't pass outside the family. So it was decided that, instead of putting the policy on the market, Edgar would make it over to Constance as a gift, which would relieve him of the burden of paying the premiums and meant he could go on living here at Howlett's. From our point of view, we benefited by acquiring collateral through which Constance could raise capital which she'd put into a company which Basil would set up to invest in a dockland development scheme. In turn, Constance would waive her legal rights to Howlett Hall, which meant Rowena, Edgar's daughter, and Claudia would be the sole beneficiaries. At today's valuations, that would be the equivalent of about a quarter of a million pounds. In addition, another £200,000 worth of shares would be set aside for them in Basil's company which would be worth at least double that amount in a few years, if not more. We also agreed to make provision for Edie, who was another of Edgar's concerns. We arranged to take out an annuity on her behalf through Basil's company and to buy her a house, the deeds of which would revert to the company on her death. By passing on the shares to Edgar's beneficiaries rather than Edgar himself,

Rowena and Claudia of course gained by avoiding paying inheritance tax on them after Edgar's death.'

'A tax dodge, in other words,' Finch said cheerfully.

Teddy Nugent had the grace to look abashed.

'Yes, I'm afraid it was, Chief Inspector, and one that involved all of us. By accepting the policy as a gift, Constance also avoided paying inheritance tax on it when Edgar died.'

At this point, Constance Nugent opened her eyes.

'It was all Basil's idea. He worked out the "scheme" as he called it and talked the three of us, Edgar, Teddy and me, into agreeing with it. The hours he spent discussing his brain-child! It became an obsession with him. He talked of nothing else.'

Teddy Nugent interrupted her in his son's defence.

'He wanted it to be fool-proof, you see, Chief Inspector. Basil has that kind of mind. He's a perfectionist. The only contingency he couldn't prepare for, of course, was the date of Edgar's death. A deed of gift has to be made at least seven years before the donor dies in order to be exempt from taxation. It was a gamble, although, as Basil pointed out, if you want to make money, you have to be prepared to take risks.'

'And where did Hal Dixon fit into all this?' Finch asked, although he thought he could guess the answer.

There was a long pause in which the Nugents exchanged glances, each appealing to the other to speak first.

It was Constance Nugent who finally broke the silence.

'Oh, for God's sake, Teddy! Let's get it over with. Sooner or later the Chief Inspector will have to know the truth.' Turning to Finch, she continued, 'Hal Dixon was to be *our* insurance in case Edgar died before the seven years were up. At the time, it didn't seem very likely. Edgar was perfectly fit. There was no reason to believe he wouldn't live on until he was into his 'eighties. But

215

we couldn't be sure. It was Basil's idea that we kept up the acquaintance with Hal Dixon although nothing was said openly, not to him certainly and not even among ourselves. We were simply to *cultivate* him.'

She put a scornful emphasis on the word as if to dissociate herself from the situation, although she'd gone along with the idea, Finch thought. But then, a million pounds is a hell of a lot of money, more than enough to buy off most people's moral scruples.

Constance Nugent was saying, 'Teddy got in touch with him at the phone number he'd given us, asking him out to dinner and telling him to order a mini-cab at our expense. After that, we used to meet him regularly.'

Which accounted for Hal Dixon's jaunts up to the West End, Finch added silently to himself. No wonder his landlady, Mrs Townsend, had thought he'd come into money.

Out loud, he merely asked, 'So Mr Dixon had no idea he might be used as a substitute for your brother, Mrs Nugent?'

'Oh, no; not then,' she began but Teddy Nugent interrupted her.

'He knew something was in the wind, Constance. Dixon was no fool. He soon realized we weren't inviting him out week after week simply for the pleasure of his company. That's when he started pumping me for a little bit more than dinner at my expense. He'd take me to one side after the meal. You can probably guess the kind of hint he'd drop. He was a bit short on the rent. Could I see my way to lending him a tenner? All done with great charm and tact; he was evidently quite an experienced scrounger but there was no disguising the fact that it was a form of blackmail.'

'You didn't tell me, Teddy!' Constance Nugent cried accusingly.

'I didn't want to worry you, my dear. But I spoke to

Basil about it. We agreed to drop the whole idea. In another few months, the seven-year period would have been up anyway. And then Edgar died. Ironic, wasn't it, Chief Inspector? We had come down here for the weekend. There were just the four of us, Edgar, Constance, Basil and myself. Claudia had already left for Italy. Edgar seemed perfectly fit. In fact, we'd taken him out for a drive only that morning. We were having coffee after lunch when he complained of feeling unwell. He said he thought he'd go upstairs and lie down. He was getting up from his chair when he collapsed. Basil and I got him on to the sofa but he was dead within minutes. It was then we decided to go ahead with the scheme.'

'Basil decided, you mean,' Constance Nugent said in a cold, clear voice.

'My dear,' Teddy corrected her gently, 'we all agreed with his decision. At the time, it seemed perfectly rational. We were just four months away from a million pounds tax free. A great deal of money, Chief Inspector. But it meant that Edie had to be brought into the plan.'

'I thought she'd refuse.' Constance Nugent sounded outraged that she hadn't, as if Edie should have acted as guardian of the collective conscience but, by accepting their proposal, had in some obscure manner let all of them down.

'We talked it over,' Teddy Nugent was saying. 'There seemed no major drawbacks that we could see. Claudia, as I said, had left for Italy. Rowena, Edgar's daughter, was living in the States and rarely came back to this country. As for Edgar himself, he had no close friends apart from Roland Saxby and they hadn't met since they'd quarrelled. There was no problem either over Edgar's doctor. Robert Callender's father, who had been Edgar's GP, had died the previous spring and his son, who took over the practice, hardly knew Edgar apart from a few social visits in the past. We were sure Dixon would agree if we put the proposal to him. It all seemed to fit in so well.'

Except for Aston's corpse, Finch thought. He wondered what the hell they'd done with that. But Teddy Nugent was hurrying on with his account, eager to finish; eager also to skirt round any awkward details such as the disposal of his brother-in-law's body and Finch let him continue. He could be brought back at some later stage to face that particular truth.

'We phoned Dixon from here and made arrangements to meet him,' Nugent continued. 'Basil drove up to London and put the plan to him. As we thought, he made no difficulties. We agreed to pay him £30 a week and he accepted the terms. He was to come down here with us every so often, stay the night and let himself be seen either in the village where Basil or I would take him for a drive, or about the house by the cleaning woman, Nancy Fuller. There was no problem there. Nancy hadn't had much to do with Edgar anyway. As long as she saw Dixon from time to time, pottering in the garden or sitting in here, reading the paper, she wouldn't know any difference. All the same, Constance was to instruct Dixon about the family background so that, if necessary, he could talk about events which had happened which would make it seem he *was* Edgar.

'There was only one hitch to the scheme although in the end it worked out to our advantage. The first winter that Dixon was here, he went down with bronchitis and Robert Callender had to be called in. Of course, there was no question that Dixon could be driven back to London as usual after a couple of days. He had to stay on at Howlett's. But he wrote a note to his landlady, enclosing a postal order for the rent on his room in Clapham which Basil posted in Bournemouth. It meant, though, that Callender got to know him as his patient and accepted him as Edgar, which was all to the good. You see, Chief

Inspector, there was only one drawback that we couldn't plan ahead for and that was how long Dixon would live. He might go on for years. On the other hand, he was in his late 'seventies and might, like Edgar, die suddenly. We had to be sure that, when he did die, it was at Howlett's.

'The other cause for concern was Claudia. She was still abroad but would no doubt return to England at some point and would want to come down to Howlett's to visit her grandfather. Dixon had to be here when she arrived.'

'Yes, I can see it could be awkward for you,' Finch murmured, with no apparent irony.

Despite himself, he was intrigued by Teddy Nugent's story. It was told with such eagerness to explain and win over the Chief Inspector's sympathy for the scheme, which was evidently of great importance to Nugent and for which the sum of money at the end was merely the prize, even if a glittering one, in a game of winner-take-all.

It was evidently not an eagerness shared by Constance Nugent, who was lying back against the sofa cushions, her eyes closed again, as if uninterested in her husband's recitation of these details.

Nugent was saying, the bright-eyed look still on his face, 'We decided in February that Dixon would have to move in here permanently. Claudia had written to say she'd be coming back to England in the summer. Besides, Dixon himself was finding the drive backwards and forwards to Howlett's more tiring. When we put the proposition to him that he should move in here, he accepted without any argument. We couldn't risk him giving up his room in Clapham. His landlady might have asked for a forwarding address. Nor did we want him to keep his room indefinitely. That might have looked suspicious as well, especially as he wasn't going to go back there. On balance we thought it better that nothing was done and that he simply moved in here and left his luggage behind. Dixon had already told his landlady that, when he went away, he was staying with friends on the south coast. We hoped that, even if she made enquiries, nothing much would be done to follow them up. After all, he had no family.'

'Dixon told you that?' Finch asked.

Teddy Nugent looked startled.

'You mean he had relations?'

Constance Nugent opened her eyes, suddenly alert and oddly triumphant.

'Didn't I warn you not to trust him, Teddy? You should have checked up on him as I told you to.'

'But he swore . . .'

'Of course he did. He told you exactly what you wanted to hear. He was as eager as you were to make sure the arrangements went smoothly. After all, he wasn't doing badly out of it himself. Once he moved in here, he was living a great deal better than he'd been doing in that room of his in Clapham – free meals, the best medical care, Edie to wait on him. If he'd stayed in London, he'd eventually have finished up in a council home for old people. Hal Dixon knew perfectly well he was on to a good thing.'

It fitted in with what Finch had learned about Hal Dixon from talking to his sister, Kitty Laud. It also explained why Dixon had failed to write to her for her birthday. He hadn't dared to. Living as he was by then in Howlett Hall and dependent on Edie or the Nugents for every aspect of his day-to-day life, he'd had neither the means nor the opportunity of going down to the village to buy a birthday card or even to post it without their knowledge.

But apart from remarking, 'There's a sister,' with more dismissiveness than he really meant, he made no other reference to Kitty Laud, simply adding, 'Go on, Mr

Nugent. You were telling me how Mr Dixon moved in here.'

Nugent resumed his account but far less eagerly. He seemed chastened by the knowledge that Dixon had deceived him. He was also reaching that point in his statement where certain unpalatable aspects of the plan had to be faced up to and described.

He said, 'Claudia came back to England and arranged to drive down to Howlett's and visit her grandfather. Of course, Constance and I made sure we were here that weekend. But the visit went better than we'd feared. Dixon was getting quite frail by then and, naturally, in the two years since she'd been away, it was only to be expected that her grandfather, as she thought, would have changed, although Dixon put on a bit of a show and pretended to be more easily tired than he really was. We made a great deal, too, of how the attack of bronchitis had affected his chest so that he couldn't talk for long. But he was able to chat to her about family events which Constance had described to him and, apart from being concerned about his health, she seemed to accept Dixon as her grandfather. The fact that all of us, including Edie, acted as if everything was normal helped to convince her.

'The main problem was Dixon himself. Simply by being here, he made much more work for Edie who wasn't getting any younger herself. So we arranged for her nephew, Colin Knapp, to move in here as well to help with the heavier work. Then, as the weeks went by, Dixon's health began to deteriorate. Even before Claudia's first visit, he was finding it more and more difficult to manage the stairs or get in and out of bed without help. Finally, he had a stroke. Edie phoned us and we came down straight away although we put off getting in touch with Claudia for as long as we could. But, when Callender told us that he didn't think Dixon,

221

or rather Edgar, as he thought, could live much longer, we had to let her know.

'We had no idea that she'd call to see Saxby on the way here and tell him that her grandfather was very ill; or that Saxby himself would turn up later that afternoon, demanding to see Edgar and make up that ridiculous quarrel they'd had years ago. But he did. Basil was of the opinion that it was worth the risk of letting Saxby see Dixon. He was in a coma so there was no chance that he could speak and therefore it was unlikely Saxby would realize he wasn't Edgar. But Constance thought it unwise and so did I. In fact, I thought it too risky even to let Saxby stay here for the night.'

'But what could I do?' Constance Nugent demanded. 'You saw the state he was in when he arrived, Teddy! We could hardly take him back to the nursing-home that night. My idea was far the best.' She turned to address the Chief Inspector. 'If I'd had my way, Roland would have been taken to see Dixon the following morning, before we drove him back to Beechcroft. That way, one of us could have been with him to make sure he wasn't allowed too near the bedside. There was always the chance, too, that Dixon might have been dead by then. Dr Callender didn't expect him to live much longer. And if Claudia hadn't taken it on herself to interfere nothing would have been discovered. We had no idea that she'd arranged for Roland to see Dixon that evening. And, as she knew nothing about the plan, he was allowed to spend several minutes alone with him.'

'Long enough to discover what?' Finch asked.

Constance Nugent gave him a look of deep contempt as if, by admitting to his ignorance of this particular piece of information, the Chief Inspector was guilty of gross deception and had tricked them into their confession.

'The scar on his hand. It was quite noticeable. Of course, Claudia knew about it and so did Roland. In fact,

Roland had been there when the accident happened years before, when he and Edgar were boys. They were building a tree house when Edgar cut himself badly with a saw. When Claudia visited Dixon for the first time after she returned to England, Dixon was careful to keep his left hand hidden and, even when she went to see him this last time in his bedroom, we warned Colin Knapp to make sure Dixon's hand was covered up so that the scar, or rather the lack of it, couldn't be seen. Once Nurse Holden took over the nursing, we couldn't take such precautions. That's why, if Roland was to visit Dixon, I wanted to be certain that one of us was present so that the bedclothes could be arranged in such a way that Roland couldn't see Dixon's left hand.'

'But Mr Saxby noticed the scar wasn't there and spoke to you about it later that evening,' Finch said.

It was a shot in the dark but he was fairly sure it would hit its mark. According to Claudia Byrne's statement, Saxby had asked to see Dr Callender first and then Constance Nugent, not, as the Chief Inspector had believed, because he was suspicious about Aston's illness, but in order to query Aston's identity.

As soon as Mrs Nugent confirmed the Chief Inspector's supposition, Finch pushed ahead, giving her no time to deflect him from the point.

'Mr Nugent told you, didn't he, that Claudia had come downstairs looking for you? It could have been about anything at all but both you and your husband were on guard in case anything should go wrong. So, as soon as Miss Byrne was safely out of the way, you went along to Mr Saxby's room to check why he wanted to see you.'

'Yes; partly,' Constance Nugent admitted. 'I thought he'd asked Claudia to persuade me to give my permission for him to see Edgar, not realizing then that Claudia had already taken it on herself to arrange the visit. I wanted to convince Roland that, provided Edgar, or rather Dixon, wasn't too ill the following morning, Teddy or I would make sure he saw him before he left for Beechcroft. But it wasn't only for that reason. I was very fond of Roland. He'd looked so dreadfully tired when he arrived and I wanted to make certain he was feeling better and was comfortable for the night.'

She paused and looked across at her husband for help but Teddy Nugent was staring down miserably at the carpet, leaving her to complete the account.

'I went to Roland's room,' she continued, speaking rapidly as if anxious to have the matter over and done with. 'He was in bed, with the lights still on. He told me that Claudia had taken him to see Edgar; only it wasn't Edgar. He'd seen the man's hands lying on the bed covers and there was no scar. He wanted to know what was going on. I tried to explain about the insurance policy but he kept on saying, "But what's happened to Edgar? What have you done with him?" '

She broke off, lying back against the sofa cushions and putting one hand, heavy with rings, over her eyes.

'I can't go on, Teddy! You'll have to tell them.'

Teddy Nugent took up the account in such a low, hurried tone that Finch had to lean forward in order to hear him.

'Constance told me that Roland started to get out of bed. He'd pushed back the bedclothes and was struggling to get to his feet when he suddenly collapsed sideways, dragging the covers and the pillows with him and knocking over the bedside table. One pillow was behind his head, the other was lying across his chest. Constance ran to fetch Edie who was in the kitchen. She came upstairs to Roland's room and took the pillow off his chest so that she could feel for a heart-beat. She'd had some nursing experience, you see, having looked after Helen, Edgar's wife, before she died. But Roland was dead. There was no pulse, no heart-beat, nothing. While

Edie was doing that, Constance came to fetch Basil and myself. We knew we hadn't much time to come to a decision. Claudia was in her room but might at any moment come out on to the landing and see us leaving the nursery wing. Or she might take it into her head to go to Roland's room herself. We daren't take too long making up our minds.'

'And so you decided to leave Mr Saxby where he was and pretend you knew nothing?' Finch asked although it was more a statement than a question.

'We had no intention of letting Claudia find him,' Constance Nugent protested. 'Edie was supposed to do that when she took him an early morning cup of tea. But then Dixon himself died and Edie was kept so busy that, before she had time to arrange it, Claudia had already gone to Saxby's room.'

'Who changed the pillow? Miss Cole, I suppose?'

Nugent, who was no fool, glanced sharply across at the Chief Inspector.

'Is that what made Claudia suspicious? We realized things had gone wrong when Callender told us he was informing the police but we didn't know that it was because of something Claudia had seen.'

'There was no monogram on the pillowcase,' Finch told him. 'And, when I arrived, I noticed the pillow was lying too neatly on the bed. But, of course, the original pillow had to be changed. Miss Cole had left marks on it when she lifted it off Mr Saxby's chest. Fruit stains, weren't they, Mr Nugent? Blackcurrant juice to be exact.'

He might have added but didn't that he had seen that particular piece of evidence for himself the next morning, when he had interviewed Edie Cole and had noticed the pie standing on the kitchen table, ready to go into the oven, the pastry stained with the dark juice from the fruit.

'She was preparing the blackcurrants when Constance went to fetch her and came straight upstairs without stopping to wash her hands. As soon as we saw the marks on the pillow where she'd touched it, we knew we daren't leave it there. But everything had to be done so quickly. There wasn't time to plan properly. We left Edie to deal with it while we went back to our rooms. As it was, Claudia nearly caught her in Roland's bedroom. She knocked on the door and Edie only had time to switch off the light before Claudia opened the door a little way and looked inside. But she must have heard Edie breathing because she went away, assuming, I imagine, that Roland was asleep.'

'Quick thinking on Miss Cole's part, wasn't it?' Finch remarked pleasantly.

As he rose to his feet, signalling the end of the interview, Nugent asked fearfully, 'What will happen next?'

'You'll be taken to Divisional Headquarters where once you've signed a written statement, you'll be charged,' Finch told him. 'I'll also need to know your son's London address so that he can be arrested. But first of all I'd like you to point out to my Sergeant exactly where Mr Aston's body is buried. I assume it's somewhere in the garden.'

'My wife and I had nothing to do with that!' Nugent protested, his voice rising. 'Nor with Colin Knapp's murder.'

It was Constance Nugent who saved the situation. Calmly collecting up her handbag, she, too, got to her feet, smoothing down the cuffs of her silk dress as she did so.

'I'm sure the Chief Inspector is well aware of that, Teddy,' she said. 'After all, murder is hardly our style, is it? Now come along, darling, and don't make yourself look ridiculous.'

And stalking ahead of them, she led the procession out of the room, bestowing on the WPC, who opened the door for them, a gracious smile of acknowledgement.

17

They found Edie Cole sitting at the kitchen table, her hands, uncharacteristically idle, clasped on its scrubbed surface, waiting, it seemed, for them.

'I heard you arrive,' she told them, 'and I knew you'd gone into the drawing-room to speak to Miss Constance and Mr Nugent. Told you everything, did they? I guessed they might. None of them, especially Miss Constance, had the stomach for it any more after Mr Saxby died. If I'd had my way, Mr Nugent would have taken her straight back to London.'

Gesturing to Boyce to do the same, Finch drew out one of the chairs and joined her at the table. To any outside observer, they might have been three acquaintances enjoying a mid-morning tête-à-tête.

'No, they didn't tell me everything,' he said easily. 'They denied any knowledge of the murder of your nephew, Colin Knapp.'

'He wasn't my nephew,' Edie Cole corrected him with an odd little smile of triumph at having caught the Inspector out. 'He was my son. Nobody knows that; not even Miss Constance. He was born just before the war; illegitimate, of course, although I wouldn't have married the father even if he'd asked me. Which he didn't. Cleared off as soon as he found out I was expecting. It's a different matter today, isn't it, Chief Inspector? I'd've got an abortion on the National Health. Or I'd've kept it and nobody would've thought twice about it. But not in those days. I was in service, then – a solicitor's family; ever so respectable. As soon as they found out I was carrying, they told me to go. My sister took me in and brought the baby up as her own. Then the war came and, as soon as the bombing started, my sister and the baby were evacuated down here to Howlett's. I got a job at a factory just outside Chelmsford and I used to come over to visit her. And the baby, too, of course, though I never let on it was mine. I didn't even think of it as belonging to me anyway, once I'd handed it over.

'After the war, Mr and Mrs Aston asked me to stay on as housekeeper and I agreed. I liked it here. The family was good to me and it was the first proper home I'd had. They didn't interfere either. Mrs Aston's health was bad and she trusted me to run the place as I wanted. I'd never been in charge of anything before in my life. I'd always had someone behind me, giving orders. The house was beautiful then; not like it is now. There was a full-time gardener and a woman came up every day from the village to do the rough work. I used to think it was like taking part in a film – dinner parties with all the silver laid out on the table and everyone in evening dress.'

'But you kept in touch with your son?' Finch asked, bringing her back to the present inquiry.

She looked at him, her expression indifferent.

'Only as his auntie. He never knew until much later, after my sister died and he needed to look up his birth certificate, that I was really his mother. And by then it was too late.'

'Too late for what?'

'Too late to knock any sense or decency into him. My brother-in-law had been killed in North Africa and my sister never married again so there was no man about the place to discipline him properly. And Lizzie was too soft with him but she'd never had any children of her own so he was the only one. Funny, isn't it? There was me with a baby I should never have had and her, who'd have loved a family, with no kid to bring up except mine.

But it wasn't all her fault. There was bad blood there as well. As they say – like father, like son.'

She said no more, leaving Finch to imagine for himself the disastrous love affair which had caused so much bitterness that it continued to rankle after more than fifty years.

She went on, 'He started asking me for money; not much to begin with; a few pounds here, a few more there. And he was always in and out of work; couldn't hold down a steady job for more than a month or two at a time. I paid up. I had to. I didn't want him turning up here, spoiling everything.'

'But he did,' Finch pointed out. 'He was asked to help look after Mr Aston, or rather, Mr Dixon. Someone must have given his name to the Nugents and it couldn't have been anyone else except you.'

'I had to!' she cried. The colour had run up into her face, staining the cheekbones with a dull, ugly red. 'Who else could I turn to when Mr Aston died? They came to me and told me about the plan they had. All that money! "Think of it, Edie," Miss Constance said. "None of us need ever worry again." And then Mr Nugent sat down with me and explained about the insurance policy. If I kept quiet and went along with them, they'd buy me a house and see to it that I had enough to live on comfortably.' For the first time during the interview, the hard, closed expression lifted and her features became animated. 'A place of my own – me who'd lived all my life in other people's houses!'

'And where did Colin Knapp fit in?'

The moment of vivacity passed and her face again assumed its rigid look.

'They needed someone to get rid of the body. No-one in the family wanted to touch it, as if it mattered what happened to it after Mr Aston died. The dead don't care, so why should we? For all their clever talk about

229

annuities and inheritance tax and how we'd all come out of it better off, it was one part of the plan they hadn't thought about – who was going to do the dirty work for them. I suggested Colin. I knew he'd been working in a hospital but he told me he'd been a porter; not that it matters now. I knew where he was staying in London so I rang his lodgings and young Mr Nugent went round there, picked him up in the car and brought him down here. He saw to burying the body. And then, when Mr Dixon moved in and looking after him got too much for me, he had to come back to help me out.'

'Unwise wasn't it, to involve him again?' Finch suggested.

'What could we do?' Edie Cole retorted. 'There was no-one else we could trust. Besides, I didn't know then what I know now. I thought once he'd been paid off, he'd go abroad and keep his mouth shut. That was the arrangement Mr Nugent made with him. His air-fare to Spain and so much a month paid into a bank account on condition he never came back to this country. We didn't think he'd talk. He was in it as deep as the rest of us.'

'But then it all started to go wrong,' Finch suggested. 'Mr Saxby turned up and was asked to stay the night . . .'

'Miss Constance should never have suggested it!' Edie Cole flashed out. 'I knew it'd cause trouble.'

'I believe Mrs Nugent was fond of him.'

'*Fond!*' She put a wealth of bitter contempt into the word. 'He should have been packed off back to where he came from. I suppose you know what happened that night? Miss Constance would have told you. What I want to know is what went wrong. Mr Saxby died naturally – a heart attack, I should think. So why did Dr Callender call in the police?'

'The pillow,' Finch told her. 'Miss Byrne noticed it had been changed.'

She was silent for several moments, only the corners

of her lips moving as if she were chewing over this piece of information. Then she said in a flat, dry voice, 'That was my fault.'

She said nothing more, seeming to accept both the responsibility for her mistake as well as the inevitability of its consequences with a matter-of-factness which Finch found hard to accept.

Did she genuinely feel no emotions? he wondered. Apparently not. Neither guilt nor remorse seemed to affect her.

He waited but the silence continued and at last he was forced to resume the interview.

'I assume that it was Colin who attacked Miss Byrne?'

'He panicked,' Edie Cole explained. 'Once you lot turned up, asking questions, he wanted out. I told him – they can't prove anything. Mr Saxby's death was natural as they'll find out for themselves sooner or later. Then they'll have to drop the case. He wouldn't listen to me; thought I was too old and stupid to know anything. But I knew enough to realize he was planning to clear out. That time he went to Chelmsford on his day off – remember? I told him to go, just to get him out of the house so he wouldn't be here when you turned up again. He came back that evening with a bus timetable. I found it in his jacket pocket. Like a fool, he'd marked the time of the early bus which leaves the village at half past six. So I knew what he'd got in mind. He'd catch that bus into Chelmsford and then get a train up to London. After that, he could do anything – go to the police or disappear God knows where. Either way, he'd cause trouble. You lot would start asking questions and the truth would've come out. I couldn't risk it.'

'So you decided to kill him?' Finch asked, his own voice as flat and as dry as hers.

'Not then,' Edie Cole replied. 'I thought I might be able to talk him into coming back. But it didn't work . . .' She raised her shoulders, leaving the rest of the sentence unspoken.

'And that was when you went to meet him on the footpath?'

'I knew he'd go that way into Howlett; it's quicker than going round by the road. What I didn't know then was that Miss Claudia had heard him leave the house and had followed him into the garden . . .'

'Because by that time, you'd already left?'

She gave him a quick little glance, half-amused, half-admiring.

'So you worked that out, Chief Inspector. Yes, I'd already gone ahead of him so that I'd be waiting on the path for him to arrive.'

'But not by the side door? You couldn't have done because he'd've noticed that the bolts were undone.'

The look of amusement deepened.

'You don't miss much, do you? But you're right. I couldn't use the side door so I got out through the kitchen window. From there, I cut across the garden and the shrubbery to a gap that leads on to the path. I was about twenty minutes ahead of him. When he turned up, I tried talking him into coming back. It was then he told me that he couldn't. Miss Claudia had followed him and he'd panicked and hit her with the suitcase he was carrying. Once he'd told me that, I didn't have any choice, did I?'

'He had to die?'

'He had to be got rid of,' Edie Cole corrected him, folding her lips as if she disapproved of his choice of words. 'He was no good anyway; never anything but trouble since the day he was born. And then there was the stuff.'

'What stuff?' Finch enquired.

'Things he'd been stealing from the house on the quiet, thinking I'd not notice. He'd been clever about it, though. I'll give him that. It was only when I got the suitcase back

232

to the house and looked inside that I realized how much he'd taken.' Getting up from the table, she walked across to the old-fashioned built-in dresser, bending her thin back to one of the lower cupboards which she opened. Taking out a suitcase, she carried it over to the table and, lifting up the lid, displayed its contents. Packed into it, among a jumble of hastily folded clothes, was a collection of objects, mostly small items of household silver – spoons, sugar-tongs, a cream jug, but also other articles. Lifting up the top layer of crumpled shirts, Finch saw a gold watch and chain, an enamelled snuff-box, a tie-pin set with rubies.

Edie Cole stood watching as he searched, the ugly patches of red again visible on her cheeks.

'He kept the case hidden in the summer-house,' she said. 'That's where he was making for when Miss Claudia followed him. He'd put his clothes into it the night before, ready to leave early in the morning. He thought she knew about the suitcase and the things he'd stolen. She didn't, of course. She'd no idea he'd been quietly helping himself to this and that. I'd missed some of them – the sugar-tongs, for instance, and some of the spoons and I'd guessed it was him. Think of it! Stealing from the family!' Her voice rose, full of genuine outrage. 'Things that had been in the house since before Mr Aston's time. It was that which really decided me. He was standing on the footpath, the case in his hand. He said, "It's no good you keeping on nagging at me. I'm not coming back," and he turned to walk away. There was a fence post lying on the grass so I picked it up and hit him with it. He rolled sideways down the bank and fell with his face in the water. I waited for a minute or two and then, when he didn't get up, I left him there and came back to the house.'

'And you hoped to get away with it?' Finch asked. 'Didn't you realize that as soon as we'd found Colin

233

Knapp's body, everybody in the house would be suspect?'

She said calmly, 'It was a risk worth taking. I knew I couldn't trust him to keep his mouth shut, once he'd lost his nerve. It was better to have him out of the way. He was no good to anybody. Besides, I'd been careful to leave nothing on the path that could point to me. I threw the post into the water and I brought the suitcase back with me. So what could you prove? You can't accuse anybody of murder without evidence. And there wasn't any.'

'That's true,' Finch admitted, sitting back in his chair and regarding her with an unwilling respect that was close to admiration. He had underestimted her, he realized, seeing her merely as an elderly servant, poorly educated and more used to taking orders than acting on her own initiative. She was a damned sight more intelligent than he had given her credit for, a conclusion which she evidently made about him for she continued, 'I didn't think you'd realize that I'd gone ahead of Colin. I'd counted on you believing that whoever had killed him had followed him from the house. So, as I was back in my room before Mr Nugent came looking for me after he'd found Miss Claudia, I thought I'd be in the clear. I wouldn't have had the time to kill him.' She looked him up and down with a critical, appraising glance. 'You're not the fool I took you for.'

Coming from her, it was praise indeed, Finch admitted wryly as, turning away, he indicated to Boyce that the interview was over and both men got to their feet.

And it was as a kind of accolade to her that Finch himself pronounced the words of the formal arrest, intoning them with a proper sense of their solemnity.

Sitting by the open window of her bedroom, Claudia and Robert Callender were silent, listening as the cars drove away.

Then she asked, 'What will happen to them?'

It was the same question that Robert Callender had put to the Chief Inspector before their arrival at Howlett Hall and Finch's answer, though non-committal, had been clear enough in its implication that all of them would be facing serious charges without specifying their exact nature.

Robert Callender could make an informed guess himself what they were likely to be – failure to register Edgar Aston's death, the illegal burial of his body, conspiracy to defraud and, in Edie Cole's case, murder, although he assumed that as far as Constance and Teddy Nugent were conerned, the court would take into account their ages when passing sentence. About Edie Cole and Basil Nugent, he was not so sanguine.

It was impossible to keep the truth from Claudia and he replied, 'They'll have to be charged and I assume they'll plead guilty. That should weigh in their favour. But it's you I'm more concerned about. You're in no fit state to drive back to London and you certainly can't stay here on your own. In a moment, I'm going downstairs to phone Mary Holden and ask her to stay here with you. In the meantime, you must rest.'

As he turned aside to get his medical bag, she said, 'It's odd but Uncle Rollo warned me.'

'Warned you of what?'

'The Astons' attitude to money. He said they either liked it too much or spent it too quickly. But I don't really think I take after any of them.' Then breaking off, she added before he could answer, 'Robert, you idiot, why haven't you told me you love me? I'm not like Rowena either, you know. I don't have much taste for the exotic.'

In the few seconds it took him to cross the room to her, it didn't occur to him to question exactly what she had meant by those last remarks.

18

It had been a bad morning, one which Finch hoped would never be repeated. Up before sunrise, he had driven over to Howlett's where he stood in the shrubbery, at the place that Teddy Nugent had indicated, hands stuffed deep in his pockets, listening to the dawn chorus of the birds and watching while two sturdy Constables, dressed in overalls and boots, exhumed the body of Edgar Aston. Even Pardoe was affected although he did his best not to show it.

'Earth to earth,' he commented sardonically as the last spadeful of leaf mould was removed and the grave exposed.

Once McCullum had finished photographing it, he trotted forwards to examine the remains, leaving Finch to supervise the men with the coffin shell and the sheet of black plastic who were waiting at a discreet distance.

And once the body had been removed and the mortuary van had driven away, it wasn't over then. Leaving the forensic experts to examine the grave, he drove into Howlett in time to meet Kitty Laud. She had been brought from Chelmsford in the company of two WPCs and emerged, tremulous, from the back of the police car as it drew up outside the undertaker's.

It was an encounter which Finch had been dreading even more than the exhumation of Aston's body. He hadn't known Edgar Aston. But he did know Kitty and, in a strange way, he felt he also knew her brother, the charming and debonair Hal Dixon who, wearing one of

Aston's suits, lay in the silk-lined coffin in Mr Fairchild's little pine and velvet chapel of rest.

If Finch could have saved her from the ordeal of formally identifying Dixon's body, he would have done so. But there was no-one else.

It was Kitty herself who redeemed the situation. Dressed entirely in black, her cheeks, under the veiling drawn down over her face, carefully powdered, she rose to the occasion like the old trouper she was.

It might have been bizarre; ludicrous, even. Instead, clutching Finch's arm and tottering a little on her high-heeled patent leather shoes, she managed to invest the formality with her own form of dignity and to turn it into something like a ceremony.

There were no tears; no outcries of grief.

Instead, dry-eyed, she looked down into the coffin in silence for several seconds and then announced in a clear voice which could have reached to the back of the stalls, 'Yes, Chief Inspector, that's my brother, Harold George Dixon.'

'Thank you, Mrs Laud,' Finch said gravely before escorting her to the car, where he packed her as carefully into the back seat as if she had been a piece of very old and very valuable porcelain.

There would be papers to sign but he was inclined to leave that for another occasion although he intended calling on her later in an unofficial capacity to reassure himself that she really was all right. For the moment, though, solemnity was the order of the day and, as the car drew away from the kerb, he raised his hand in a salute which she acknowledged with a gracious turn of the wrist which wouldn't have disgraced the Queen Mother.

In the event, it was early evening before he found time to call on her and discovered her sitting alone in the hot little back room, alone apart from a middle-aged neighbour who had the sense to withdraw as soon as Finch arrived. The WPC whom he had assigned to sit with Kitty had evidently been dismissed.

'Not that I had anything against her personally, dear,' Kitty explained. 'She was ever so kind and sympathetic. She was just so *young*. Anybody under the age of thirty, especially women, gets on my nerves after a while. They remind me too much of the past. Silly of me but there you are.'

She seemed to be grateful for his company, though, and perked up as soon as he entered. She was still wearing her black dress but had cheered it up with a paste brooch and a pink and mauve scarf which she had tucked into the neck.

Seeing he had noticed it, she added, fingering the silk, 'It's one of Hal's presents. Sent it to me for my birthday a couple of years ago. Pretty, isn't it? But he always had good taste, had Hal.'

She smiled at him and he smiled back, trying to match her mood of determined gaiety despite his own low spirits, brought on by the meeting he had had earlier that afternoon at Howlett Hall with Claudia Byrne. She was up and was dressed but had not properly recovered and had been seated in the drawing room, hand in hand with Robert Callender. As he entered the room, there had been no need for them to tell him the reason for their obvious happiness. It had been blazoned in their faces.

He had congratulated them awkwardly when Robert Callender had broken the news of their impending engagement and then, feeling like a skeleton at their feast, had gone on to give them a brief report of what he felt they ought to know, skirting round the delicate issue of the likely charges to be brought against the Nugents and Edie Cole, before arranging for them both to make formal written statements.

He had seen the light in them die a little although he

consoled himself with the thought that they'd no doubt rekindle it again for one another in the days ahead. In Kitty's case, there was no such hope and he was acutely aware that he must not let his own sense of loss cast a shadow over her.

So he chatted and smiled and lugged in from the boot of the car the boxes of lino tiles which he had made a special effort to stop off and buy for her on his way back from Howlett.

'Lovely, dear,' she said. 'I like red. Nice and cheerful. And you'll be back tomorrow, you said, to lay them? Shan't I be smart?'

To repay him, she in turn fetched out as her offering an album of photographs and press-cuttings from the bedroom which she spread out on his knees.

Looking through them and making the right appreciative noises, he thought that for Kitty, happiness lay in the past, captured in black and white images and print. For Robert Callender and Claudia Byrne it lay in the future. As for himself, he felt suspended in an emotional limbo from which he daren't look either forwards or back. He could only thank God that there'd be enough paperwork involved in the Howlett case to keep him fully occupied for the next few weeks.

Kitty was saying as they reached the last page, 'You'll come to Hal's funeral, won't you?'

'Of course,' Finch assured her.

'I'd like to make sure he has a good send-off. He'd've liked that.' Breaking off, she added unexpectedly, peering up at him sideways with her bright little dark eyes, 'You look tired, dear.'

He tried to rouse himself.

'Do I? It's been a long day.'

She patted his knee as she got up.

'You want cheering up.' Going over to the sideboard, she produced a bottle of brandy and two glasses which she set out on the low table. 'Liquid sunshine, as Hal always called it.' Filling their glasses to the brim, she raised her own. 'Well, cheers, darling. Here's to the future.'

'To the future,' he echoed.

It was an absurd situation to be seated there among Kitty's mementoes, sharing the sofa with that bloody silly pierrot doll. As he raised his own glass in return and sipped at its contents he felt a small bubble of involuntary laughter begin to form somewhere in his chest.

To the future!

And why the hell not?

THE END